A LOVELY MURDER

First Edition
ISBN: 978-1-68313-064-2
Printed and bound in the United States of America.

Cover and interior design by Kelsey Rice

A LOVELY MURDER

~ A DANNI DEADLINE THRILLER ~

BY
LORI ERICSON

P
Pen-L Publishing
Fayetteville, Arkansas
Pen-L.com

For Lloyd, always

PROLOGUE

His presence surprised the hell out of me.

The stereo played Simon & Garfunkel's *The Concert in Central Park* album, one of Tracey's favorites. I got out of the car and stood there listening for a minute. Had the last year been just a nightmare? Maybe Tracey was inside, dancing on the wood floor in her stocking feet. I came to my senses. I knew better. The solid ache in my heart reminded me. The pain was too deep to be imagined.

She had loved the lakeside cabin. The bastard bought it for her, even put it in her name. The privacy, the beauty, the lake, and the surrounding tree-covered hills were Utopia for her. She was so happy every minute she was able to get away to the secluded retreat, like a kid relishing the first ice cream cone of the summer.

"Just enjoying the sun and sounds," she'd say, her pretty blue eyes sparkling with a big smile.

She'd been such a beauty. My precious little sister. Mama's baby girl.

The music played, but the cabin was empty. On the patio, I found the man she'd foolishly loved.

What right did he have to be here now? Acting like he mourned her. Like he'd lost something, someone special.

The rage raced to my extremities when I saw him. I gritted my teeth and shook my head. He looked so relaxed, gazing out on the lake. Unclenching my fist, I pulled the long butcher knife from the magnetic strip on the cabinet backsplash. I took a deep breath and clutched the blade against my thigh.

It was obvious it was him, although I couldn't see anything but the top of his head over the back of the lawn chair.

My chest rose and fell with seething anger as I stared through the patio door. I watched his hand reach out and wrap around a tumbler full of dark liquid. The scotch he liked to sip.

Calm sank into me. I could do this.

My fist tightened around the black grip. The sharp blade pressed against my leg, the tip sinking into the skin just below the hem of my shorts. My leg tingled as a thin line of blood meandered through the hair on my calf.

He didn't turn when I pushed the door open. He didn't say anything when I eased into the cushioned lounge chair next to his. Eyes slid sideways, but no words were spoken.

I leaned back, dropping the knife beside my outstretched leg, and listened to the music while I watched the sun glisten on the far side of the lake.

"Bridge Over Troubled Waters" played through the outdoor speakers.

As the song approached its end, I stood and glared down at him.

I wanted to ask why he'd done what he had—why he'd betrayed Tracey, made her suffer for his own guilt. But it didn't matter anymore.

She was gone.

It was over.

Over for her, months and months ago.

Over for him now.

The bastard's gaze came up and met my own.

I raised the knife and plunged it in. I'd thought it would be like carving a ham, but it was more like cutting a melon.

His eyes bulged and stared up, the brow knotting in confusion.

The rage seethed inside me, sunk into the knife, and flowed out with the red liquid, spraying in all directions and glistening in the evening sun, as if from a lawn sprinkler. I smiled with a sudden rush of joy.

My heart lifted and sang as the music blended with the sucking sound the knife made as I plunged it in and pulled it free, the flesh pulling and giving way around the blood-soaked blade. I grew giddy on the sweet, metallic odor mixed with the pine from the nearby grove of trees.

Life was gone, but I kept at it. The eyes glazed and stared ahead. Empty.

"That's for Tracey, you son of a bitch."

I stuck the blade in and twisted.

The body quivered in an after-death shudder.

"This is for Mama."

I couldn't help it. I smiled and stabbed again.

Blood covered my hands, my wrists. Pulling the knife out one last time, I tossed it aside. More crimson raindrops sprayed from its edge. I dropped to the side of the lounger and gripped my knees.

Blood dripped to the patio and pooled in the shadow beneath the chair beside me. Red spatter ran down the sliding glass doors. The stainless steel grill and the bright-yellow cushions of the lawn furniture were speckled with it. His blue swim shorts had turned a sort of deep purple, nearly black below the slashed open abdomen. The front of my polo and shorts were soaked in the sticky mess as well.

I surveyed the damage, then leaned back in the lounge chair and took a drink of his precious scotch. It burned going down. I squeezed my eyes shut, smiled to myself, and looked out toward the lake. The tumbler rolled from my fingers and shattered on the patio.

Mama walked toward me. She wore her usual plaid cotton dress that buttoned up the front and black lace-up shoes with white ankle socks.

"So proud. So proud of you, son." She clasped her palms together, bunching her ample bosom tight against her with a look of pure joy on her face. "He deserved it, deserved it all. You did good, boy. Real good. He's the first, and you'll do just as good with the rest."

The edges of my mouth turned up, then I threw back my head and laughed. She was gone by the time my chuckle was over.

I pulled myself from the chair and got to work. I rolled the body in a tarp I dug out of the garage, dragged it into the woods, and buried the bastard. Next came tackling the bloody mess on the patio.

His white Miata was in the garage. I drove it up the road about a mile where the cliffs towered over the deeper end of the lake and it would miss any big trees that might halt its plunge. I watched from behind the tree line until a fishing boat left the cove below. It took some effort to do it on my own, but I popped the car in neutral and pushed it off the cliff. Falling backward on my ass, I listened for the splash. It came loud and quick, followed by a round of gurgles.

Walking the gravel road back to the cabin, I sang to myself as the sun set on the far side of the lake.

"Hello payback, my new friend . . ."

Danni tried to explain why she felt a tug to stay loyal to *The Lovely County Sun*. Leaving the weekly newspaper that had given her a chance to redeem herself would be tough, but that was the goal when she'd returned to her hometown.

"Well, it is what it is."

"I get that, but I think you'll regret it if you don't jump on this opportunity." Rick held Bruno's leash while they walked along the top of the dam with the Jack Russell terrier. "I know Paul's a good friend and a great guy to work for, but this is what you wanted since you came home. You've got to take the job. You deserve it."

A small breeze from the lake pushed a strand of hair into her eyes. She tucked it behind her ear.

"I know I need to get on with my career, but I think it's my decision to make."

"I understand that. I just want you to be happy."

She sighed. "I know you do, but *I* have to be the one to decide."

"I get it. Didn't mean to step on your toes."

"Leaving *The County Sun* is hard, but I know going to the daily is what I want. I love the rhythm of working for a daily newspaper. Plus, I definitely need the money. Certainly want to pull my own weight once we get married."

He chuckled and grabbed her hand, entwining his fingers with hers.

"That's right. I want to marry you for all the big bucks you'll be bringing in. Maybe I'll resign from the D.A.'s office and hang a shingle, not even stress too much about building a client list."

"Both of us switching careers just as we make the biggest personal change of our lives might cause a little stress on the relationship, don't you think?"

Rick stopped and wrapped his arms around her. Smiling, he leaned in and kissed her.

"No stress here. Ever."

"Sure." She snorted.

Bruno tugged on the leash. Releasing the embrace, Rick followed the dog to the edge of the dirt path where something in the grassy area off the trail had his attention.

"Hey, buddy, don't go too far. You'll take a tumble down that slope, and I'm not going with you."

Danni admired the view of Rick in his blue T-shirt and long khaki shorts before she jogged toward him, put a hand on his shoulder, and looked down the hillside.

"What's he after?"

"I'm not sure, but it smells like something's dead down there."

Bruno's stubby white-and-brown tail stuck straight up amid the weeds as he sniffed around.

"Ooh, it does stink. Probably a dead opossum or something." She clapped her hands. "Come on, Bruno, you don't need to be near whatever that is."

The dog came bounding out of the weeds. Rick took Danni's hand in his again, and they continued along the trail. The sound of a boat motor caught her attention. An aluminum fishing boat that had been trolling along the shoreline near the end of the dam pulled away and started toward the docks.

"I guess I should tell Paul this week. He's got Becky now, anyway. She's not a bad reporter for someone with an accounting degree." She chuckled. "I can give him a two-week notice, be off a week before the wedding, and then start the new job after we get back."

Rick squeezed her hand. "Now you're talking. The *Bloomington Daily Times* is where you belong. You should have taken the job the first time they offered it."

"I don't know." She shrugged. "It just didn't seem right. I needed to stay with the weekly for a while after Sheriff Doyle was ousted. I'd started writing that series of stories there. Just couldn't abandon Paul right then."

"But now's your chance to do something for you."

"I know you're right. It's just hard."

They fell silent again.

An older couple in matching green hiking shorts and tan T-shirts passed in the opposite direction. Bruno stood on his hind legs when the man reached out and patted him on the head.

"Cute little dog," the woman said.

"Thank you." Danni nodded.

Bruno let out a yip as the couple moved on.

"How was your mom this morning?" Rick asked.

Danni took the leash to prevent it from wrapping around her legs when Bruno changed sides of the trail.

"Not bad. She sang a little bit while she sewed. She's made nearly a hundred of those seat cushions."

"I wish it was different for you, Danni. A woman, I would think, needs her mother during a time like this."

"She's been suffering so long, I don't know anything different anymore."

The sun reflected off some sort of shiny metal object in the woods at the end of the dam, making her squint, but it vanished quickly.

She stopped to let the dog pee in the weeds.

"Think she'll get two hundred cushions made in time for the wedding?" he asked.

He squeezed her hand, let go, and took the leash back.

Bruno sniffed something in the rocks on the lake side of the dam.

"We'll cover as many seats as we can and not worry about it. The chairs are fine without them, but they will add a nice touch. It's been great seeing her come to life a little. I can tell she likes contributing to the wedding."

"Maybe we can get a discount from the rental place in exchange for all those cushions afterward."

"I'd thought of that myself. What else are we going to do with them?" She laughed. "Besides, I'm all about making this thing as cheap as possible."

"Me too. I can't believe Addison won't let me chip in."

She smiled. "Dad's a traditionalist. You know that. It's the bride's family that's supposed to pay."

A whoosh sang past her ear.

Rick, a few steps behind her, grunted.

She turned in time to see him collapse.

A white rod with bright-green and yellow feathers protruded from his chest.

The breath that entered her lungs burned and didn't want to let out.

A scream rattled her ears.

It was hers.

She shuddered. Shaking her head, she tried to make sense of what was happening. The arrow must have come from the wooded hillside at the end of the dam, but she couldn't see anyone among the trees.

She knelt next to him and cradled his face in her hands. His eyes filled with tears.

"I love you." He mouthed the words and clutched her thigh.

She sucked in her breath. "I love you too. Hold on. I'm here, baby." Her voice caught. "I'm here."

The cell phone dropped to the ground as she struggled to pull it from the back pocket of her jean shorts and keep her grip on Rick. She grabbed it and punched in 911.

"Hold on, baby. Don't move."

She began to shake. His arm fell from her thigh and stretched out on the ground beside him. Blood pooled between them. A tear slowly rolled from one eye and made its way to his hairline.

"Don't leave me, Rick. Don't, please."

He squeezed her hand, then went limp. His eyes closed.

She put a hand to his cheek. "No, no, no, no."

A voice behind her gave directions to their location. A hand touched her shoulder. She looked up to see the tear-filled eyes of the woman who had passed them on the trail. Her husband talked into a cell phone in a frantic voice, words Danni didn't quite comprehend as she turned back to Rick.

It all felt muffled, like she was watching it from her couch as it played out on the big-screen television.

Danni looked up toward the end of the dam and saw the sun reflect off something in the trees again.

She dropped Rick's hand to his chest and shuddered. With another glance at the hillside, she sprang to her feet and tore off toward the trees. There was no choice. There was no helping him. She'd do the only thing she could and maybe find out who shot him.

At the end of the dam, climbing over a line of massive boulders, she stumbled and scraped her knee. Blood trickled down her left leg as she plunged into the brush, searching for movement ahead.

Who would do that? Why? Where was the son of a bitch? Was she quick enough to catch him? Her? Could it have been an accident?

Her mind raced faster than her feet. Her heart pounded in her ears. She darted around trees. Leapt over a fallen trunk. Dodged low branches, making her way up the hillside. Briars caught and ripped at her bare legs. She ignored it.

Run. Run was all she could think. The reason why tried to seep in, but she pushed it back.

Focus on plunging faster up the hill.

Focus on what was ahead.

Each tree. Each sapling.

Run.

Where? Where had that arrow come from?

Who? And where had he gone?

Out of breath, she stopped, searching the forest around her. To her left, farther up the hillside, brush rustled. Someone moved fast through the undergrowth.

Taking off again, she pushed a young tree to the side only to have a branch whip back at her, smacking her across the cheek and barely missing her right eye. The hillside grew steep. She grabbed branches. Pulled herself up. Scrambled as fast as she could. Stopped again to listen.

Nothing.

She waited.

A distant siren.

Rick. Oh, Rick.

She shook her head and scanned the area around her. There was nothing but trees and brush between her and the lake. Whoever had shot Rick had to be up the hill. Had to be trying to get out of the woods.

Running again, she tripped on something hard and fell face first to the ground. Her clothes snagged on a sapling as she went down. The cotton T-shirt yanked to the side. It ripped but held and helped to break her fall, or at least slow the momentum of the tumble.

She pulled the shirt loose from the tree, rolled over on her back, and fought to catch her breath.

Her heart pounded.

The siren grew louder, then stopped.

A turkey vulture circled in the window of sky in the canopy of leaves above her. The bird arced to one side, disappeared for a few seconds above the trees, and came back into view, its graceful flight similar to a ballerina, with arms wide open, gliding silently across a stage.

Silence.

Only her own breathing.

"Who are you?" she screamed.

Silence.

"Why?" she screamed louder.

"Oh my God, why?"

A lump caught in her throat, but she didn't cry, wouldn't cry. Tears would make it real, not a nightmare. It had to all be a nightmare.

Holding her breath, she listened.

Nothing for a minute.

She exhaled.

A car ignition started from somewhere up the hill. Then the sound of gravel spraying behind it as it sped away.

She lay still, watching the vulture.

I had watched this happy, sappy couple for days on end before I took action. They made me sick.

The first time I followed them to their newly built house just outside of Bloomington, my thirst to exact revenge grew. I liked them even less when I saw how they lived. The SUV had pulled into the garage of the two-story modern house at the end of the cul-de-sac. The house had big panel windows in front, framed in black to match the sleek metal roof. Iron fencing surrounded the property with twin block pillars at the end of the front sidewalk in cream-colored stucco like the house.

It was impressive. Two nights before, when it was lit up, it was especially impressive.

It wasn't fair they were living in such a swanky place and, from all appearances, so happy and lucky. If things hadn't happened the way they did, if someone hadn't stuck their nose in where it didn't belong . . .

If. If. If.

I slapped the steering wheel and stared out the windshield. The blinds were up. I saw movement inside but couldn't make out more. I was too far away, parked halfway down the block in front of a house with enough teenagers in and out that my nondescript car wasn't noticed on the street.

The wide wooden door opened. The woman, her auburn hair swaying around her shoulders, brought a broom with her and swept the porch, then down the front path. She stopped at the edge of the street and looked up at the sky for a few minutes, then turned and started to sweep her way back to the house. The door opened again, and the man trotted toward her. He tried to take the broom. She stuck it behind her back, but he wrapped his arms around her and took it from her. After a kiss, she stood with her hands on her hips and watched him sweep the walk before following him up to the porch. A playful swat on her behind had them both laughing and struggling for the broom again before they went inside.

God, how I hated those people. They had everything, while so much had been robbed from me—from me and my family.

A small pickup with its radio cranked up and thumping bass pulled up behind me. I slumped down in the seat and watched in the rearview mirror. Two teenagers, both dressed in baggy dark clothes, looking like wannabe gangbangers, got out and swaggered up to the front porch of the house to my right. One of them had to hitch up his low-hanging black jeans twice before he made it across the lawn. They didn't even look my way.

I focused my attention back on the house at the end of the street and gripped the steering wheel so fiercely my knuckles ached and turned white.

"Look at that place." Mama's raspy voice made me jump. "They got it really nice there, son."

"I know, Mama. I know."

"You need to take care of this. It ain't over yet, you know it ain't." She sat, staring ahead, with one elbow hanging out the open window. She wore her blue dress with the tiny yellow flowers and a red bib-front apron. A white cotton dishtowel, wrapped around one of the shoulder straps, looked like it was stained with spaghetti sauce. "You're the only one to do it. The only one to make sure this wrong is righted."

I turned back toward the house.

"I know, Mama."

She had mourned my sister beyond belief. It was nothing like my father's death a decade before, a passing with no feeling of great loss.

That had been a blessing to us, the ones left in the wake of the son of a bitch's brutal control. Mama wouldn't have admitted that, but I knew.

It had been Tracey, Mama, and me all those years—struggling to live with the man of the house, the one who had to put his approval on everything: every decision, every purchase, every meal, everything. We all worked to keep him satisfied. We all suffered when he wasn't. But Mama bore the heaviest burden. She tried her best to protect us from his wrath. Tracey and I loved her for it, ached for her pain, and did anything we could to ease her burden. It had been the three of us against him. After he was gone, it was the three of us creating a life we never dreamed of before.

When Tracey decided to leave us, chose to take her own life, the pain hurt too much.

Mama howled at the viewing, curled up next to the coffin on the blue carpet, like a toddler throwing a fit. I'd carried her out of there, found a room in back, and laid her on a couch. Standing alone next to the casket, I clenched my jaw while friends and family shuffled through, giving me a hug or a handshake, expressing some small condolence with no knowledge of the burden I carried.

The funeral proved worse. Mama didn't say a thing to anyone. She sat with her head bowed, tears dripping atop her fisted hands in her lap, at times shaking with silent sobs.

I handled all the mourners at the graveside, then took her home and refused to accept visitors that afternoon. Mama and I needed time to deal with it on our own. They all understood, offered a few condolences, and left their casseroles and cakes, most with names written on masking tape attached to the bottom of the plate.

Mama stayed in her room with the door closed until late that night. I heated up a spaghetti casserole for her. Stirring more than nibbling, she rocked back and forth in the vinyl kitchen chair. I worried she wouldn't get past the loss.

"Mama, I'm sorry she did this," I whispered.

The fork hit the edge of the plate with a loud clink.

"Sorry? You're sorry *she* did this?"

She blew a breath out between clenched teeth, her seething anger evident in her glare.

I tried to swallow the lump in my throat. "Yes, Mama. I'm sorry Tracey gave up. We could have worked this out. It would have all been okay eventually."

I jumped at her scream of anguish.

"Don't you ever say anything like that again. Don't you ever blame her. Tracey didn't do this. Tracey didn't make this happen."

Her eyes were full of hate. Her stare pierced me to my heart from across the table. I lowered my head, ashamed.

"I'm sorry, Mama. I didn't mean to upset you."

A throaty sob made me look up again. She clutched the tablecloth on each side of her plate. Her head thrown back, she shook with grief. Raising both fists, the burnt-orange cloth still gripped in her fingers, the plate jumped as she pounded the table. In one swift movement, she yanked the tablecloth and pitched it to the floor. The plate hit the cupboard and shattered. Spaghetti covered in red marinara slid down the white front of the lower cupboard, like worms clinging to the side of a bucket.

She fell to the floor and clutched her chest. I rushed to her side. My knees slammed against the tile.

"Mama, Mama."

"Tracey." The name, a whisper that hung between us.

"Hang on, Mama. I'm calling an ambulance."

I started to rise, but she clutched my arm, her nails digging into my skin.

"Stay." A whisper. "It's too late."

A gasp for breath.

"Listen to me, son." Her voice so low.

Trembling, I leaned closer to hear.

"You got to take care of this."

I wasn't sure what I was supposed to do, but I couldn't deny her anything. Not now.

Her deep-blue eyes filled with tears, yet the stare she fastened on me was clear.

"Yes, Mama. I'm here."

How could I lose her now too? There would be no one left but me. No one. It wasn't fair. The two people I cared about most, gone because of someone else. Someone else's callous, ego-driven ambitions.

Mama gasped, then spat out the words in a breathy whisper. "You have to set this right. You have to, boy. You got to do right by her."

"I will, Mama. I promise." My voice caught.

Her fingernails dug deeper into my arm and then released. Her hand landed on the tile with a clank from the rings on three fingers. Her palm lay open, as if waiting for something to fill it.

Rising from the floor, I stared at the lines on the inside of her hand, the calloused ridges, the curl of her long fingers. That hand had fed me many times, mended my clothing, clung to the seat of my bike while I tried time and time again to stay upright, turned the pages of books as she patiently read the words. That hand had clutched my chin to make me look into her eyes as she scolded me, swatted my backside when need be. That hand once covered mine, guiding the razor to show me how to glide it across my chin without skinning myself alive. That hand wiped tears from my face when I left home for good.

Both gentle and strong, her hand lay open and still.

"Mama."

I sobbed and sank back to my knees. I dropped my chin to my chest and shuddered. Anger bubbled up, stopping my tears cold. There was no more time to mourn. It was time to take action. I slammed my fist into my thigh.

"I will take care of this. I will. I promise. For Tracey. For you, Mama. I'll make them *all* pay for what they've done."

The sun faded over the hillside at the end of the dam in a blaze of pink and orange. The wisps of colors glistened across the lake and mixed with the red and blue strobes coming from the emergency vehicles. They usually didn't walk this late in the evening, but maybe they should. The air felt crisp, but not cold. Rick would love it.

Rick. Oh, God, Rick.

Danni sat on the bumper of the ambulance. She hadn't moved in nearly an hour, but her heart pounded. She tried to focus on the flashlights that bobbed among the trees in the distance, like fireflies in the evening light. Sheriff James sent the deputies to search for any sign of an archer, some clue of the killer.

A few months before, when the nights were still cold enough she had to wear a hat and heavy coat, she and Rick had searched the same hillside for a lost little girl. They had bought the house not far from the dam the previous fall but hadn't met the neighbors yet when they heard a woman yelling outside. They threw on their coats and grabbed flashlights after learning that a six-year-old autistic child had disappeared. The mother had been frightened she'd fallen in the lake. They combed the dam, the shoreline, and the woods with a group of neighbors and sheriff's deputies. To everyone's relief, the child was found on a back porch a few doors down, playing with a puppy.

The following night, Rick had teased her and suggested they tromp around in the woods again, maybe take a blanket to spread out and enjoy each other in the moonlight. It was too cold for that, but she would be game next summer, she'd said.

A night like this would've been perfect. She bit her lip and sniffled.

Flashlights continued to flicker among the trees. Were they covering the same areas she'd searched with Rick at her side? The overturned tree he'd rushed to, thinking it would be a perfect spot for the young girl to hide? The rocky cliff where they'd concentrated the flashlights together to see if she'd gone over the edge?

Had someone sat on those rocks to watch them walk along the dam and taken aim at the man she was supposed to marry? Why? Who? She trembled.

A photographer with equipment bouncing off each hip walked toward her. He glanced at Danni as he passed. The blanket wrapped around her slid off one shoulder.

The rattle of metal and a crunch of gravel caught her attention. The EMTs had finally loaded Rick's body on the stretcher and made their way toward her. A white sheet covered him. Two EMTs, one with her back to Danni, jostled the stretcher across the loose rocks.

"Slow down a little bit," the one on the far end of the stretcher said.

The woman EMT cocked her head, looked behind her, and nodded at Danni.

They hit what must have been a large stone and came to a stop. Rick's left arm slid out from beneath the sheet with the jolt. His hand dangled from the stretcher. Danni sucked in a breath.

That hand was supposed include a white gold band in just a few weeks. She twisted the engagement ring on her own finger.

He'd picked out the perfect ring for her. A respectable stone that wasn't too big, didn't stick out too much so she wouldn't catch it on sweaters and nylons. Just one diamond in a square setting. Her eyes had filled with tears when he went down on his knee and pulled it from his pocket. No need to even ask.

"Yes, yes."

The twinkle in his eyes. The smile. She'd never forget that moment.

She ran her fingers across the ring again and jumped to her feet, leaving the blanket that was half on her shoulders to fall to the ground. She grabbed his hand, clutched it against her chest, then pulled it away and looked at it for just a second before tucking it gently beneath the white sheet. The woman EMT nodded before moving backward again.

They pushed the stretcher a little closer to the black van while the coroner, who had been following, shoved a clipboard under one arm, opened the two rear doors, then stepped aside.

The wheels folded beneath the stretcher as they pushed it into place. Danni jumped when the two doors closed. The coroner, a badge hanging from a lanyard around his neck, turned to her.

"I'm sorry, Danni."

She stared up at him, looking through his Coke-bottle-thick lenses into his eyes. He patted her on the shoulder, then turned and spoke briefly to the EMTs before he walked around the end of the van and disappeared.

A minute later, the coroner's van pulled away. She watched it make its way down the dam's access road.

"Danni."

She didn't turn around.

The van traveled around the side of the small park below the dam and slowly meandered past the backside of the baseball field, the red glow of the taillights briefly obscured by the tall chain-link backstop. It came to a stop at the road, the red lights brightening for a few seconds. She sucked in a breath when the van took a left and disappeared from sight.

"Danni."

Dropping her chin to her chest, she shut her eyes.

A hand wrapped around her shoulder, turned her around, and pulled her into a chest. She recognized the tan county deputy's uniform. The back of her head was stroked.

She didn't cry. Tears wouldn't come. She should cry but couldn't think of how or why.

Rick was gone. She'd never hear him laugh again, never hear him lecture her about her smoking or not to spoil the dog, never feel his fingers entwined in hers or his arms around her. He was just gone. No goodbye. No kiss. Just gone. Like a vacuum had sucked him out of her life, leaving no trace that he stood next to her a few hours before.

"Is she okay?"

The chest that held her moved. A muffled, soft voice said, "She'll be all right. She just needs some time. Let me get her out of here."

"Where? We haven't questioned her yet."

The chest shifted toward the other voice. "She's just not ready to talk yet, sir. I think it's shock. We've already questioned the couple that saw him go down. They didn't see any signs of an archer. She probably didn't either."

No, she hadn't seen anything. She tried to shake her head to tell them, but couldn't make the effort.

Rick.

They'd taken him away.

A muffled voice. ". . . having problems with anyone, any known enemies? You know the drill."

"Yes, sir, will do," the chest replied.

She was pulled away, then helped into the back of a car. Someone tucked a blanket around her.

"It's okay, Danni. I'm going to take you home." The voice sounded familiar, but she couldn't place it and didn't bother to look up.

She stared out the window, hoping to see the lights of the van that took him away. It was gone.

He was gone.

The door next to her opened again. The chest reached in and put something beside her. She felt the seatbelt wrapping around. She stared ahead.

Bruno whimpered and gently laid his paw on her thigh. He nuzzled up against her and lowered his head to her lap as the car moved down the hillside. She stroked his back but just let her hand lie across his shoulders.

A police radio crackled. The driver leaned to the right and lowered the volume.

Then his voice, "Addison, it's Ben."

The car pulled out on the road and sped up.

"I'm fine, but I have some bad news." A pause. "Yes, sir, Danni is okay. Well, okay physically. I have her here with me. I'm bringing her home to you. I'm afraid Rick is dead."

Rick is dead.

Rick is dead.

Rick is dead.

She let out a long breath and collapsed against the door of the car, her head thumping the window.

Cool fingers traced her hairline. Danni rolled over and looked up at her mother, then pushed the covers back and sat up. Her head ached. Her throat felt dry.

"I'm okay, Mom. I'm okay."

Taking a robe from the hook on the door, she wrapped it around her and went to the kitchen. Feet shuffled behind her.

"Hey, sweetie, how are you feeling?" Her father leaned against the counter, a half-eaten sandwich in his hand. "Can I get you something? You need to eat."

She shook her head.

"I think I want a shower."

"Good, baby. You do that. When you get out, though, let's try to eat something. I'll get you anything you want."

She nodded, then patted her mother's shoulder on her way to the shower.

The water was as hot as tolerable. She leaned against the tile wall and let it stream over her. When it started to cool, she quickly washed her hair and got out. With a towel wrapped around her head, she went back to her room. Her father sat at the dining room table and talked on the phone.

"We'll need to cancel all the rentals. Yes, well, thank you. Yes, a real tragedy." He paused and offered a slight smile to her as she passed. "No, you can send me a bill for the cancellation fee."

Danni hung her robe back on its hook, pulled on a T-shirt, and combed out her hair, then climbed back in bed. Her childhood bear Theodore stared at her. He knew she was hurting but didn't offer any sympathy. "Tough it up, girl," he seemed to say. Those button eyes had always seen right through her.

She rolled over and pulled the covers up to her chin.

Rick called to her. A dense fog covered the dam, making it hard to see even the trail in front of her.

"Where are you, baby?"

"Rick?"

Bruno pulled at the leash, wanting to investigate something in the weeds off the side of the trail, but Rick called from farther ahead.

"Danni, Danni."

The fog grew thicker. She couldn't even see the dog at the end of the stretched out leash.

She jerked awake.

"Danni, honey, you need to get up." It was her father's voice. "You've got someone here to see you."

He shook her shoulder gently. She couldn't feel her right arm tucked under her. It must have gone to sleep. Rolling onto her stomach, she dangled the arm off the bed and shook it.

"Go to sleep on you, sweetie?"

She nodded.

"The sheriff and Ben Sizemore are here to talk to you. You okay with that?"

She sat up. "Yeah, I guess I better be."

"Good. I'll tell them you're getting dressed and will be out in a minute."

A laundry basket filled with a variety of her clothes, neatly folded, sat atop her old cedar trunk. She pulled out a pair of jeans and a T-shirt. Her hair looked ghastly. She'd gone to sleep with it still wet. She ran a brush through it and pulled it back with a purple hair tie she found on top of the dresser. No makeup, but it didn't matter. She slipped on a pair of socks and sighed as she looked in the mirror. That would have to do.

The sheriff and Ben—a tall, thin, white-blond deputy, whose dad was a childhood buddy of her father's—sat at opposite ends of the green velour couch, matching mugs of coffee in front of them. Ben had become a good friend since he'd made a point of warning her that someone was out to get her more than a year before.

Both officers moved to stand when she came in the room, but she waved for them to stay seated and shook her head. Ben pursed his lips and nodded to her once she took a seat in the leather armchair across from them, her feet curled beneath her.

"Danni, I sure am sorry for your loss, and sorry to have to intrude here while you're grieving." Sheriff James raked his thick gray hair. Dressed in a blue button-down shirt, tucked into jeans with a sharp crease ironed down the front, his eyes shot between Danni and her father as he sat forward on the couch and rubbed his knees. "Since this happened at your place just outside of Bloomington, it's our case. We want to get to the bottom of this as soon as feasibly possible."

He'd been sheriff of Lovely County less than a year. The former sheriff had left office in disgrace after a scandal Danni broke in the weekly county paper. She was nearly killed in the process. Sheriff James was recruited from Savaton County, where he was known for his integrity and earning the respect of his deputies.

"We've got a few questions, if you're up to it."

He pulled himself forward, perching on the edge of the couch. She nodded. Ben took a small notebook from his front pocket, along with a pen. He gave Danni a sympathetic smile.

"Thanks for bringing me here last night, Ben." Her voice sounded foreign and a little too high-pitched.

"That wasn't a problem. Glad to do it."

She looked back at the sheriff and nodded.

"Did you see anything, or anyone, before Rick was shot?" the sheriff asked.

Shaking her head, she bit her lip. "Nothing."

"Can you tell us what happened leading up to the, um, incident?"

Her mouth was dry. She didn't want to think about the day before.

It had been good up until then. A Saturday. They'd lingered in bed, then eaten bagels and cream cheese with strawberries, fighting over sections of the newspaper, and then, like always, ended up reading the good parts to each other. She had mopped the kitchen while Rick gave Bruno a bath. They had gone to her parents' house with a pizza for lunch, stayed until midafternoon. After that, they went back to the new house and took a walk around the park and up on the dam.

The new house.

How could she ever go back there without him?

"Can you tell us anything about what happened?" the sheriff asked again.

She closed her eyes for a few seconds, opened them, and leaned forward.

"Rick said he wanted to walk off his lunch. We went down to the park, did two loops around the lower trail, and then went up on the dam. We do that a lot."

"Did you see anyone on the trail?"

She swallowed. "There was an older man and his dog, some kind of brown mutt, on the lower trail. I've seen him there before, but I don't know his name. I think the dog is Charlie. There were a few teenagers at the gazebo. One of them was the girl who lives two doors down from us. That was about it in the park.

"I didn't see that older couple until we passed them up on the dam. They were the ones who called 911." She paused. "There was a guy fishing out on the lake, but he'd headed toward the docks before Rick was . . . " *Oh, God.* It was hard to say it aloud. A golf ball gathered in her throat, and her heart pounded.

"It's okay. I understand." The sheriff took a drink from his mug and put it back on the table, all the while keeping an eye on her.

Her father started to get up. She shook her head, and he sat back down. They all stared at her. She swallowed.

"I didn't see anyone on the hillside. Didn't see anyone up there but that old couple, and they couldn't have done it. They were behind us, going the other way. I bet they didn't see anything either."

"The old man saw Rick fall. They'd turned around, watching a pair of cardinals, when he was struck."

Ben looked at his notepad, then flipped pages and readied his pen to take more notes.

Sheriff James cleared his throat. "Danni, do you know of any trouble Rick was having? Any threats? Anyone he thought might have been out to get him?"

She shook her head and concentrated on answering in a steady voice. "Of course, as a prosecutor, that's always a possibility. But he hadn't mentioned anything in particular. His boss, Terry Butler, might be able to tell you more."

"We've talked to Terry. He's going through Rick's files. He's plenty angry, as you might guess, and doing everything he can to help in this investigation. Now, Danni, did Rick ever mention the Viney boys to you?"

The name sounded familiar.

Think.

Yes, he had told her about the case. She couldn't remember the details.

"Some kind of meth ring family operation, if I remember right."

Sheriff James sat back against the couch.

"That's right. Rick sent the youngest to Cummins Prison about a year ago. I guess the kid, just barely twenty-one, became a prime target down there. Got in some trouble right off and hung himself from the top bunk of his cell using a torn up sheet about a month after he went in."

Danni nodded.

"Had Rick mentioned any threats from the family?"

Threats? No. She knitted her brow and tried to think. "No. Had they threatened him?"

"That's what we're hearing. The oldest, Billy Tom Viney, he's nowhere to be found and, from all accounts, is quite handy with a compound bow. We don't know that it's him, but we're looking into it." Sheriff James ran his thumbs over the crease in his jeans on each knee.

"We talked to the other two boys this morning. They claim to have been at the White Star shooting pool all afternoon. We're checking out that alibi, but the boys said they didn't know anything about Billy Tom's whereabouts."

Danni pushed a loose strand of hair behind her ear. She wasn't sure how to respond to that. She'd never laid eyes on the Viney boys, as far as she knew. Rick hadn't mentioned any trouble, nothing he seemed to fear. He had a couple of handguns and had even given one to her. They'd gone to a gun range and shot it a few times. They also had a security system and were careful to activate the alarm at night and when they left. It was already installed when they bought the house. Rick didn't seem to be worried any more than usual about their safety.

The sheriff stood, and Ben followed.

"We'll get out of your hair and let you rest, but we'll keep you up to speed if anything develops."

"Did they find anything in the woods?" she asked without looking up at the sheriff.

"No, afraid not. We've got a pretty good idea of the direction the arrow came from, and we've got deputies out there again today in the daylight looking for any trace of evidence, but nothing so far."

"Okay."

Ben came around the table and put his hand on her shoulder.

"Danni, we'll figure this out."

She looked up. "Thank you."

Her father followed them out the back door. Danni stayed curled up in the chair, staring at the two mugs they'd left on the table.

Why Rick? Why now? Why did it happen?

6

The day I planned to knock another one off my list was beautiful.

The hillside forest grew thick with green foliage and was still a little moist from the lingering morning dew. It wouldn't take long to dry out. The sun was up and poking through the canopy in streams of light and shadows. A pungent smell of composting leaves and forest debris came in waves, alternating with a strong scent of lilacs. Birds chirped and a squirrel clung to a nearby tree, barking a disjointed alarm while eyeing my camouflage clothing.

Avoiding the thickest briars and the steepest part of the hillside, I inched toward the shoreline. A couple of fishing boats bobbed side by side on the far end of the lake. I heard the mumble of voices, but they were too far away to catch the fish tales. Gentle waves lapped against the rocky shore below me.

I turned and noted the route I'd taken down the hill. Staying behind the line of trees that leaned toward the lake, I made my way to the end of the dam. The best spot would be no more than thirty yards from the trail.

I was good, but I didn't want to miss.

A fallen tree, ten feet or so from the boulders that blocked the end of the trail, seemed perfect. A good view and hidden just enough. Afterward, I'd have to run along the base of the hill the way I'd come and then back up the sharp incline. It was the clearest path.

I swung a small backpack off my shoulders and dropped it between my feet, removing a bottle of water and a package of cheese crackers. It could be a long day, maybe a wasted day. But maybe, just maybe, I'd get a chance.

I had to get this right. The first time, anger took over. With this one, I'd have to be precise, use my skill, and make a point.

Mama always told me I could do anything, be anything I wanted. School was a cinch. Professional success came easy. I excelled at every hobby or sport I bothered to try. Chess, swimming, track, wrestling—nothing too team-oriented. I wanted to be the champ.

Relationships, women, no problem. A little sweet talk, the allure of a possible commitment, and I had them eating out of my palm. Play a while and move on. I lost interest pretty quickly. It was the game, not the girl. One had lasted just about a year, but she'd played her own game. Made me think she wasn't that interested. Yet, eventually, she succumbed just like the others. I had her snagged for sure and then moved on. Like everything I put my mind to, I was good at it.

I knew Mama watched as I exacted this revenge. She'd want it to be perfect, not let my anger generate sloppy mistakes. I had to demonstrate *my* superiority to these self-righteous, moralist hypocrites. They had judged my family, and they'd meted out their own justice. They'd pay. Mama wanted them to pay. They'd pay.

My fingers ran along the edges of the grip on the bow leaning against the tree trunk beside me. I'd have to think of it like a hunt. Zero in on the target, and do what needed to be done. I took a deep breath.

"Come on, now. Have some confidence, boy."

She sat with her back against a big oak, her legs stretched out in front of her, her long dress nearly covering her ankles. Reaching down to her feet, she attached a loose Velcro strap on one of her white tennis shoes.

"Yes, Mama." I swallowed.

"Don't let me down, and don't talk with your mouth full."

I wrapped the plastic packaging around the crackers and shoved the remainder into my backpack, then took a long swig from the water bottle.

"I'll get this right, Mama."

I glanced sideways toward her, then looked away.

"You better. You're the only one who can do anything." Her voice was sharp and loud.

I held my palm up toward her. "I know, Mama. I know," I whispered.

"You don't have to worry." She raised her voice again. "If anyone was even down there on that trail, they ain't gonna hear me talkin.'"

I cringed at the grammar. I'd never correct Mama, but it still bothered me. I had to break myself of some of her bad habits years ago. I knew I wouldn't be respected professionally if I talked like a hick. I may have been raised in Arkansas, but I was taught the importance of making the best of what I had. Mama drilled that into me. Even if she didn't have good grammar, she knew to push me to get an education, better myself. Sometimes the pushing went too far.

I sighed. There was no one in sight other than the fishermen on the only two boats across the lake. The trail looked empty.

"Maybe they're not going to go for a walk today. Maybe today's not the day."

"You know it is, boy. We've been watching them. They always take that mutt for a walk come Saturday." She turned and looked over her shoulder. "It's a pretty day. They'll be here. Just have some patience. You ain't having no bellyache over the first one, are ya? It was brutal but had to be."

"No, Mama."

I stared out toward the lake but could feel her eyes burning into the side of my face, watching for weakness. She was always waiting for me to look weak.

"I know what you got up in that head of yours," she said. "Me and Tracey are gone. We ain't gonna know if you do what's right, if you take care of all of 'em. But that's not so. Deep down, you see the truth of it, and you know what needs to be done. You got one. Don't have no regrets on that. It was good, but there's more needs doin.' Let's get the rest. Ain't a one of 'em needs sparin.'"

"I'll try, Mama."

"Now, boy, I've always tried to be there for ya, tried to encourage you to be the best you can. Remember how I called you a special boy, my special boy. You could do anything you put your mind to. I made you go off to that school and get the learnin' to make something of yourself. You did good, real good. I was proud then and always. Now you've growed. You have to do what's right here, be the man of the family. Take care of this." Her words came out fierce, aimed at me, like the arrows strapped to my bow.

I glanced toward her. "Yes, Mama. I am a man."

"That's right, son. You remember that when you aim that thing. You remember what they did to our Tracey. And this one's the worst of 'em. The worst. You remember, and be the man."

"I remember, Mama."

- - -

After it was done and I raced back up the hill, I felt her bearing down at my heels.

"That's a good son," she called out, then whooped and hollered. "Ya did it. Ya did it!"

The wind had picked up and swept through the flowers heaped atop the new grave. The long end of a maroon ribbon danced straight up, collapsed to the ground, and came up again, like a ballerina rising and falling to the orchestra.

Danni's father would come looking for her soon. She had spent nearly every waking minute of the last two days sitting on that granite bench. Her brother, Shane, who'd died in a car accident when she was a teenager, was buried not far from Rick's spot. Her eyes moved from his granite memorial to the small, metal, temporary marker for Rick.

Her father kept a dozen burial spots reserved for their family in the prettiest, most private corner of the cemetery. She was raised in the house next to the sprawling grounds. Her family had run the funeral home and cemetery for generations, but familiarity with the business of death didn't make it any easier when you had to bury one of your own.

The previous week was a blur. She'd gone through the motions of making arrangements for Rick's funeral, sat quietly staring ahead throughout the church service, shook hands with more than a hundred people who attended, and collapsed afterward back at her parents' house without shedding a tear.

Her mind raced from memory to memory of Rick. She couldn't think about the day he died and couldn't think about the future. She desperately wanted to hold on to his scent, the sound of his voice, the feel of his touch, the way his laughter made her smile, no matter what was going on. He had a way of lightly running his fingertips along her forearm when she talked, all the while listening intently. Not trying to distract her, but letting her know he couldn't keep his hands off her. He'd even reach out in the middle of the night and find her hand, pulling it between them and entwining his fingers in hers.

It was all gone. Gone in a flash. Gone with the tip of an arrow ripping through his flesh.

Danni ran both hands through her hair, clutched the back of her neck, gripped her head between her bent arms, and pulled it toward her lap. She sat hunched over for a minute, then straightened and shivered. It was time to go back to the house, maybe try to help her dad with supper.

She stood and turned toward the house but was surprised to see Michelle, a fellow reporter and good friend, walking her way. She wore bright-green, yellow, and purple paisley pants with wide legs that swept around her as she walked. Her top was a matching purple wraparound with a plunging neckline. A long, yellow beaded necklace draped in two strands down to her waist and matched the yellow wedge heels she teetered on as she crossed the lawn. Danni loved her style, but she could never pull off that kind of wild clothing.

"Hey, girl."

Michelle's long, blonde hair whipped across her face in the wind. She pulled it aside.

"Hi." She smiled.

"I hear you're needing to get out of here for a little bit. Want to go for some pizza or sushi? My treat." Michelle came up beside her and wrapped an arm around one elbow. "I'm not taking a 'no' on this, unless there's some great excuse. I'm talking asteroid heading for Earth, got to save a baby from drowning, kind of excuse."

Danni shook her head and snorted a chuckle, the closest she'd come to laughing in a week.

"There we go. I'm thinking a bottle of wine or maybe a margarita, or three, is definitely in order."

Michelle stood a few inches taller than her, most of it in her long legs. Clutching Danni's arm the way she was, she forced her to walk a little faster than her feet wanted to shuffle. Her legs warmed up to it.

Back at the house, she changed into a button-down shirt, tucking it into a clean pair of jeans, and put on a pair of black ankle boots. Someone had retrieved her makeup from the house. She dabbed cover stick under her eyes and added a little mascara before combing out her hair and calling it good.

At the closed bedroom door, she twirled her engagement ring a few rounds, then took a deep breath before opening the door.

"She'll be okay. She's strong, just needs to get past this and realize life has to go on." Her father talked in a hushed voice. "I can't have her slipping away mentally, like her mother. I don't know what I'd do."

She stopped in the hallway and listened.

"Does she want to go back to the house? She can't just leave everything behind, Addison. She's supposed to be starting at the *Daily Times* soon, but I don't think she's even told Paul at *The County Sun* yet." Michelle's voice sounded a little panicky.

"Well, that's up to her. She may not want to change jobs just yet. That might be too much." Her father paused. "I told the realtor to take the sign down in front of the house downtown. She could want to go back there. The new place is so big, may have too many memories. But we'll have to let her make the decision."

They both turned when she stepped into the living room.

"Well, lookie there. She has risen from the dead." Michelle's mouth hung open. "Oh, shit. I'm so sorry, honey. I didn't mean . . . Dammit."

"It is what it is." She smiled and shook her head. "Let's get out of here."

They sat in a high-backed booth at Casa Sushi, listening to oriental instrumental music as they read the menu and ordered. After the waitress brought the small cups of sake and bowls of clam miso soup, Michelle batted her big brown eyes and cocked her head to one side, as if posing a question but not saying a thing.

"What?" Danni asked.

"You tell me. I know this is hard, but girl, you're strong. You can and you will get past this, get on with your life."

"What am I supposed to be doing? It's just been a week."

She slumped against the back of the red vinyl bench seat. Michelle sighed.

"You know exactly what you're supposed to be doing. Get up off your ass, get back to work. We don't call you 'Danni Deadline' for nothing." Michelle offered a quick grin with raised eyebrows. "You also need to figure out where you're going to live, and get it done. It's exactly what Rick would want for you. You keep going like you are, a week becomes two, three, a month, and on."

Danni took a drink from the tiny ceramic cup with no handles. The sake tasted strong. The warmth spread down her throat and went right to her head. She sipped again, put down the cup, and twiddled her fingertips against the side.

"I know."

She stared at the cup.

"You know. Well, that's good. So when are you going to do something?"

Michelle leaned closer.

Her best friend obviously just wanted the best for her and probably hurt to see her grieving, but she could never understand. No one could. There was more pain than even she could really comprehend. How could she go on? How was there another day with the sun coming up? How could people laugh and go on—run errands, go to work, carry on with their lives as if the world hadn't changed?

A loud clatter of dishes forced her to look up. In the far corner of the restaurant, a busboy in a white bib apron looked embarrassed. He had knocked his tub full of dirty plates and glasses off the edge of a table but caught it sideways before it hit the floor. He tilted it back up on the table and dabbed at the liquid that had sloshed across the front of his apron.

The commotion apparently didn't draw Michelle's attention. She still stared at Danni.

"No one's saying you have a time limit on mourning someone. I'm not trying to get you to forget about Rick, or forget what the two of you had together. But you can't just hide out at your parent's house and not move forward."

"I know," she muttered and stirred the soup she hadn't tasted.

She glanced at Michelle, who sipped soup from her own spoon.

"You know I only want good things for you, girl. I hate that this has happened. You're supposed to be starting a new life, starting a new job pretty soon, and a big chunk of its been yanked away. But you got to pick up and go on, figure it out from here."

She sighed. "Maybe I should move back to my place. The new house is great. It's beautiful, but there's so much of Rick there, so much of our life together, and Dad has a point. It's too big for just me."

Michelle reached across the table and patted her hand.

"Whatever you want, Danni. But see there, you've made a decision on something at least. That's one step forward. Now what about the job?"

She pursed her lips. "I haven't given notice to Paul yet, but I guess. It's a good opportunity. Rick wanted me to take it. I just don't know."

Michelle gave her a wide-eyed "what gives?" look.

Before she could respond, the waitress shuffled toward the table and placed two long plates in front of them. They declined more sake. Danni removed the paper wrapping on her wood chopsticks and pulled them apart. Michelle was already plopping a piece in her mouth while she picked at her own, moving a sushi roll to its side and pushing it through the orange sauce drizzled in loops across the plate.

"Have you heard they have a suspect?" Danni asked without looking up.

Michelle put down her chopsticks and dabbed at her mouth with the white cotton napkin she pulled from her lap.

"I've heard. I'm not covering the story. The editorial board thinks I'm too close to it. But I've heard."

"I guess they can't find the guy. They think he threatened Rick over some meth bust. His name's Viney. I can't remember his first name. Actually, it's one of those two-word country names. Billy Bob or something."

Michelle twisted in the booth. "You shouldn't worry about it, Danni. Just let the police handle that."

She nodded and took another sip of her sake. It had cooled and wasn't as good.

"I wonder why they call this place Casa Sushi. What a stupid name. You'd think they had sushi tacos on the menu."

Michelle looked around at the oriental decorations and snorted. Danni shrugged and took a bite of her roll. She was still chewing on the tempura shrimp when Michelle dropped her chopsticks and clapped her hands together.

"Trevor." She put her napkin on the table and slid out of the booth, a big grin on her face. A tall, thin man in jeans and a brown blazer gave her a hug. "Trevor, you remember Danni, don't you?"

Trevor who? He looked familiar, but she couldn't place him.

"Danni, yes, it's good to see you. I'm sure sorry about your loss. I hadn't had the pleasure of meeting the assistant district attorney, but I understand you were engaged." He patted her on the shoulder.

She *was* engaged? Her hands curled in her lap. She fingered her ring.

"Maybe you don't remember me. Trevor Daniel, from Little Rock."

"Oh, Trevor. Political reporter, right?" She made an effort at a smile. "How are you?"

"That's right. Yes, I'm good. I'm getting settled, taking things as they come."

Michelle had a grip on his elbow. "Trevor's covering politics for us now. I thought I told you. I think he's been here almost a month."

He must be covering more than politics the way she is grinning and clutching on the guy.

"Well, don't let me disturb your lunch, I've got an interview meeting me here." He looked toward the entrance, then turned to Danni. "Oh, Danni. Did you hear about Ronnie P. Hutchens? I know you wrote some stories about him in Little Rock."

Danni shook her head.

"He's missing. Wife reported it. They're not sure what happened. Might have taken off for some beach somewhere, I guess." Trevor stared down at her.

"I hadn't heard." She shrugged.

"She's been a little preoccupied, Trevor."

Michelle clasped his arm. He patted her hand.

"Sorry, Danni. I guess it doesn't matter. He'll turn up."

Michelle released her grip on his arm and smiled at Danni.

"Here's my interview now." Trevor waved at a rotund man in a three-piece suit coming in the door. "I'll call you later." He kissed Michelle on the cheek. "Nice to see you, Danni." He headed toward an empty table with his guest.

Michelle slid back into the booth. "Sorry he got into that stuff about Hutchens."

"No worries. I hadn't heard, though. I didn't think his marriage would last, anyway, after all the scandal. Didn't expect him to just disappear, but I guess he doesn't have a job holding him to Little Rock anymore."

"I doubt the state would hire him back after everything that happened while he was at the Highway Department."

Michelle took a drink of her margarita and glanced across the room toward Trevor.

"So, I guess you two are an item?" Danni asked.

"Let the cat out of the bag, didn't we? I meant to tell you, but I hadn't had a chance with everything that's happened." She looked down at her lap and blew out a breath.

"It's okay. You don't have to worry about me." Danni picked up her chopsticks, put another piece of her tempura roll in her mouth, and chewed. "I'm glad if you're happy."

Michelle smiled and shrugged. "So far, so good."

"I worked with Trevor but really didn't know him beyond the newsroom."

Michelle grabbed a piece of sushi roll between her chopsticks and held it in midair as she talked.

"Well, I don't know where it's going, but I'm having fun. We've got a lot in common. The job, of course, but more than that. He likes art, and we both *love* to listen to live music, about any kind. He actually plays the violin. Mostly highbrow stuff, but I like to watch him play. He gets such a serious look on his face." She popped the sushi in her mouth.

"You've been seeing each other a while then?"

"We met two years ago at the Associated Press annual banquet in Hot Springs. He's kept in touch, Facebook and email mostly. Then, when he came up here to interview for the position on our staff, we went out and, well . . ." She shrugged and waved her chopsticks in the air before stealing a glance toward Trevor on the other side of the dining room.

"I can't believe you didn't tell me before."

Michelle leaned over her plate. "You were so busy with the wedding, and I really wasn't sure how much of a thing it would be. You know me and men. Then, with what happened to Rick. I didn't want to tout my happiness while you're so miserable."

"I'm going to be okay, Michelle." She put her napkin on top of the half-eaten sushi and pushed the plate aside. "I just need some time to figure out where to go from here."

"I know you're stronger than you think you are."

She sighed, nodding her head but not as confident as her friend.

"Danni."

The bed dipped as her father sat down on the edge. Blinking a couple of times, she finally opened her eyes.

"Good morning."

"Morning," she muttered. "What time is it?"

The room was dark. Rain pelted against the window.

"Technically, still morning, but it's after eleven." He stood up and looked down at her. "Why don't you get up and eat some lunch with me? You've been in this bed since yesterday afternoon. No dinner, no breakfast. It's time to get up. Aren't you hungry?"

She shrugged and pushed her fingers through her hair.

"I need to go to the bathroom."

"Okay, that's a start." He pulled open the top drawer of the bureau next to the bed, then tossed his hands in the air and turned back toward her. "I don't know what you need here, but take some clothes with you. Get a shower, and then come have some lunch. I want to talk with you."

She sat up and just looked at him.

"Come on. Put your feet on the floor, and let's get a move on. I insist, will stay here until you're moving."

He hadn't talked to her like that since she was a teenager. The stern look on his face just reiterated the point. He turned toward the door and waited until she stood up, then he walked out, leaving the door wide open.

After grabbing some clothes and shuffling off for a shower, Danni eventually joined him in the kitchen.

"Thanks," she said when he placed a bowl of tomato soup in front of her. She crumbled a handful of crackers into the steaming bowl and stirred.

"Want some tuna?"

"This is fine."

"I made it with sweet pickles and toasted the bread, just the way you like it."

She smiled. "Okay, maybe a half."

He cut a sandwich in half on a paper plate and slid it toward her.

"Just eat half if you want."

Neither of them spoke as they ate. Her father dipped his toasted sandwich in the soup and tilted his head to one side, taking a bite from a dripping corner. He grabbed the roll of paper towels from the middle of the table and yanked one off, then wiped his chin where tomato soup had dribbled.

"Whooee, that's good comfort food for a miserable day like we got going on here."

She took a sip of the milk he'd sat out for her. Stealing a glance at him, she found him staring at her and turned away, bumping her front tooth on the edge of the glass.

"Danni, this has to stop. You need to go get some help. It's breaking my heart to see you like this."

Avoiding his eyes, she took another sip. He was right. She needed to get out of that house, stop sleeping all the time, and figure out what to do from there. How could she go on? What was the point? A lump grew in her throat. She took a deep breath and looked up at the ceiling, trying to keep from crying.

"I love you to pieces, Sis. You know that. And I understand that it's hard to think about a future without him, but you have to. It's been two weeks now. The longer you stay like this, the harder it will be to move on."

Thunder rolled in the distance, and they both looked toward the window over the kitchen sink where the rain ran in streams against the glass. Her father put his hand over hers and squeezed.

"You know Rick wouldn't want this. He wouldn't want you staying in bed."

She nodded. She'd tried a few days before to think of what Rick would want her to do, but she'd made the mistake of looking at a calendar and realized it should have been their wedding day. She'd hardly crawled from the bed since then.

"You've got to pull it together. Heck, next thing you know, I'm going have to set up another sewing machine."

"I'm not that bad, am I?" She snorted.

He shrugged. "I hope not. I'm not sure I could deal with it, but I certainly don't want to try."

"Oh, Dad. I know you're right. I just can't think about it, not sure I'm ready yet to think about it." She let out a heavy breath, sputtering her lips.

He squeezed her hand again and let go. "Well, the only way to know is to start by putting one foot in front of the other. Take some baby steps."

"Baby steps." She sighed. "Yes, baby steps."

"Okay." He grinned.

Throwing her head back and running both hands through her still damp hair, she sighed.

"Where should I start?"

"Well, let's figure out where you want to go. Your old house, or the new one?"

She snorted. "That doesn't seem like a baby step."

"Well, maybe not, but first things first."

"You just want to get rid of me," she teased.

He shook his head. "Never in a million years. I just know you're not going to move on if I allow you to keep staying here in that bed."

"Okay, then I guess I'll go to the new house for now. All my things are there."

She hesitated, a million thoughts running through her head. Rick's things were there too. She'd need to do something with his clothes. Maybe she should go to her old house. There were fewer memories. They hadn't lived in the new house long, but long enough that she'd always think of it as theirs—the place where they were going to live out their married life together.

"Do you need help packing up and going home? I don't want you to be alone there if you're not ready for it."

He began clearing off the table.

"I think I can manage that, but I'm really not sure I want to stay for long. It would probably be best if I go back to the house downtown. I was close to everything, and the new house is really too big for me on my own." She sighed. "I still have plenty of furniture at my old place. It's sort of staged for the sale."

He leaned back against the counter and wiped his hands on a dishtowel.

"Okay, good. We can get you some boxes and start moving you back over there. Now, Sis, you are absolutely welcome to stay here a while longer until you get things moved over there, if you like. I'm not kicking you out." He grinned. "Just kicking your butt in gear."

"I know, Dad. Probably should stay there a day or two so I can see what all I need to get done and just do it."

She brushed some bread crumbs from the table, pushed her chair back, stood up, and stretched.

"Lookie there, the rain has stopped. We're going to get some sunshine today after all."

He gave her a hug.

The sun was shining when Danni pulled out of the driveway and onto the highway. The white cemetery gates in the rearview mirror looked like soldiers watching over her passage. The car was loaded down with her clothes and everything that had migrated to her parents' home over the past couple of weeks.

It would be hard, but her dad was right. Baby steps. One task after another, and pretty soon she'd be getting through the days. Getting through the days, the best she could do for now. That's what it would take.

She came to the light at Maple Street and planned to go straight, toward the house, and get things organized. Instead, she turned left and found herself headed to the courthouse.

"It is what it is," she mumbled to herself.

Pale skin and dark circles under her eyes greeted her when she pulled down the visor mirror after parking. She ran a brush through her hair, dabbed on some cover stick to hide the raccoon eyes, and swiped her lips with a light lipstick.

Better. Presentable at least.

The third floor bustled when she stepped out of the elevator. A small conference was going on in one corner of the reception area. A young woman Danni didn't recognize sat behind the desk.

"I can ask him to call you again. That's the best I can do." The girl, a phone tucked into her shoulder and her hair swept to one side in a long brunette braid, rolled her eyes when Danni stepped up to the counter. "You can try to send him an email if you like, but I can't force him to call you back."

The receptionist tossed her pen down on the desk blotter.

"Ma'am, I understand you're frustrated, but maybe, just maybe, this *is* his response, and you should talk with your own attorney about it."

She paused and held up a finger signaling she was almost done with the call. Danni gave her a sympathetic smile.

"Ma'am, I do understand. Yes, I will give him the message. You have a nice—" Holding the phone out, she looked at it, raising her eyebrows. "Or not, I guess." She put the receiver back in its cradle more gently than Danni would have and shrugged. "And how may I help you?"

"Is Terry Butler available?"

"Let me check. Can I tell him who's asking?"

"Danni Edens. He knows me."

The girl's eyes widened. She ran her fingers over a green rubber Gumby toy next to the desk pad, then picked up the phone again and pushed a button.

"Mr. Butler, Danni Edens is here to see you." She smiled up at her. "Yes, sir." She pointed down the hall as the phone buzzed again. "He said you can come on in. His office is the last door on the left."

"Thank you."

Danni wasn't sure the girl heard her. She was already answering the next call.

A strong odor of lilac air freshener, or maybe a scented candle, hit her as she passed an open door. She paused in front of Terry's office, staring at the closed door across the hall. How many times had she come down this corridor and traipsed in there? How could things have changed so fast?

Taking a deep breath, she reminded herself: *baby steps.* She turned and entered the county prosecutor's office.

"Danni, it's so good to see you."

Terry came around his massive dark-mahogany desk and wrapped his arms around her shoulders. Her purse slid down her arm and hit the floor as she tried to hug him back.

"Oh, sorry about that." He bent as much as his round, short body would let him but managed to pick up her bag and hand it back to her. "Here you go. Now, sit, sit."

He waved at the two leather chairs facing his desk and waddled back to his own chair, plopping down and pulling himself forward. He looked taller sitting on the other side. He probably kept the chair at its maximum height just for that purpose, but he might need a footstool under the desk if he did.

"Can I get you anything? Coffee? Soda?"

She shook her head. "No, I'm good."

With his elbows on the desk, he steepled his fingers in front of his lips and then pulled them away.

"I guess you're wondering what's going on with the investigation."

"I am."

He leaned back in his chair. "We've finally got Billy Tom Viney in custody. Caught him with all the makings of a meth lab in the trunk of his car. No surprise there. He doesn't claim any big love for Rick Turner but says he wouldn't have hurt him. Claims he doesn't even own a compound bow anymore, and that he's got an alibi." He sighed, then continued. "We're having a little trouble confirming that alibi, but we're holding him on the meth charge anyway. We've got two detectives working this hard. Should know something regarding the alibi shortly, possibly today."

"What's your gut feeling about him?"

"I haven't interviewed him myself. I will if the alibi doesn't shake out, but one of the detectives isn't sure this guy cares enough about anything to take the time to act. He agrees Viney has spouted off about Rick in the past, but he's convinced it's all blow, and he's being honest about not being involved. Apparently, the alibi might net his buddy in the meth operation. Our detective Don Nelson said he doesn't think

Viney would rat on the guy if it wasn't for a possible murder charge hanging over his head."

Terry sat up, slipped his reading glasses on, and pulled a file folder from beneath a couple of others on a stack to his left.

Danni twisted her mouth to one side and chewed on her bottom lip, the waxy taste of lipstick surprising her. It had been a while since she'd worn any. She ran her tongue over her teeth in case any lipstick had rubbed off there.

"We are looking into other leads. Rick was a fair prosecutor, yet you can't help but make a few enemies in this business."

"I'm sure," she muttered.

Terry eyed her over the top of his wire framed glasses. "I'm sure it's the same for reporters. Just part of the job."

She didn't respond.

He flipped a couple of pages in the file.

"We do have another possibility we're looking into. There's a father whose daughter was allegedly raped last year. Rick made a plea bargain with the accused that didn't sit well with Daddy. Honestly, Rick was right in taking the plea. There just wasn't enough evidence. And the daughter didn't have the most stellar reputation. That shouldn't be a factor, but it is. Unfortunately, when it comes to rape cases, the defense almost always attacks the victim. Her credibility wouldn't have stood up. Rick did his best to pursue it anyway, but then her story started changing, and we were forced to get what we could."

"So you think the father would kill Rick for taking a plea and not going to trial on it?"

He nodded. "It's possible. Seems an extreme reaction, but we're checking on any archery connection. Half the deer hunters up here have compound bows. There's an archery course, Arrow Dynamics, east of town that has a substantial clientele, from what I understand."

"An archery course?"

"They have close to forty acres with trails and fake targets for bow-hunting practice. They say it's quite a set up. They offer classes and have a big retail shop where you can get all sorts of bows and other paraphernalia for hunting."

Danni sat forward on her seat. "Was the arrow unique? Would they recognize it, know who might use that kind?"

"Now, Danni." He took off his glasses, tossed them on the desk, and leaned forward. "You don't need to worry about all that. We have the two best detectives in the county working on it. They're on top of it. And I've told the sheriff to give them all the support they need to make sure this investigation ends in a successful prosecution. You need to trust that's happening and know that I'll accept nothing less. The entire sheriff's department is in agreement on this. They considered Rick one of their own."

"I'm sure they did, Terry." She slumped against the back of the chair. "I just, well, I just want to, I want to know what's going on. I want to know everything that can be done is being done."

Terry nodded, then pulled himself out of his chair and tottered over to her side of the desk. Leaning against one corner, he crossed his arms, resting them across his ballooned middle.

"You know I'm not going to keep anything from you. As soon as we know anything for sure, you'll be the first person I'll notify."

She took a deep breath and closed her eyes. Running her fingertips across her forehead, she said, "I know you will. I just want it to be over and whoever did this rotting in jail."

Terry patted her on the shoulder. She opened her eyes.

"You can count on that, Danni. We want to make sure we cover all the bases on this one, so it will take some time."

Pursing her lips, she nodded.

"Now, would you like to get any of his personal things from his office? We've been going through the files, so it's kind of a mess in there, but you're welcome to get anything personal you'd like."

She shot a look toward the door over her left shoulder but wasn't sure she was ready for that yet. Moving his things from the place where he'd spent each workday seemed so final.

"Ummm. I really, well, okay. I guess I could gather up some of his things. I'm headed to the house."

"It's up to you. If you're not ready, it can certainly wait."

She stood, clutching her leather bag against her chest.

"No, I need to do it and might as well."

Baby steps.

She really didn't want to walk in that room and not see his face light up, not see him with his feet on the desk and a file in his lap as he held the phone with a raised shoulder and waved to her to come in.

She had to do this. She *could* do this. She could box up his photos and personal things.

Don't think. Just take another step. Baby steps.

11

Rick's office chair creaked as Danni rocked back. She picked at some loose stitching on one of the brown leather arms. He'd probably absentmindedly pulled the thread. He was always doing something like that—keeping his hands busy, fiddling with some gadget, often playing with a yo-yo or bouncing a ball against a wall. She pulled the desk drawer open and smiled. Sure enough, a yellow yo-yo, a couple of small rubber balls, and a Bill Clinton bobblehead doll were among the pens and paperclips.

She closed the drawer and opened it again, pulling out a string of paperclips linked together. Running her fingers along the links, her stomach knotted. She took a deep breath, then tossed the paperclip chain back in the drawer.

Terry had left her alone to gather Rick's personal items. The file drawers were empty, along with the bins on the side of his desk that were usually stacked nearly a foot high with case folders. The staff had apparently pulled his files to go through as part of the investigation or to finish up work left undone.

She swiveled around in the chair, then tossed one of the balls against the wall between the window and Rick's framed law degree. It bounced back higher than she expected. She had to stretch to catch it, grabbing the edge of the desk with the other hand in fear she would tip over. Cradling the rubber ball in her hand, she stared at it, then squeezed down hard enough that her knuckles turned white, the red rubber bulging between her fingers. She swallowed hard and closed her eyes.

How can this be happening? Rick should be sitting here tossing the ball, casually catching it on the return, the phone on his shoulder, in a verbal spar with some lawyer about a possible plea bargain.

She relaxed her hand and let the ball fall to the floor, then clutched both arms of the chair and shook it several times before letting go. *Baby steps.* She sighed, stood up, and surveyed the room. It wouldn't take much to pack up Rick's things. As if reading her thoughts, the receptionist with the long braid peeked in.

"Sorry to disturb you."

"Oh, it's okay. I'm trying to figure out where to begin."

"These might help."

The girl pushed the door open, bringing with her a couple of file boxes that she sat on a side chair.

"Yes, thanks."

"I'm Kendra, by the way. Kendra Carter. I just started here a few weeks ago. Right before, umm, well, I met Rick but didn't get to work with him for long."

Her face turned red.

Danni nodded.

"Sorry for your loss," Kendra mumbled and took a step backward.

"It's okay." Danni picked up one of the boxes. Placing it on the desk blotter, she began loading the balls and other toys. "Other than the stuff on the wall, it may all fit in this."

The girl picked up a framed photo. "This is a gorgeous picture of the two of you."

She turned it so Danni could see it.

"Thank you. That was several months ago. We were celebrating buying our house. Good day."

She reached out to take the picture, but Kendra held on, staring at it. She tugged a little harder. *What the hell, girl?* Kendra let it go.

"Oh, sorry. I bet it was a great day."

Danni laid the photo on the desk and moved the box to a wooden chair against the wall. Then she pulled a big piece of paper off the blotter and wrapped it around the picture. Rick had loved that shot of the two of them. They'd shared a meal on a blanket in the middle of the living room that night, then made love on the floor. "Christening the house," he'd called it. She was a little giddy from a glass of wine when he took the picture, holding one arm up with his smartphone as they lay on the blanket, their faces cheek to cheek.

She pulled open the remaining desk drawers, adding more of Rick's things to the box. A tie he'd stashed in one gave off a whiff of his cologne. She clutched it to her nose a second before dropping it in the box.

"I, um, well, I wanted you to know everyone here seemed to really like Rick. It's been awful since it happened. I wish I'd had a chance to get to know him better. He was so busy that week I started working here, I barely talked to him. But he seemed like such a great guy."

Kendra twisted her long braid around her fingers, like a pair of brass knuckles.

Danni looked at the girl. There was something familiar about her. Maybe she'd seen her in the office.

"Have I met you before? You look familiar to me."

Kendra blushed a little and absently rubbed her palms together.

"I don't think we ever met, but I'm from Little Rock. I worked in classifieds at the paper there. I used to see you coming and going with the other reporters."

That was it. One of the "downstairs crew," as they used to call the advertising people who worked on the lower floors at the newspaper office.

"Yes, I do remember you. I think your hair was shorter."

"I like it better long." She smiled and flipped her braid over her shoulder. "Well, I guess I better get back to my desk."

They both turned as someone shouted in the hallway.

"You son of a bitch. Y'all don't do anything about that bastard, then you accuse my baby. Who the hell do you think you are?"

The man stood in the doorway to Terry's office, his back filling the space. He waved his arms as he spoke. Terry said something, but Danni couldn't hear it.

"I don't give a fuck what you think. She didn't do a damn thing, but you can bet your ass *I* sure thought about it. Chickenshit lawyer, made my little girl feel like some kind of whore."

Terry talked again, and the man stepped farther into his office.

"Mr. Lendo?" Another voice from the hallway.

The angry father had light-colored hair in a short butch cut that let his scalp show through. Dressed in a khaki coverall with a black belt running around his massive waist, he turned, saw Kendra and Danni, then glanced down the hall before taking a step back and slamming Terry's door.

Kendra reached to close the door to Rick's office, but Danni came around the desk and snatched it from her. Two county deputies rushed down the hall, but she beat them to Terry's office. Lendo swung around when she pulled the door open.

"Who the hell are you?"

"Danni Edens." With hands on her hips, she looked up into the man's angry eyes. "So, did you kill my fiancé?"

12

Mr. Lendo's brows furrowed, and he took a step toward Danni. Terry, who looked tiny next to the massive man, moved between the two of them.

"Mr. Lendo, now let's not get too excited here. We can all sit down and talk things out."

Terry, his back to Danni, waved his palms at the man.

"Who is she? She his girlfriend?" He nearly hissed the questions, then snarled at Danni.

"His fiancée, soon to be wife," she said. "We were supposed to get married by now. That is, until someone killed him." She moved around to Terry's side. "Do you have a compound bow, Mr. Lendo?"

Terry put a hand on her shoulder. "Danni, you need to leave the questions to me and our investigators."

"I ain't afraid to answer." Mr. Lendo cocked his head to the side.

"Everything okay in here? Need some help, Mr. Butler?" one of the officers asked from the doorway.

Terry turned. "I think we've got it under control. Don't we, Mr. Lendo?"

"Name's Barry, and I ain't here to hurt nobody. I just want to make sure they stop bothering Leslie and accusin' her of a bunch of bullshit." He waved his hands in the air again.

"No one's been accused of anything. We're conducting an investigation and questioning a lot of people." Terry turned back to the two deputies. "Officers, if you'd wait out in the hallway, I think we'll be done here shortly. We're going to sit down and have a discussion, a peaceful discussion, and then Barry here is going to be on his way."

The taller of the two cops eyed the man, like he was sizing him up for a tuxedo fitting, then nodded at Terry.

"Yes, sir. We'll be right here if you need anything."

They retreated but left the door open.

"Now, Mr. Lendo, if you'd have a seat, we can talk about this calmly." Terry motioned to a couch and two chairs at one end of his office.

"What's she doing here? She gotta be in on this?"

"She's here collecting Rick's personal items from his office. Is it a problem for you if she sits in on this discussion?"

"I'm not going anywhere." Danni raised her eyebrows and crossed her arms across her chest. They'd have to drag her from the room.

Terry rolled his eyes. Mr. Lendo waved his arms in an exasperated motion, then took a seat in one of the chairs. Danni plopped down on one end of the couch, and Terry sat in the other chair.

"We may be able to clear this up pretty quick. Do you use, have you ever used, and do you now own a compound bow?" Terry asked.

"Ain't got a thing to hide. I'll tell you right now, it was me. You leave my Leslie alone. She had nothing to do with it. I killed him."

He slapped himself on his chest, folded his hands in his lap, and glared from Terry to Danni with his eyebrows raised in a *challenge me* kind of look.

The room spun for a few seconds. Closing her eyes didn't help. She took a deep breath and leaned back against the couch, splaying a hand out in the soft velveteen of the cushion and gripping her thigh with the other.

Terry leaned forward, his hands on his knees, and his belly hanging down just enough to rest between his thighs.

"We can't have you confessing to a crime you didn't commit just to protect your daughter, Mr. Lendo. Are you honestly stating that you killed Rick Turner?"

"Yep. Handcuff my ass, and haul me outta here. I ain't saying anything else cuz I want a lawyer. Y'all gotta get me one. I'm as poor as a cattle farmer in the downtown projects."

He pushed himself out of the chair and held his wrists together at his waist.

Terry struggled out of his own chair and let out a heavy breath, sputtering his lips. When he got to his feet, he put his knuckles on his hips and looked up at Barry Lendo.

"This isn't going to stop us from looking into the possibility that your daughter was involved. I don't think that's the case. We've been crossing our Ts and dotting our Is in this investigation, but this confession might make us take a harder look in that direction. Maybe there is some connection between her and this murder, and you're trying to stop us from looking into it."

"I told you I want a lawyer. Ain't saying another thing."

"Officers." Terry nodded at the two county deputies who had stepped farther into the office. "I guess we need to book this gentleman. The charge is murder. Murder in the first degree."

13

Barry Lendo's confession bothered Danni as much as it seemed to irritate Terry. He assured her the man's ownership of the murder was bogus, and he would be freed within hours. Terry had already called the jail and told them not to officially book him, just hold him until he cooled off and came to his senses.

Nonetheless, she felt a seething hatred that had her shaking. She sat in her car in the courthouse parking lot, the air conditioner blowing her hair back as she leaned against the steering wheel and closed her eyes. Questions had wanted to pour out of her, but maybe Terry was right that it was a waste of time giving any credence to the confession. They hadn't confirmed Lendo's whereabouts to know if he could have even been there at the time.

Consciously trying to slow her breath, she leaned back in the car seat, turned the air down a notch, and watched as people flowed in and out of the courthouse. A sprinkler system in a landscape island in front of her car sent water dancing in a short stream perfectly adjusted to go no farther than the curb that framed the tight cluster of purple and white flowers.

A lump caught in her throat. She swallowed and sighed, then dug in her bag for her sunglasses. Her head ached, and the sun reflecting off the white concrete wasn't helping. As she put the car in reverse, a sharp slap on the window made her jump. Michelle twiddled her fingers when Danni looked up.

"Jeez, you about scared the pee out of me," she said after hitting the automatic window.

"Well, I hope not. That'd make for a stinky car seat."

Michelle smiled, her eyes hidden behind huge black sunglasses. She wore a short white skirt and a black silky top with sleeves that were draped in more flowing fabric than her entire skirt.

"I guess it would. What are you up to?"

"Just the job. Checking for new court filings."

"How's my dog? I was going to holler at you today and maybe come get him. Think he's ready to come home?"

Michelle nodded. "Yep, I'm sure he is. He's just fine. Seems to like the country life. Though, he is a little mopey. I think he misses you."

A woman who'd just pulled herself out of a blue sedan slammed her door so hard they both turned and watched her waddle away.

"I see you're loaded down. I guess headed to your house. Glad to see it, Danni."

Michelle pulled off her glasses and cocked her head to one side.

"It's time. I need to figure out what I'm doing."

"Do you need any help?"

Danni shook her head.

"At least let me bring Bruno down to you this afternoon. Save you a trip up the mountain." Reaching through the window, Michelle patted her shoulder a couple of times, then slipped her glasses back on. "Just give me a call, and I'll swing by with the pooch."

Danni took a deep breath in through her nose and stared ahead.

"You okay, really okay?" her friend asked.

"Getting there, I think." Danni looked up at Michelle. "I guess I need to get home and clear out the cobwebs."

"I tell you what. You get settled. I'll finish up here as quick as can be and go by the office for a while. Then I'll run to the house, pick him up, grab a bottle of wine and some take out. We'll make a girl's night of it. How's that sound?"

"Michelle, you are the best."

"Oh, girl, don't I know it."

She arched a shoulder up, grinned, then turned toward the courthouse, waving over her shoulder as she sashayed off.

Her hand gripped the keys that still hung in the ignition. Danni stared at the house in front of her. *Remember, baby steps.* She turned off the car, grabbed her bag, and headed toward the front door.

The grass was freshly mowed and looked nice. Thanks probably needed to be extended to the neighbors for that. Her hand trembled, and the keys jingled as she slid them into the lock. It clicked, but she didn't push it open. She leaned her forehead against the heavy wooden front door and took a deep breath.

Baby steps. Hell, no, this isn't a baby step. A leap forward, more likely. It still needed to be done.

She pushed the door open and stepped into the house.

It didn't smell right. Something was rotten. Her dad and Michelle had both been in the house over the last few weeks—collecting things for her, watering the plants, and just checking on it. She put her bag down on the sofa and went to the kitchen. Sniffing, she opened the refrigerator, but it was fine. She kept sniffing until she discovered a bag of potatoes in the pantry that had gone bad. After tossing them in the trash, she gathered the bag and her keys and went back outside.

Just keep moving forward. More baby steps.

She dropped the small bag into the bottom of the empty trashcan at the side of the house and then held down the button on the key-bob to her Subaru. The rear door popped up. With a box tucked under one arm, she pulled a rolling suitcase behind her. She went back to the house, taking the long way around the front rather than the stepping-stones that cut across the lawn.

Stopping, she pulled open the mailbox embedded in one of the square stucco columns on either side of the walkway leading to the house. The Post Office was supposed to be holding her mail, but there was a single plain envelope inside. Maybe a note from the neighbors. With the envelope between her lips, she grabbed the suitcase handle and went back in the house. She put the letter on a side table in the entryway and noted that the houseplant in the middle of the table had missed some water and was nearly dead.

It took her three trips to get everything from the car. She dumped the suitcase on her bed and began sorting through her clothes, folding some and putting them away in the dresser. It was hard to keep pushing herself to move forward, but she did it and tried to avoid Rick's tall chest of drawers. She knew what was on top of it without looking. There were three different bottles of cologne (even though he only ever wore one), a black-and-white picture of her in a silver frame, and a wooden tray filled with a couple of watches, two sets of cufflinks, a pin from the Arkansas Bar Association he sometimes put on his suit lapel, and one stray light-blue button she'd promised to sew back on a dress shirt.

No, she wouldn't let her eyes wander that way. She didn't need to.

But then it was time to put clothes in the closet. She opened the door and reached up to grab some hangers from her side, but she turned and looked at his row of dress shirts, his tie rack crowded with colors, his suit jackets at the far end, separated by shelves from floor to ceiling, each wide enough for one pair of shoes. Some held hats, mostly ball caps, instead.

His favorite light jacket hung from a hook to one side. She pulled the sleeve up to her face, breathed in, and closed her eyes.

Oh, Rick.

It was too hard to believe he was gone. She took the cotton jacket from the hook and sank to the floor, clutching the ribbed collar against her face.

His smell. His wonderful smell. It'd be gone eventually, something she couldn't hold on to. Something so Rick, it hurt.

The sobs came in sudden spasms that shook her body. She curled up in a ball on the wood floor and finally let the reality of her loss out in tears, some soaking into the jacket and others forming a puddle beneath her. She sobbed for herself, for Rick, for the release she'd denied since that day she stood on the dam with a blanket wrapped around her shoulders watching the coroner's van pull away. That van had taken what remained of the love of her life.

15

The doorbell rang repeatedly. It didn't register. Danni's frantic sobs had subsided, but she still lay curled in the floor of the closet, tears seeping. All her hopes and dreams for the future had been wrapped up in a life planned with Rick. Now it was gone. He was gone.

The simple tasks of putting away her things, cleaning the house, and taking care of herself needed to be done. That's what Rick would want her to do.

Baby steps.

She wiped at her tears, rolled over on her back, and stared at the closet ceiling.

Big decisions needed to be made as well. All the things she'd tried not to think about over the last few weeks rushed through her head.

Where did she really want to live? This big beautiful home or her old place? Her grandparents had left that house to her. It was smaller and probably the best place for her now. She'd been happy there for the last couple of years. The yard was fenced for Bruno, something she and Rick had planned to do at the new place but had never decided what kind to install. With its three bedrooms and massive kitchen, the house would be perfect for a family. They had planned to wait a few years before trying for a baby—get settled in each other first, they'd agreed. That wouldn't be part of her future now.

A decision also needed to be made about her job. It would be easy to go back to work at the weekly. *The Lovely County Sun* needed her and valued her but could never pay what the daily newspaper could. The benefits were better at the *Daily Times,* and the office was just blocks from her house—the other house.

Rick's voice telling her she deserved the job echoed in her head.

He'd had so much faith in her. Even after she'd told him about her big mistake in Little Rock, the one that got her fired and nearly sued for libel, he'd told her she would go places as a reporter. There was no other place she really wanted to be but Bloomington anymore. Since she'd come home from Little Rock, she'd realized the value in being close to her family. And now, since Rick's death, there was no denying how quickly things can change.

Oh God, Rick's death.

In the blink of an eye, or the flash of an arrow in flight, the world could shift.

The job at the Bloomington paper would be the best choice. She'd have to make an appointment to see the editor. Michelle would be thrilled to have her in the same newsroom. They could encourage each other, like they'd done in college. Never competing, but sharing in the excitement of a good story.

Tears streamed from her eyes again as she thought of how Rick wouldn't be there to share in the thrill of big bylines down the road. She held his jacket to her face again and tried to stop the tears.

"Girl, what the hell are you doing?"

Danni gasped and sat up, dropping the jacket in her lap. Michelle leaned against the closet door.

"I'm, umm, well. I was putting away my clothes." She sniffled.

"I can see that." Michelle smiled. "Looks like you're trying to wash that jacket the hard way."

The jacket was a mess. Wadded up in her lap, it was covered in big wet blotches. She held it up in front of her, then folded it in half and laid it across her legs. There was no way it would go in the wash. She shrugged.

"Well, maybe this is a good thing?" Michelle dropped her big orange purse on the floor behind her and squatted down. "This is the first time I've seen you cry. I was worried you weren't really dealing with all this shit."

She nodded and tears fell again. She wiped at them with her palm, but it didn't help that more came.

Michelle reached out with both hands and pushed Danni's hair back behind her ears.

"You're a mess, but that's okay. You let it out until you're done, and then we'll get you cleaned up."

She sighed, and swallowed, trying to stop the flood.

Michelle dropped to her knees and threw her arms around her. "It's okay. It's okay."

"I know. I'm all right," she mumbled into her friend's hair. She took a deep breath, pulled back, and wiped at her face again. "I'm going to mess up all your blonde curls."

"Pshaw." Michelle rocked backward and waved a hand. "All done for now?"

She hiccupped.

"Well, let's get you up on your feet. How about a bath?" Michelle stood up and held out a hand to help her to her feet.

"I think washing my face is good for now. Maybe a soak later."

She hung the jacket back on its hook and hiccupped again.

"Then it's your choice of hot tea or wine. I brought a big bottle of chilled Riesling. I left it at the bottom of the stairs, and it's not going to be chilled for long if we don't get downstairs soon."

Bruno whimpered from the bedroom behind Michelle. They both turned, and Danni rushed past her friend, picking up the Jack Russell, wrapping him in her arms, spinning, and dropping to the edge of the bed. Bruno licked her face.

"Oh, baby. I missed you too." She giggled and closed her eyes as the dog continued to lick at her face. "Okay, okay. I know. You're home. We're home." Laughing, she fell on her back and let the dog bounce around on top of her, his tail wagging.

"You two need me to leave?"

"Ha. Ha. No. I think we're done. Let's go have a glass of that wine."

She set Bruno to the floor and followed Michelle out of the room.

Downstairs, she first sprayed the kitchen with pine-scented air freshener, explaining to Michelle about the rotten potatoes. She leaned over the kitchen island with a glass of wine in her hand and surveyed the adjoining living room.

"I've got to make some decisions about my life." She sighed. "I could stay here, but it's so big. I mean, come on. I don't need all these bedrooms. I don't need a den and a living room and an office, much less a three-car garage."

Michelle stood at the French doors looking into the backyard.

"The pool is nice though."

She giggled. "We don't have a pool."

"But you could add one."

Michelle turned from the windows and took a seat on a stool.

"I could add a pool at my place downtown if I wanted one. That's a lot of work." She twirled the stem of the wineglass between her finger and thumb. "Besides, you've got a pool. I can go there any time I want, and that's no work for me."

"Ha. Ha. But true. You're welcome anytime."

"Honestly, it's really a better backyard over there. It's more level, better for Bruno, and already fenced. The only thing that's missing is a garage, and maybe I'll have one built."

"Can you afford that? You're down to one income again."

She nodded. "That I am. Well, not even. I haven't gone back to work yet. But Rick took good care of me. Had insurance on this place, so it's essentially paid off, plus he had a life insurance policy. I don't know all the details, but I'll be good for a while. Quite a while."

"And your other place is paid off too." Michelle whistled. "Wow, girl, you are set up. Sell one, and retire if you want. At least go for a long vacation."

She stared out the patio doors. "I need to get busy doing something soon. I have a few things to deal with to get my life in order. After that, I guess, maybe, I'll see your editor about a job."

"Good." Michelle held up her wine for a toast, and they clinked their glasses together. "I'm glad to hear that."

Danni took a drink, sighed, and looked around the room. The way the kitchen opened up into a massive living room was impressive. Sunshine streamed in the floor-to-ceiling windows, highlighting the light wood flooring, the glass tables, the overstuffed comfy chairs and matching brown leather couch.

"I'll have to sell some furniture. My house downtown has a lot of mine still there. We got rid of a few things but left it staged for the realtor to sell it. Now I've got this houseful too. I'll want some of this, but there's no way I'll get it all in my place." Moving into the living room, she pointed at the couch. "That I'm taking for sure. I love that couch. And at least one of the chairs, but I'm not sure both will fit in my living room."

"Those are awesome. Maybe they'll both fit, but if not, you can give one to me."

She laughed. "You got it."

"Oh, goody. These are soooo comfortable." Michelle sank into one. "You really did a great job with this house. It's beautiful."

"Rick actually had a tasteful eye and liked good quality."

She took a sip of her wine and set it down on the glass coffee table.

"Take this stereo with you too. It has a great sound."

"That might be hard. The sound system is built into the walls."

"Nice."

The doorbell rang, and they looked at each other. Danni shrugged and made her way to the front door, Michelle trailing behind her.

It was Trevor. Michelle stepped around her and gave him a quick hug.

"What are you doing here? Trying to horn in on our girls' night?"

"Not exactly. It's only four o'clock anyway. I tried to call you. Got some news that I thought you ladies would appreciate hearing, so I assumed a quick visit wouldn't be a problem." Trevor smiled at Danni.

"Come on in, and have a glass of wine with us, if you like." She stepped back, holding the door open.

"I better steer clear of the wine. I've got a column to finish before deadline." He patted Michelle's hand linked around his elbow. "Nice place." He looked around the living room and nodded.

"Well, it's probably going to be on the market soon, if you're interested." Danni picked up her wine and ran her finger through the condensation on the side of the glass. "I think I'm going to switch to iced tea. Would you like a glass of tea or some ice water, Trevor? I bet I even have some Diet Dr. Pepper in the fridge."

"No, thanks. I'm not staying long."

"Well, I think I'll have more of that wine." Michelle poured a little in her glass. "So, what's the news?"

He took a seat on one of the barstools.

"I was in the newsroom, and Patty came back from the sheriff's office. Apparently, that Viney guy's alibi is a bust. They've officially charged him with Rick's murder."

16

Danni put down the pitcher of tea she'd just pulled from the refrigerator.

"Really?"

"That's what I heard."

Michelle came around the bar and put an arm around her.

"You okay?"

"Yeah, yeah. I'm fine." She pulled another stool out from beneath the island and sat down. "Just surprised. Terry didn't think he could be the guy."

"I wonder what changed," Michelle said.

"I don't know any more than what I've told you," Trevor said.

"They must have already released Barry Lendo. I figured his confession wouldn't last long. He was only trying to protect his daughter."

She ran her fingers through her hair, then clutched the back of her neck with both hands for a few seconds.

It had been a shock to hear Mr. Lendo confess to the murder, and she'd known at the time that Terry was right about him. Still, she'd had a lot of hatred for the man when she left the courthouse. If he truly killed Rick, she had a right to hate him. And if he was lying just because he thought it the best way to protect his daughter, the misdirection had the potential of delaying the investigation and the search for the real killer. Now, it seemed the issue was already resolved. She needed to talk to Terry.

"Terry said he'd call. I wonder what's going on."

Michelle shrugged. "Maybe he just hasn't had a chance yet."

"Sorry, Danni, for all you're going through," Trevor said. "Hope I haven't aggravated your situation by coming here to tell you this news."

"No, no. Glad you did. I need to know what's going on."

Trevor nodded and stood up. "I better get back to the office. Still have a column to finish."

"Call me later?" Michelle gave him a peck on the cheek.

"I tried to call you twice earlier, before I headed this way."

"Oops, I bet my cell's been on silent since I was at the courthouse." Michelle went to the couch for her bag. With one hand stuck down in her purse digging for the phone, she stopped and turned back toward Trevor. "Hey, how did you know how to find this place?"

Trevor shrugged. "You told me what neighborhood she lived in. It didn't take long to find your Jeep. That bright yellow is hard to miss, sweetheart."

Looking puzzled, Michelle said, "Hmmm, I guess the color does stand out a bit."

"Got to go, ladies. Enjoy the evening." Trevor waved.

Danni came around the counter, following him into the entryway. "Trevor."

"Yes?" He stopped in front of the accent table next to the front door.

"Can you let us know if you hear anything more? I'd really appreciate it. Terry Butler will call me eventually, but he may be tied up for a while this afternoon with everything coming to a head so quickly."

Trevor hesitated, looked like he was distracted, and stared at the nearly dead plant on the table.

"Sure. I'll give Michelle a ring if I hear anything. But she better keep that phone on." He smiled and opened the front door.

"The ringer's on now." Michelle waved her cell phone in the air.

Trevor nodded at her and shut the door.

Michelle plopped down on the couch and scrolled through her cell phone.

"Want to take this dog for a walk with me?" Danni pulled Bruno's leash off a hook in the entryway closet and was greeted by a happy dog dancing on hind legs. "I think he wants to go."

"Sure." Michelle stood up and shoved the phone in the back pocket of her bright-red Capri pants. "But I'll have to stop at the Jeep and get my sandals. I'm not about to walk far on concrete in these high heels."

Danni looked at her four-inch heels and shook her head. "I don't know why not."

Once Michelle's feet were properly attired, they started up the street. Danni hesitated at the corner.

"What's wrong?"

"I, umm, I'm not sure I want to walk to the park. We could just walk around here in the subdivision, get him a little exercise."

She stared up the hillside to her left, toward the park and the dam. Would she ever be able to go there without it all coming back to her? She pulled on the leash and turned right. Bruno tried to pull her in the opposite direction. He knew which way he wanted to go.

"I didn't even think about that. You definitely should move back to the other house. Living too close to the scene of the . . ." Michelle stopped and shook her head. "Sorry, Danni. Living too close to the lake and dam would probably be too much of a reminder. I know it would be for me."

"It's okay. But you're right. I thought the same thing."

Bruno gave up on going to the park and trotted ahead, tugging on the leash.

"Come on," Danni said. "Let's go a few blocks and back home. He'll be happy just to get out."

"You know you can always stay with me for a while." Michelle walked backward a few steps, looking at her before turning around and getting in stride again. "I'd love to have you and the pooch. You could enjoy some country air, take long walks along the creek, sit on the deck by the pool, enjoy the mountain view. It might be just the ticket before you go back to work and move, or whatever you decide to do. You wouldn't have to be at the house with all these memories and wouldn't be under your dad's constant eye."

"Thanks, Michelle. I don't know. That does sound kind of nice, but let me think about it."

They spent the next twenty minutes walking and critiquing the houses in the neighborhood, agreeing that hers and Rick's was the nicest.

Her cell phone went off when they got back to the house.

"Terry, I hoped I'd get a call from you tonight. I heard that you've charged Viney."

"We have charged him with the murder."

She took a seat on the staircase. "What changed?"

"His witness isn't supporting his story. Our investigators searched his home and found a compound bow with arrows matching what was used in Rick's murder." Terry took a breath. "Between you and I, I think we need more evidence before this gets to trial, but there's enough to hold him over for an arraignment. We were concerned he might be able to post bail on the drug charges, and he might run. We might never get him on murder."

"You need more evidence? Does that mean you're not sure he did it?" She switched the cell phone from one ear to the other.

"Our team is confident enough to file the charge against him. They're hoping to get a full confession. He's talking but denying it at this point. We'll have to see if that holds out."

"When's his arraignment?"

"Eight a.m."

"I'll be there."

"Now, Danni, you know that's not necessary."

"I want to look him in the eye, Terry. If he killed Rick, I want him to know that I'm going to be there every day he appears in court from arraignment to sentencing. I'll see you in the morning." She pursed her lips and hung up.

"What?" Michelle leaned against the banister, her eyebrows raised.

"Let's eat. I need to be up early for court. I want Billy Tom Viney to see my face when he makes his plea."

Something didn't feel right about Viney. The guy had claimed to have an alibi that Terry thought was legitimate that morning. There had to be more to it. The arrow used was fairly common. There had to be something Terry wasn't saying. What else did the prosecutor have on the guy?

17

Sleep came easier than Danni expected. When she opened her eyes, the sun poured through the window. She pulled back the covers and stretched, then smiled to herself. She'd slept the night in their bed—slept soundly and hadn't even dreamed of Rick.

She left a note for Michelle, who was still out cold in the guest room, and rushed to make it to the courthouse in time for Viney's hearing.

The wooden pew-style bench that lined the hallway outside of the courtroom was packed when she arrived. The echo of voices and at least one not-so-happy baby were nearly deafening. She tried to ignore it all as she shuffled around people on her way to the courtroom.

"Danni. Hey, Danni," a female voice called behind her.

Her mouth fell open when she turned and saw who flagged her down. Elizabeth, her cousin, stood just a few feet away.

"Lizzie, I, uh, I wasn't expecting to see you here." She stepped closer and gave her a brief hug.

"Sorry you are. Sorry I'm here."

Lizzie's blonde hair was frizzier than ever and pulled back with a headband that left it bunched up behind her head, but what was really shocking was her weight. The girl must have lost at least forty pounds, maybe fifty. She was rail thin, her arms looked boney, and her skin pale. Tears welled in her eyes.

It was hard for Danni to remember the last time she'd been around her cousin. Had she been at the funeral?

"What's going on?" Danni asked.

"It's Josh. They arrested him for meth." She sniffled and wiped at her wet cheeks. "And it's all my fault."

"What? Meth? How?"

Lizzie's eyes darted from her to the crowd around them. "I, um. Oh, Danni, it's all just awful."

She buried her face in her hands, her purse sliding off her shoulder and catching in her elbow. Danni wrapped an arm around her trembling shoulders and pulled her into a corner near the elevators.

"It's going to be okay. You and Josh will get through this. Tell me what happened."

Lizzie pulled a tissue from her purse, dabbed at her face, and blew her nose.

"I was so stupid. Shoulda never tried the stuff. He was mad when I did, but I just wanted to lose some weight. I turned into a tubbo after little Shane was born and couldn't get it off. Was hatin' myself. Some of my friends had tried it. Once I got him off the tit, I figured it was safe. Stuff keeps you going, and you're not hungry. But man, after the first time, had to have it all the time."

"That's what meth does to you."

She stroked her cousin's arm while the girl dabbed at a new set of tears.

"I know, I know." She blew her nose again and struggled to find another tissue in the worn brown bag hanging from one shoulder. "Never touch it again. Swear to God, never will, never will."

"What happened with Josh? Did he start doing meth too?"

Shaking her head, she sniffled. "He got pulled over in Little Brook. He was just going way too fast, and the cop had a drug dog. I didn't even know the stuff was in there. Musta slipped under the . . ." Lizzie covered her face with her palms again, the tissue sticking out between her fingers.

The elevator next to them binged, and several people shuffled out of it, none of them paying any attention to Lizzie or her. The lingering odor of secondhand smoke followed the group.

"He wouldn't let me tell them it's mine. He's takin' the blame for me. Says I gotta not go to jail cuza Shane. Oh, Danni, what am I gonna do? This ain't right."

Danni pursed her lips and took a deep breath. "He's a good man, Lizzie, and he may be right. Has he ever been in trouble before?"

Lizzie shook her head. "Never. Had a coupla speeding tickets, but that's about it."

"Good. Well, first thing you've got to do is quit that shit. No more. It's bad stuff and ruining people's lives all over the place."

Lizzie bobbed her head up and down, tears streaming down her face. "Don't have to tell me that. I won't never touch it again, never. I hurt the love of my entire life, and he's the one been tellin' me to stop all along."

"That's the first thing, and you get some help if you need it. Don't try and not make it. There are plenty of programs and support for this, Lizzie. Don't even hesitate to get help if you need it. You could lose that baby. You know that, don't you?"

She nodded again and bit her trembling lip. "I could lose everything. Josh. Little Shane. Everything."

"You need to sit back down and just wait. It's probably not a good idea for you to even go in the courtroom. Let me handle this." She blew out a breath, puffing her cheeks. "Let me see what's going on with Josh. Maybe they'll set bail today."

Lizzie's eyes widened, then a new wave of tears flooded down her cheeks.

"I can't afford bail. At least not more than a couple hundred bucks. I'd have to ask Momma. She doesn't know. Oh, God."

"Don't worry about that yet. You can hire a bondsman who'll take care of most of it. You just put up a little. I can help with that. We're not going to let Josh sit in jail."

"Okay." Lizzie let out a breath. "Thanks for anything you can do to help us. I can't lose Josh. I can't."

Danni patted her on the shoulder. "This is the first time he's been in trouble, so with a drug offense, even meth, as long as he's not charged with manufacturing or sales, he can probably get sentenced to drug court."

"Oh, God. He has to go through that when he's never taken any drugs, and it's my fault." She trembled and gnawed on her bottom lip.

"Let's take one step at a time and figure this out. Now sit back down and try not to worry too much until we know something."

Danni led her by the elbow to an empty spot on the hallway bench while Lizzie wiped at a new batch of tears streaming down her cheeks.

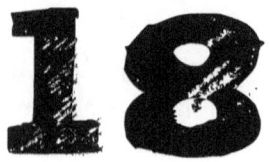

Glancing back at Lizzie when she opened the courtroom door, Danni could see the bones along the girl's spine as she bent over and sobbed quietly. Meth was a terrible drug.

The hearings hadn't started yet. The jury box was full of hand-cuffed inmates in orange jumpsuits. Josh wasn't among them. They were brought to the courtroom in stages, and he was likely waiting in a courthouse holding cell for his turn before the judge. Several attorneys were gathered around a long wooden table, including a couple of public defenders.

She leaned over the hip-high wooden fence that separated the spectators from the attorney tables and judge's bench.

"Excuse me."

A brunette in a black skirt and a sleeveless orange top turned around. "Yes, oh, hello. Danni Edens, right?"

She nodded. "Yes. Just Danni is fine. And you're a public defender, right?"

"Still am today. I don't know about tomorrow." She stuck out her hand for a shake. "Laura Thompson, just Laura. What do you need?"

"Well, Laura. If you don't mind, I need to know who's handling the Josh Dempsey case. It's not for a story. It's personal."

Laura picked up a clipboard and flipped through the pages pinned to it.

"That's one of Albert's cases. Want to talk to him?"

"Yes, if I may."

Laura stared at her for a few seconds, clenched her jaw, as if holding back something she wasn't sure about saying, then turned and pointed to a man talking to one of the inmates in the front row of the jury box.

"There he is. Just a minute. Let me get his attention."

Albert was a short, thin man in a three-piece gray suit with a shiny look to it. He wore wire frame glasses on the end of his nose, which he constantly crinkled up as he talked to the inmate. Laura tapped him on the shoulder and said something to him, pointing with her thumb over her shoulder. He glanced at Danni and nodded, then said something more to the inmate before making his way over toward the courtroom divider. Shuffling through some files he carried in one arm, he said in a surprisingly soft voice, "So you're wanting to know about Mr. Dempsey?"

"Yes, please." She bit her lip. "I'm Danni Edens with *The Lovely County Sun*, but this isn't for a story. It's personal."

"Let's see here." He pushed his glasses up higher on his nose. "We're going to plead not guilty today and see if we can get bail. First offense. It shouldn't be too high, maybe ten grand. He a boyfriend or something?"

"No. He's the husband of my cousin. Look, Mr. uh, Albert. Is that okay?"

"Sure, sure. Albert's fine." He continued to look at his paperwork. "Looks like there wasn't a lot there, but it's still a felony. Nature of the drug and all."

"That's just it. He doesn't do drugs."

Albert looked up at her, wrinkling his nose as the glasses slid forward.

"I know." She gave him a pleading look. "Everyone says that, right? But in this case, believe me, they can test him. He'll be clean. Please, is there any way you can make this go away?"

Twitching his mouth to one side, Albert clicked his tongue. Amazingly, that was the loudest sound she had heard from the man.

"Well, let me see if we can't work something out. Bail may be needed for now, though. Have a seat. He'll probably be in the next round of pleas."

"Thank you, Albert. Thank you."

The public defender nodded, glanced down at her chest, then turned back toward the jury box.

She took a seat but had to stand up immediately when the bailiff called the court in session. She sat through several pleas. All of them pronounced themselves "not guilty" and were taken away, still in cuffs, until they could post bail or wait for their next hearing.

"The court calls Billy Tom Viney. Charge is murder in the first degree." The bailiff's voice boomed.

She gasped and sat up. The reason she'd come that morning had nearly slipped her mind with the worries over Lizzie and Josh.

"I'll represent." Laura stood at the attorney's table.

"And just who are you representing? Mr. Viney, if you're here, you need to stand," the judge roared.

Laura waved her hand, palm up, signaling her client to stand, and a bailiff looked ready to climb in the jury box to force someone to get up.

A man in the second row of the jury box with a smirk on his face moved forward in his seat. Viney, a chunky guy for a meth dealer, finally stood. His dirty-brown hair curled around his ears, and the right side of his face was scarred from what looked like a bad burn.

"Glad for you to join us here, Mr. Viney. Miss Thompson. Do you want to waive the reading of the charges?"

"Yes, your honor, we'll waive."

"What will Mr. Viney plea to these charges?"

"Not guilty."

"Why am I not surprised?"

"Your honor." Terry Butler stood up at a table on the other side of the courtroom.

She hadn't even noticed him before.

"Yes, Mr. Butler?"

"The state would ask that Mr. Viney be held without bond due to the serious nature of this crime. Also, I'd like to point out that Mr. Viney is charged with murdering a member of my staff and has a clear disdain for authority, particularly the police. He was on the run for some time before we were able to track him down for this most recent arrest." Terry slapped a folder down on the table.

"Objection. The prosecution is already implying that my client has a history of such offenses, and his statement about alleged disdain for law enforcement is inflammatory and absolutely beyond the scope of this hearing."

Laura's head shook in short, quick flinches when she spoke, the words spitting from her mouth.

"Your honor—" Terry leaned forward, his hands clutching the back of the wooden banker's chair at the prosecutor's table.

"Hold on here, Mr. Butler. I think we can just put this all aside for this hearing and get on with it for today." The judge took a pen to a document that couldn't be seen from the courtroom side of the bench. "Mr. Viney, we will hold you without bail, and with your plea of not guilty in mind, we'll set a jury trial to begin September fifteenth. That's a Monday. I'm going to reserve this courtroom for that entire week, and we better be done by the end of it. Is that understood, Miss Thompson? Mr. Butler?"

"Yes, your honor. I think the state will have no problem presenting its case and getting a guilty verdict in five days."

Terry made a note on the front of the manila folder he'd slammed on the table earlier.

Laura rolled her eyes. "Your honor, if you don't mind."

"Yes, Miss Thompson?"

"We will be filing for a change of venue. We don't believe Mr. Butler, nor any member of his staff, would or can be fair in this prosecution considering their relationship with the victim in this case."

"File away. Next case."

The judge slammed his gavel.

19

The sound of the gavel still echoed in Danni's head, but the court had moved on to the next case.

Billy Tom Viney plopped back down and slouched in his seat in the jury box, ignoring the bailiff who signaled for him to follow. The bailiff, obviously irritated, stepped up into the jury box and wrapped his hand around Viney's arm, clad in jailhouse orange. Viney gave him a dirty look, shrugged, and struggled to his feet. His hands were cuffed in front of him, and he wore ankle shackles as well, forcing him to move slowly in an odd shuffle.

Danni rose in a stupor, unaware of a discussion between the judge and the attorneys about the next case or the low rumble of whispers and movement coming from the spectators and others crowded in the courtroom—her mind a vacuum focused on Viney, her senses tuned just on him. The sound of his feet moving in the orange rubber sandals. His neck cracking as he tilted it from side to side while shuffling in front of the deputy. The smell of sweat and lingering cigarette smoke.

The deputy pushed open the swinging wooden door, allowing Viney to step through.

She shook her head when it swung shut, realizing she was the only one standing in the rows of spectator benches. Her leather bag had dropped from her shoulder, slid down her arm, and lay on the floor at her feet. A few people around her stared, but the court proceeded with no regard for her stunned reaction. She gathered her purse and picked up an ink pen and a pack of gum that had fallen out.

Exploding from the courtroom, she smacked into someone just reaching for the door.

"Danni?" Michelle stepped back and frowned. "Are you okay?"

Without answering, she turned and pointed down the hall but couldn't say anything for several seconds. Her hand shook in midair. Viney was being escorted by the bailiff toward the holding area next to the judge's chambers.

"Viney," she finally said in a whispered squeak.

"What?" Michelle asked.

She didn't respond but took off toward the other end of the hall, nearly colliding with a woman that had stood up and was headed in the same direction.

"Excuse you, bitch," she snarled at Danni.

The woman wore a short jean skirt, a sleeveless green top, and a pair of wedge sandals.

Danni ignored her.

Viney turned toward them. "Sheila?"

The bailiff pushed on his shoulder, but he shook it off.

"One second, dammit. Let me talk to her."

"I want to talk to him." Danni came up short in front of the shackled inmate.

He looked at her, drew his head back, and frowned. "Who the fuck are you?"

"Hey, now." The bailiff nudged him on the shoulder.

"Yeah, who the fuck are you?" The woman she'd ignored coming down the hallway tried to wedge herself between her and Viney.

"Come on now. We need to move on," the bailiff said.

"Just a minute, Deputy. I really want to ask this guy something," Danni said.

"Reporters can request an interview with an inmate through jail admin."

"I'm not here as a reporter. I want to know why he shot Rick. Why he killed my fiancé."

She glared into Viney's eyes, ignoring the bailiff as she spoke.

The woman stepped into Danni's space, eye to eye, their chests almost touching.

"He ain't kilt nobody. Shut your face, bitch."

"She's right. I didn't kill him. He was a sorry sumbitch, but I didn't do it." Viney glared at her.

"Okay, that's it. You ladies need to move on."

The bailiff grabbed Viney by the arm and pushed him down the hall toward the holding area.

"Come see me, Sheila. These bastards won't give me bail, so come see me," Viney shouted over his shoulder.

"I love you, baby. I will. I will."

Sheila stood on her tiptoes, watching him through the crowded hallway.

Danni glared at her, then turned to leave only to be whirled around when Sheila grabbed her upper arm and yanked.

"Don't you be accusin' him. He don't need to be locked up. Didn't kill nobody."

The woman reeked of cheap, flowery perfume. She stood a little shorter than Danni. Her blonde hair was streaked with several bright-pink dyed strands, and she wore no makeup other than too much eyeliner and a heavy coat of mascara.

"Let me go, *now*," Danni snarled at her.

"Fu—" Sheila started to respond but was yanked away before she could finish, dropping Danni's arm and falling to the floor on her butt.

"She said let go, you dumb bitch." Michelle towered over her with one hand on her hip.

Snickering and light chuckles came from some of the spectators seated in the bench seats outside the courtroom.

"Hey, you got no right pushing me," Sheila shouted, jumping to her feet.

The bailiff who'd taken Viney away rushed back down the hall.

"Ladies, this needs to stop or someone's going to jail," he shouted.

"What's going on out here?" Another deputy poked his head out of the courtroom. "The judge says quiet down or you'll get hauled in here, charged with interfering with the court."

"No problem from us, officers."

Michelle took Danni by the arm and pulled her down the hallway.

"You ain't heard the last from me, bitch!" Sheila shouted behind them.

Michelle hit the button for the elevator. "Oh, brother."

Danni blew out a breath then wiped a palm across her forehead.

"You okay?" Michelle asked.

"Yeah, since you keep rescuing me. Guess I am. Thanks."

They both laughed when the elevator door shut.

"That was hilarious. Who's the skank?"

"Viney's skank, I guess. You sure threw her to the floor."

Danni hit the button for the lobby.

"And damn near got myself arrested doing it."

"Oh, shit," she said and pressed the button for the second floor again before the door opened for the lobby. "I forgot about my cousin. Lizzie's up there. Josh got arrested. I need to help her."

"What? Josh? For what?"

"Long story. I'll tell you later, but I need go back up there. I need to talk to Lizzie and see what's happening with Josh. Let's just hope that crazy ho is gone."

The television blared from the front room. I didn't need to see the images. It was my favorite movie, and I knew exactly what scene was playing just from the sound effects and dialogue. There was enough time to get my sandwich and catch the final scene.

The toast popped up, and I rushed to put together the turkey bacon, lettuce, and tomato. With the plate in one hand and a glass of lemonade in the other, I made it back to the living room just in time.

"Shane, come back."

Tears rolled down the on-screen boy's dirty face while he watched the cowboy ride off into the sunset.

"Good movie. Damn good movie." I bit into my sandwich. With my mouth full, "Damn good sandwich."

I flipped to the news. A camera focused on a shackled man being led down a sidewalk by a Lovely County deputy who had him by the elbow. Another deputy followed.

"Billy Tom Viney, arrested on charges of manufacturing a controlled substance, was arraigned this morning for the murder of Assistant Prosecuting Attorney Rick Turner."

The broadcast cut back to the news desk and a female reporter with thick blonde hair. A photo of Rick Turner was displayed on a screen to the right of the reporter.

"July twenty-first, Turner was struck and killed instantly with an arrow from a compound bow. Viney pleaded not guilty to the crime, but authorities claim to have enough evidence to prove their case. According to a statement of probable cause, Viney, whose brother was prosecuted by Turner and sent to prison where he later committed suicide, had a clear motive for the murder. Viney is being held at the Lovely County Jail. No bond was allowed in the case. A tentative trial date was set for mid-September."

My mouth hung open. I didn't feel the plate slip between my knees and barely registered the clatter when it hit the floor. The second half of my sandwich came apart—tomato slices, lettuce, and bacon sliding to one side.

"Dammit. Dammit all."

I gripped the padded arms of the recliner. A high-pitched laugh that was more of a cackle erupted to my left. I sighed and bent to pick up the sandwich pieces.

"Funny. Yes. Very funny."

"Well, son, if I could, I'd make you a new one."

"I know, Mama. I know you would."

"I ain't done nothing. I ain't," a voice pleaded from the newscast.

I turned back to the screen where the handcuffed Viney spoke into a microphone at his chin.

"You gotta believe me."

The deputy jerked him away from the camera, pulled the door open on the county cruiser, and shoved him into the backseat.

"I ain't!" the man yelled as the door shut. He continued to mouth something, his eyes pleading through the closed window.

"Someone else is taking the blame. That's okay. You know that, right?" Mama nodded.

"I suppose so. I just want her to suffer, Mama." I sucked in a breath through my clenched teeth. "She should be the one sitting in that police car. She should be the one going to jail."

"It's better for you this way, son."

She rocked back and forth a couple of times while smoothing out the cotton apron fanned across her lap.

"But I want her to know she's to blame, that this is her fault."

I wanted her to understand that, if she hadn't made the selfish choices she did for her own career, she'd still have that man in her life. She should be dead, but I got him instead. I just want her to hurt for a while before I get her.

"She's hurting over what you took from her. That's a pain she wouldn't have had if you killed her first."

I wiped a smear of mayonnaise from the wood floor with a napkin.

"That's true, Mama. Maybe I need to make her suffer some more before I kill her too."

"That's my boy."

I hummed a little of the *Shane* theme song and took my plate back to the kitchen for a new sandwich.

Things were good when Mama was happy.

21

Later that morning, Danni leaned against the brick edge of a raised flowerbed, watching a mom and her two young daughters enjoy the gardens on the Bloomington Square. The youngest, a toddler, was a giggler. She smiled and laughed at everything her older sister did. Their antics were so entertaining, Danni didn't notice the county cruiser that had pulled up.

"How are you doing?"

She jumped.

"Oh, sorry. Didn't mean to startle you."

Ben Sizemore touched her on the shoulder and smiled. The sun glinted off his blond hair, making it appear whiter than it normally did.

"You okay?"

She smiled. "Yes, actually, I am. What are you up to, Ben?"

"Shift's coming to an end. I was headed back to the department when I saw you sittin' here."

They both turned when giggles erupted from across the square. The two young girls were chasing after a chipmunk, who scurried back and forth on a stone path that meandered through the flowerbeds, as if it wasn't sure where to go.

"They're having fun," Ben said.

"Yes, they are."

"So, what's been going on? Are you back to work?"

He took a seat next to her on the short brick wall.

"No, not back to work yet, but soon. I just came from the court-house." She sighed. "Sat in on the arraignment for Billy Tom Viney."

Ben nodded.

"He says he's innocent. I don't know what to think."

"You know they all say they're innocent." He cocked his head to one side.

He was right. She couldn't think of an arraignment she'd ever attended where the accused admitted to the crime.

"I know, but Terry Butler didn't think he was the guy yesterday, and now they've found a couple of arrows matching what was used and he's suddenly guilty. Terry said those arrows are pretty common, and Viney's a bowhunter, so it stands to reason he might have that kind."

"Well—"

"I just don't want the wrong guy to be accused of this and the investigation to come to a halt when the real killer is out there wandering around free as a bird."

An old truck rumbled past, leaving a trail of gas fumes that lingered in the air.

"I don't think you need to worry about that." Ben swatted at a cricket that had leaped up on his thigh. "There's a little more to it, and it looks like he's the guy."

"Really? What?"

He pursed his lips. "Probably not supposed to tell you, but, well, there's a cellmate of his says he told him he did it."

She sucked in a breath. "Oh?"

"Let us handle this. You know the sheriff and Terry Butler are gonna make sure this is done right." He patted her shoulder.

"Don't patronize me." She stood up and put her hands on her hips.

"Come on, Danni. I'm not. This is Rick we're talking about. Everybody in the county wants to make sure this is done right. He was one of the best prosecutors around. Demanded what he needed and worked us hard sometimes, but he was always respectful and knew what he was doing. Got the job done. Everybody loved the guy."

She sighed and watched people stroll by before responding. "Yes, well, I guess somebody didn't love him so much. Just hope it *was* Viney, and the arrest sticks."

"Billy Viney did it. And he had no business hatin' Rick. His brother, like that whole damn family, was cookin' meth and got what he deserved. Just cuz he couldn't handle being in prison and took the chicken-ass way out doesn't mean Rick's to blame."

She looked down at a line of ants crawling across the sidewalk between them. Ben stood, placed a hand on each of her shoulders, and turned her to face him.

"Don't worry, we got the right guy. We've been friends a long time. I would tell you if I had any doubts."

She nodded. "Okay. Thanks for reassuring me. I just don't want this to be a mistake."

"It's not."

He wrapped his arms around her, pulling her face against his chest. The smell and feel of him brought back the night she stood on the dam. He'd held her to his chest that night. She shuddered and sucked in a breath. Ben pulled back and dropped his arms.

"I'm sorry. Didn't mean to make you uncomfortable."

She waved a hand. "No, no. You're okay, Ben. I'm just, well, you know."

"Sorry, Danni."

He looked away.

She grabbed him and hugged him.

"It's okay. You're a good friend. Thank you," she mumbled into his chest.

"I better get out of here." He pulled back again and blushed. "They'll end up having to pay me overtime for hugging on you. Do you need a ride or something? I got time for that, if you need a lift."

"Oh, no. I'm waiting for Michelle. We're going to have lunch."

"Sounds nice, but watch out for that one. She's a handful." He grinned.

"Tell me about it." She smiled. "Thanks for stopping to talk to me, and stay in touch. Come by Dad's sometime. He loves seeing you."

"I will. I will." Ben nodded and retreated to his county cruiser.

She waved and watched him back out.

The two little girls scurried past, headed back to the rock path amid the flowers. Their mother followed and rolled her eyes when Danni looked up.

"They are adorable," Danni said.

"Thanks. They're something today, that's for sure." The mom laughed and then hollered at the youngest, "Get your hands off that! No picking!"

The girl had her fist wrapped around a white lily, but she looked at her mom and dropped it. She giggled and ran off, her spiral curls in pigtails bobbing up and down as she bounced away.

Would the children she might have had with Rick have gotten his dark-blond hair or auburn, like hers? It was something she'd never know. It was too late. Too late for so much.

"Danni?"

She let out a deep breath, trying to shake off the thoughts, and turned to see Michelle approaching.

"Hey, girl. You ready for lunch?"

Michelle, dressed in a paisley purple and green dress that hugged her curves, was stunning.

"You bet, but I'm not dressed for anything fancy." She ran her hands along the front of her denim Capri pants. "Nice dress."

"Don't be silly. We're just going to the café. I had to go home and put on something decent for my interview with the mayor. Come on. I'm starving."

"I'm hungry too. Let's go."

During lunch, she told Michelle that she had helped arrange bail for Josh and that, when she left her at the jail, Lizzie was waiting to pick him up.

"When did he start having problems with meth?" Michelle asked.

"Lizzie says that Josh never touched the stuff. Cops found it under a seat of his pickup after a traffic stop for speeding. She said it's hers."

"Good gravy. I can't believe she'd get involved with that shit. What was she thinking? She has a baby, for God's sake."

Danni nodded. "I know. I couldn't believe it either. She's just sick at the thought that she's hurt Josh this way. I guess she tried it in an attempt to lose weight and didn't realize how quickly you can get addicted to it."

They sat in silence for few minutes. She fingered the butter knife next to her plate and hoped her cousin could kick her addiction. Lizzie had been so stupid. Now she could lose everything important in her life with one mistake. Danni could tell her all about the pain of losing what was most important. For Lizzie to lose Josh over her own mistake would probably kill her.

Could she take it if Rick's death had been her fault? She'd rather die herself.

"So, what's your game plan for the rest of the day? Got any other skanks you need me to tackle?"

Michelle took a sip of her iced tea, her eyebrows raised.

Danni laughed. "No, I think I'll steer clear of any and all skanks this afternoon."

"Good thing."

"I thought I might move some boxes tonight, just get some basics from the house. I'm going stay at my place downtown tonight. I'll get help later with moving the bigger stuff."

"Good. Get on with your life."

"I know. It's time. He's gone." Tears welled in her eyes. "I have to make a life on my own again."

Michelle reached across the table and squeezed her hand.

"You'll be okay. You're strong. I know this has set you back. It's been an awful shock."

Using her napkin to dab at her tears, Danni took a deep breath.

"I guess life is full of surprises. Sometimes, though, it feels like, as soon as I get really settled into something good, it gets yanked out from underneath me."

"Oh, honey."

"Really, Michelle. It's not just Rick, but even with my brother, Shane. Just when we were getting close, no longer kids competing for everything under the sun, but growing up and enjoying, supporting each other, and then the car accident, and he's gone." She swallowed hard.

"Then my job," she continued. "When I finally got the position I'd always wanted at the biggest newspaper in the state, I screwed it up and lost everything. Now Rick. Geez."

The male waiter, dressed in a black jeans and a red T-shirt with the café name across the front, stopped and filled up Michelle's water glass.

Once he'd left them alone, she said, "You know things happen in life that we don't expect. Losing people we love is the worst, but you've had a great love. You've enjoyed the adoration of a big brother. Without those memories, without the experiences from both, your life would be less in so many ways. You know that. I'm sure you do."

Danni combed through her hair with both hands, then leaned forward in the booth.

"I wouldn't give anything for the memories of my brother and what we meant to each other. I wouldn't trade anything, either, for the memories I built with Rick. I wouldn't. I won't have him for my husband. I won't have him to love and cherish and make all those promises in marriage. But I will have the knowledge I'll hold in my heart forever that he wanted a life with me, that I was everything to him, and that we made each other happy. I'd never had that before and won't ever again."

Michelle smiled. "Oh, time will tell. There's so much could happen that you can't even imagine right now."

"I know. But we were going to start a family. I wanted to have kids with him, take 'em camping, put a swing set in the backyard, join the PTA. All that."

She looked away, more tears trying to brew.

"Well, you won't have kids with Rick, but kids could still be in your future." Michelle put her napkin on her plate and pushed it aside. "And as far as that job you lost. We both know that wasn't your fault, and you can go to work at a great daily newspaper right here in your hometown whenever you're ready."

Danni dabbed at the corners of each eye.

"Don't know what I'd do without you right now. You've been such a good friend."

"Ah, shucks. You're gonna make me blush."

Michelle batted her eyes and grinned.

22

Her cell phone rang, but Danni couldn't find it among the boxes stashed all over the dining room. She missed the call. It was her dad. He picked up on the first ring when she called back.

"Hey, Dad."

"What's up, honey? I haven't heard from you. Wanted to make sure you weren't mad at me for kicking you out."

She laughed. "No. I needed kicking out."

"Glad you see it that way. How are things going?"

"It's going. Going good, actually." She held one hand on her hip and looked around the room. "I'm at my place. I got some boxes and made several trips since yesterday afternoon. I've got the stuff I really need moved over. I'm going to stay here tonight."

The phone was silent.

"What? That's not a good idea?" she asked.

"Oh, no, no. I was just thinking a minute. Yes, absolutely, a good idea. Do you need any help?"

"Not a bad idea, but not today. I'm done for the day. I'm exhausted."

"I'll tell you what. I'll come by in the morning and help you move whatever else you want to get moved for now. We don't have any services or anything going on this weekend. I'm good to go."

"Thanks, Dad."

"You eating? You've got to take care of yourself."

She laughed. "Yes, *Daddy*. I'm eating. I had lunch with Michelle, and I'm thinking about ordering a pizza or something here shortly."

"Good. Call me tomorrow when you're ready, and I'll bring the truck. We'll get this done."

She moved the phone from one ear to the other. "Okay, Dad."

"Oh, what about Bruno? He still with Michelle?"

"No. He's running around the yard right now." She peeked out the back window.

"I guess it's good you're moving back in over there. I thought I was going to have to build you a fence for the mutt."

She laughed. "Yeah, he's definitely enjoying his freedom to run. Lots of freedom. He's barking at something right now. Better go get him in before the neighbors call animal control."

"Okay. Well, don't forget to order that pizza."

"Don't worry. I'll eat." She laughed. "Love ya."

"I love you too, sweetie. Mom says she loves you too."

"Give her a hug."

She hung up and smiled to herself, doubting her mother had said a word. That thought was interrupted by more barking from the backyard.

"What the hell?" she muttered to herself.

It was darker than she expected. The sun was nearly set, sending a warm, orange-colored glow over the trees at the back of the lot.

"Bruno. Bruno. What's up, boy?" She couldn't see him, but he barked again from the far side of the yard. "Come on, boy."

The fence was set into the side yard about fifteen feet, so she couldn't see him until she came around the corner of the house. He was on his hind legs, barking at Rick's old Scout in the driveway.

"There a kitty cat out there, boy?"

The Jack Russell ran up to her, hopped up, putting his paws on her legs, and then ran back to the fence to bark some more.

"I don't see a thing, boy. Let's go in the house. Here, Bruno, *now*."

He ran back to her, and she picked him up. She didn't see anything he could be barking at, but there could be a cat, or maybe someone had just walked by on their way to a bar on Watson Street. She turned back toward the house but heard a shuffling in the gravel driveway. She held Bruno close to her with a hand clasped on his muzzle, trying to keep him from barking again, and eased her way back over to the fence. Standing on her tiptoes, she could see over the top of the wood privacy rails. Bruno squirmed. She bent and dropped him to the grass. He immediately hopped up on his hind legs again and barked.

A shadowy figure darted out from the other side of the Scout and took off up the street.

She gasped, grabbed Bruno, and hurried back into the house. After locking the door behind her, she set the dog on the floor. It could be someone trying to get whatever they could from unlocked cars. That had happened in the neighborhood before. She would have to look into building a garage sooner rather than later.

The experience brought back memories of a problem with a stalker the year before. The prowler who ran off was probably nothing to worry about. After all, she'd survived a stalker who had made threats and eventually attacked her on her porch in an attempt to make her back away from a corruption investigation.

Rick had come into her life about the same time. She smiled, thinking of his protective nature, how he'd hovered over her when she was hurt.

Pulling the blinds closed, she shivered.

There was no one to hover over her now.

23

Standing to one side of the window, I watched her use a white cloth to dust, tossing it over one shoulder as she manipulated the furniture. Boxes were scattered around the floor and piled on the dining room table and chairs.

God, she is cute as hell. That auburn hair and button nose, and my, my, what a body. Not too thin, but certainly not a fatty. I would love to have some of that, but no way it's happening.

The bitch doesn't deserve me.

I pulled back and leaned against the outside of the house when she came toward the window. Sweat gathered on my brow. I wiped it away and peeked around the edge of the trim.

Music came on. A soft jazz. She appeared to be happy. Dammit. She didn't deserve happiness. She deserved a sharp knife to the gut, or maybe a not-so-sharp knife. Make her suffer. I'd meant to kill her that day on the dam. I'd missed and took the life of the man she loved. It had worked out better than I imagined. She was so close to marrying him, and their happiness had made me sick to watch, but that was gone. I'd let her suffer a while longer and then get her the next time. She'd never know happiness again.

"No, not a lick of happiness." Mama's voice came from behind me. "You know she ain't done nothing but ruin things. Ruined it all."

The woman sat down then, as if she'd overheard the conversation, even though I knew she hadn't. A framed photo in her hands, she stared at it and sighed, then looked up toward the ceiling. She seemed to be trying to stave off a wave of tears. I couldn't see the picture but assumed it was her boyfriend, the ever-popular assistant district attorney turned martyr.

"A few tears. Hmmm, not enough. That girl needs to know some real pain."

"Yes, Mama. She will suffer the most. I'll make sure of that."

The dog sidled up to her, stood on his hind legs, and put his head on her thigh. She patted him on the head, then got up and went into the kitchen. The sound of the back door opening made me jump and press my back against the side of the house again. The door slammed shut. I could hear the dog panting and running around the fenced-in yard.

From the corner of the window, I watched her come back into the dining room and pick up the picture again. She placed it on a side table, bent, and wiped at her cheeks with the tail of her shirt. Lifting and pushing boxes around in a sudden hurry, she found a cell phone, stared at it for a few seconds, then hit a button and started talking to someone.

"Look at her. Just going on with her life. No stick-in-the-gut worries for her."

Mama put her hands on the windowsill and nearly pressed her nose against the glass.

"Looks like she's doing just fine, doesn't she?" I whispered.

"Yes, son, it does. It sure does. And you got to do something about it."

"I know, Mama."

I wiped at the sweat running down the side of my face.

"Don't tell me you know. You need to be *doing* it. You need to take care of this. It's your responsibility, boy."

"I know, Mama."

My words came out louder than I expected, and the dog must have heard me. The mutt started barking, drawing the woman's attention.

She put down her phone and headed for the back of the house.

Mama was already gone.

I dodged behind the older model Scout in the driveway and held my breath.

An edge of a screen panel on the front porch was loose. Danni wondered if such a thing could be fixed as her father pulled up to the curb out front. She held the door open, still gripping the straw broom she'd been using to clear the cobwebs and dust from the porch.

He hesitated before coming inside, staring at the copper-colored Scout in the driveway.

"You've got a flat tire."

"Great."

She leaned the broom against the wood post of the door and followed him to take a look.

"Hmmm." Crouching next to the tire, he picked something up out of the gravel. "This isn't good."

"What?"

"Looks like someone let the air out. Here's the valve stem cover." He held up the tiny black cap.

"What?" *Geez, is that all I can say?* "Good grief. I need some caffeine. Want a cup of tea?"

"Sure. Then I'll run over to the shop and get my compressor to air it up." He followed her back toward the house. "Probably just a kid. You're going to get that sort of stuff living so close to the university."

"Yeah, well, true. I was just thinking that, if I'm going to stay here, maybe I should put a garage in."

She held the screen door open for him.

"That's a good idea, Sis."

They made their way to the kitchen, dodging the mostly empty boxes scattered around the dining room.

"I know you'd rather have coffee. I'll make you some. I left a pot here, just in case the realtor needed it."

She pulled out the machine's filter cup and loaded it with grounds. He took a seat at the small wooden table and looked out the window.

"May need to mow that grass again this weekend."

She heard him carrying on about the yard but didn't pay much attention while filling her teapot with water. Whoever was outside last night when Bruno was barking must have let the air out of her tire. *What a pain in the ass.*

"Hello, Danni?"

"What? Oh, sorry, Dad. I was thinking about that stupid tire and who would pull a stupid prank like that."

"You were young once. Kids are always up to something. At least it's not slashed. But I think the garage is a good idea. You've got plenty of room on that side of the house. Probably get a two-car in there and create a breezeway between the house and there so you wouldn't have to go outside to come in."

"You think?"

"Yep. Let me call Bruce. He'll give you a fair price and get it done quick if he's not too wrapped up in another project right now."

She nodded and poured hot water in a cup over a bag of Earl Grey. The coffee pot let out a groan.

"Always loved that sound."

He smiled and started to get up.

"I'll get it."

She waved a hand at him and grabbed a mug from several that were turned upside down on a towel next to the coffeepot. Just as she sat down, his cell phone rang.

"Hello." He nodded. "Well, hey, Josh. How are you and your little family getting along?"

She took a sip of tea and waited for the conversation to end.

"What's up with him?" she asked after her dad put the phone back in his pocket.

"He's finally quit that job and wants to come work for me at the cemetery. Not sure why, but I'm pleased. Been hoping he'd make that decision for some time. Boy does a fine job at landscaping, and I think he'd be good for us. Wonder what happened to bring this on."

Josh had probably lost his job over the arrest. And he obviously hadn't told her dad that part, but he would have to tell him if he was coming to work at Resthaven. He'd need time off for court dates and maybe the rehab he would have assigned if he went through the drug court system.

"That's good timing. You were just saying you needed more help out there."

"Always do this time of year."

He sipped his coffee, and they sat in silence for a few minutes, both of them watching Bruno rolling a half-deflated soccer ball around the backyard.

"Want to go with me over to the house and get the compressor be-fore we go get some of your things? You could see your mother. She's doing pretty good today. Even heard her humming earlier while she was sewing."

"More pillows?" she asked.

"No, chair cushions. Nothing new."

She put down her cup.

"What? Why is she still doing that? Surely she understands Rick's gone. There's no wedding."

He nodded. "Yeah, she knows, but that's one reason it'd be good for her to get her eyes on you. Know you're okay. She looks sad every time your name comes up. I think she's worried."

"Sure, Dad. I'll come with you. But why in the heck is she still mak-ing cushions?"

He chuckled. "Well, I've put her to work. The lady from the party rental agency liked them. She came and picked up the ones Mom had put together already. Made a trade with me on the cancellation fee. I told her about your mother's situation. Mom actually talked a little with the lady, by the way. The next thing I know, she's bringing her some silvery-looking fabric and other stuff to make more."

She laughed. "Wow. Mom's got a job."

25

Danni's cell phone rang as she meandered along the mountain route to Michelle's. She ignored it. Depending on who it was, she'd call back once she arrived. Cell service was hit and miss on the way up anyway.

Living way out in the sticks as a single woman was a little nuts in her opinion, but Michelle claimed to love it. And the girl certainly had plenty of privacy, peace, and an absolutely stunning view.

There were peeks of that view on the way up—lush, green, rolling hills as far as the eye could see. The south end of Lovely County had gotten rain off and on the previous couple of days, making everything appear a deeper green under the cloudless blue sky. She was looking forward to floating around in the pool and enjoying the promised barbecue lunch.

She drove Rick's Scout, knowing it would do better the last mile or so to Michelle's, where the road was gravel and little more than two ruts in the weeds. It was a struggle to put Rick out of her mind while gripping the steering wheel, knowing his strong hands had held it last. She did the best she could and continued to concentrate on the surroundings.

Still on asphalt, she came around a corner, startling a turkey vulture that took immediate flight and surprised her. She jerked the Scout to the right, nearly ran off the road, but was able to correct, stay on the pavement, and avoid a steep drop off. She slowed. Her heart pounded and her hands shook.

Another vulture stood in the road, its claws clamped on some kind of dead animal, probably an opossum. The bird's head turned, and tiny black eyes watched her drive past, as if she were a parade float on display. Looking in her side mirror, she saw the bird dip its head, grab some of the roadkill with a jerk, straighten back up, and nod as it savored the meal. A second vulture, possibly the one that flew at her car, gracefully landed a few feet away and watched the dining, awaiting his own chance at the asphalt fare.

With a shudder, she turned her full attention back to the road. Those were some of the ugliest and biggest birds around. They served an important purpose in nature, but she hated them.

Not far from the roadkill feast, she made a left on a dirt drive. Michelle's was one of only four or five driveways off the road before it looped back to asphalt. Trees, thicker here, created a shadowed path.

A small white pickup, hugging the opposite ditch, crept along and nearly stopped when the two cars met. The driver's window was rolled down. An arm rested on the door, the elbow pointing out. A dark-haired man stared and didn't return her wave of fingers.

"Hey, dude, I have a right to drive this road too," she muttered and turned in to the driveway.

She came to a stop behind Michelle's Jeep. A newer-model, gray Toyota Camry she didn't recognize was parked next to it. Who else had been invited?

Her cell phone rang again when she climbed out of the Scout. *Terry Butler.*

"Hey, Terry."

"Danni, I need you to come by my office early next week, Monday morning if you can, to discuss the case."

"Do you have news?"

"Best if we talk about it Monday."

"Nine o'clock?"

"That'll be fine."

"You sure you can't tell me more? Is there a problem with Viney?"

"Relax. Enjoy the weekend."

"Sure."

She hung up and leaned her head back against the headrest. *Dammit.* It wasn't going to do her good to stew on the investigation.

"Baby steps, girl. It is what it is," she muttered to herself, grabbed her purse and overnight bag, climbed out, and smacked her butt against the door, closing it behind her.

She heard music from the backyard and walked around the side of the house. The side yard was checkered with holes. Her heel caught in one, and she stumbled just before she reached the covered patio. She grabbed the back of a chair holding a big bag of dog food to keep from falling on her face. The bag started to tumble out of the chair, but she caught it before kibble was scattered across the patio.

"Danni! Are you okay?"

Michelle lay stretched out in a lounge chair, sipping a tall glass of something with an orange tint to it, while Trevor floated in a big black inner tube. His white legs bobbing in front of him looked to be appropriately greased down with sunscreen but were still turning pink. That explained the extra car in the driveway.

"Yes, I'm fine. Just caught my foot in one of these blasted holes."

"Oh, those are from the armadillos. They're making a mess of my lawn this year." Michelle got to her feet. She looked stunning in a paisley print one-piece with a neckline that plunged to her belly button, a small gold clasp between her breasts. "By the way, that dog food is Bruno's. I forgot to take it home with him."

"Thanks. I'll have to take it home unless, that is, you're planning to get a dog. A big dog. This'll last Bruno a month." Danni came around the edge of the pool toward her. "You look amazing."

"Well, thank you." Michelle hugged her then whispered. "Got some new bathing suits this year. Showing off my new figure since I've lost so much."

"You did good. It shows," she whispered back.

"Hey, you two, cut out the gossip. I feel shunned." Trevor paddled toward the ladder. "I bet you girls are about ready for me to start the grill. Michelle says I have to man the barbecue since I showed up unexpected and crashed the party. Hope you don't mind, Danni."

"Not at all. Cook away. We can sit and chat."

Michelle grabbed her by the elbow and pulled open the sliding glass door.

"Come on. Let's get you one of these peach margaritas. They're yummy. It's a little early, but what the hell."

"I think I'd rather have just a smoothie."

"Really? Turning pious on me?"

"Never. I haven't been feeling too great today. A little queasy. Not sure I need alcohol so early in the day. Maybe later. I'm going to get on my bathing suit first."

She took her bags to the spare bedroom, changed, and came back to find Michelle running the blender at full blast.

Handing her a nearly full glass of the frozen concoction, Michelle said, "Drink it slow. You don't want a brain freeze."

The doorbell rang. She put down her glass.

"I didn't know this was going to be a party."

"Not supposed to be."

Michelle shrugged and headed down the hall, her flip-flops slapping the hardwood. She was gone a few minutes and shrugged again when she returned.

"Poor guy looked like he could use a margarita. Some electrician at the wrong house. Think he's on the wrong dirt road."

"Hot day to be lost in the sticks. Must not have heard of GPS." Danni chuckled.

"Don't need it when you can charge the customer for travel time, not to mention the weekend rate," Michelle added.

"Hey, did you tell her the juicy news?" Trevor rubbed spices on three thick steaks.

"What juicy news?" she asked.

Trevor and Michelle exchanged a smile. A party for three was likely planned all along. And he seemed exceptionally comfortable in the kitchen, opening cupboards for spices and plates like he'd done it many times before. Michelle had been holding out. The relationship between the two of them appeared to be closer than her friend had let on.

With both elbows on the counter, Michelle rested her chin on two fists and clicked her tongue.

"You're not going to believe it. We've got a feature writer, been with us a little less than a year, Cole Terryson. He's green, but been doing some decent stuff. Nothing outstanding. Then he comes up with a story about a month ago, in-depth piece about the murder of those twins over in Memphis. Story's from the family's point of view. Anyway, the editorial board is tickled shitless with it. They run it on the front page, Sunday edition."

"Okay."

She ran a finger through the condensation on the side of her smoothie glass and waited for Michelle to finish sipping her own drink and continue the story.

"Go on. Tell her the rest," Trevor chimed in.

"Well, turns out, he stole the whole damn thing, word for friggin' word, from a weekly paper in Memphis."

Danni nearly spit out the drink she'd just taken. Instead, she swallowed and gagged on it.

"Good God, girl. I didn't mean to get you all choked up," Michelle said.

"Went down the wrong pipe," she squeaked.

"They've fired him, and the paper may get sued. The publisher is trying to work out something to settle it right now."

"Plagiarism? I can't believe it. You'd have to be pretty stupid in this digital world to think you could get away with that."

She took a napkin and dabbed at her mouth.

"Really. You should have seen the commotion in the newsroom when they got that call. All the bigwigs huddled in the back office for hours."

Michelle pulled out a cutting board and a knife.

"He needs to never work in journalism again." Danni sighed. "That's the kind of shit that gives all reporters a bad name."

"I agree with that." Trevor put the lids back on the spices and loaded them in the under-cabinet rack. "That goes for libel too. Readers lose their trust. It can really destroy a newspaper, the entire industry, truly."

The two girls didn't respond, but both put down their drinks.

"What?" Trevor looked from one to the other. "Oh, sorry. I forgot. Uh, I didn't mean you, Danni. Sorry."

"It's okay," she mumbled. "And I didn't really libel anyone."

26

Trevor's comment about libel brought back all the feelings of failure, anger, and even embarrassment Danni had experienced when she was fired from the Little Rock newspaper. She ran a trembling finger around the rim of her glass.

"I still don't know what all happened," he said, "but there were rumors that you were falsely accused in the mess, among other things."

He leaned back against the counter and wiped his hands on a bright-yellow towel.

"She doesn't want to talk about that."

Michelle swatted him on the shoulder.

"It's fine. Truth's better than the rumor mill any day." Danni sighed. "I'm sure you heard a lot after I left."

He shrugged. "Management wasn't saying much, so I didn't know what was really going on."

"Well, I will say that I learned a lot through it all. I back up everything now. Photos, recorded interviews, everything. My own ignorance caught me. Somehow, all my materials and proof of the truth were stolen. I had nothing to fight the accusation that my story was false. I could have rebuilt the evidence, but why bother if the paper was so willing to throw me under the bus."

"You've never said much about it." Michelle shrugged. "I was always afraid to ask, but I knew something wasn't right. You're too good of a reporter to libel someone."

"Thanks, Michelle. I'll tell you the whole sordid mess." She took a deep breath. "At the time, I was covering a scandal at the Highway Department. The director was accused of taking some kickbacks."

"That's the guy that's missing, right? Hudgens?" Michelle asked.

"Yeah, Ronnie P. Hudgens. That's what I hear." She shrugged one shoulder and went on. "Anyway, turns out it wasn't a great deal of money involved, but enough Hudgens lost his job, got some charges filed against him, and his wife took off. While he was still waiting for trial, his wife calls me, says she wants to talk. She rats him out for an affair—alleges, I guess I should say, that he was using his state credit card for overnight visits with the mistress."

"Nice, ethical government employee."

Michelle piled sliced tomatoes on a plate.

"Tell me about it. Anyway, he denied it. I got copies of his travel receipts. Pretty clear he had entertained a companion fairly frequently on the state's dime. King rooms everywhere he went. Dinner for two, etcetera. The wife says she'd never traveled with him for business trips. She doesn't want to be quoted but gives me a phone number for the girlfriend. It was good timing because the girlfriend was not a happy camper at the time either. He'd dumped her. Said he had to get his wife back, clear up his reputation, and get rid of the charges. She spilled her guts to me. Confirmed all the travel dates, where they stayed, dined, and more. He still denied it all.

"We had documents, an unnamed source in the wife, and the girlfriend who was willing to go on the record." She shook her head and ran a palm across her forehead. "So the story runs, and a week later he threatens to sue for libel. He and the wife had kissed and made up. She denied ever giving me the information. The girlfriend disappeared, and so did all my notes, the documents, and the tapes I had of the interviews. Somebody had taken all my materials. Like I said, I could have dug up copies of his travel receipts again, but the documents didn't tell the whole story. Without the witnesses, it simply looked like he went overboard a little on travel expenses."

"So he sued, and you lost your job?" Trevor asked.

"Not quite. He threatened to sue, and the publisher agreed to fire me and retract the story. I think, if push came to shove, he would have backed off, and the paper would have won a lawsuit anyway. For a libel case, he'd have to prove malice on our part. He was a public figure. You both know you can only win a libel suit as a public figure if you can prove the paper had malicious intent. I have no doubt he would have backed off, knowing it was all true, and he wouldn't have wanted to see it splashed all over the front page."

"Sounds like the paper rolled over, didn't fight it." Michelle twisted her mouth to one side in a smirk.

"I think so. Of course, I was the one losing my job. My dream job. I'd worked my ass off to get on at the *Arkansas Republican Journal*, then worked my way up from general assignment reporter to government affairs. It was a bad situation."

Trevor pulled a beer out of the refrigerator and twisted off the cap.

"That's too bad. If that's all true, the paper should have fought it. I don't remember ever seeing a retraction."

"They buried it pretty good. He squawked about it, but they weren't about to put a retraction on the front page. What bothered me about the whole mess, other than losing my job, was that everything that went missing had been in my desk in the newsroom. Someone inside the paper had to have taken it, or let someone have access to my desk that shouldn't have been in there. The editorial board didn't seem to care about that either."

"Who would have done that?" Michelle asked.

"I don't know. I suspected that Teresa Hillburn. She never liked me. She wrote features and had the hots for Matt Dodson, one of the city reporters. He and I were just friends, but she didn't see it that way. Matt was always teasing me, throwing balls of paper my way, stuff like that. It didn't help that he mostly tried to ignore her."

"Got her claws out over a guy that wasn't hers anyway? Pathetic." Michelle rolled her eyes.

"Yeah, you would have loved it the day she bought a new Mustang." Danni shook her head and took a sip of her drink. "She bebops into the newsroom and wants him to come outside and see it. He finally relented and walks over to the window and looks down at it in the parking lot. He goes, 'Yellow. I hate yellow cars.' She was crushed. He notices, doesn't want to be too rude, and tells her he likes Mustangs, though, and 'nice car.' She did a one-eighty. I don't think she stopped grinning the rest of the day. I couldn't help myself. Told her she should have bought a red one, and then maybe he would go outside to look it over. She flipped me off.

"Then, the day I was packing up my stuff, she stopped everything she was doing and sat there with a smirk. I tried not to even look at her."

"Bitch." Michelle slapped the counter. "Hell, you're better off not working for an outfit like that anyway. A paper needs to stand behind its reporters, but it sounds like more than one person stabbed you in the back on that one, girl."

Danni nodded and took a long pull of her drink. The slushy mix stung her throat with a frozen clump of fruit.

"That the same Matt Dodson who works for the *Northwest Arkansas Business Bugle*?" Michelle asked.

"I haven't kept up with him since I left Little Rock, but probably. Dark hair with a big cowlick in front? He's early thirties."

"Yep, that sounds like Matt."

"He's at the *Business Bugle*? I had no idea he was even working up here."

Michelle nodded.

"That's quite a story, Danni." Trevor pointed at her with two fingers extended from his grip around the neck of a beer bottle. "She's right. The newspaper should have been more loyal to you."

"I heard that Hudgens's wife is having a fit. I guess the Little Rock cops aren't doing anything about his disappearance. Probably think he took off to Mexico or somewhere with a new girlfriend." Michelle giggled.

"Hmmm, well, he can't be with the girlfriend from back then. I heard she killed herself," Danni said.

Michelle grimaced.

Trevor held up the tray of steaks he'd seasoned.

"Enough shop talk, ladies. Let's go put these on the grill."

"Good thing I didn't let the electrician stay. Those steaks look yummy. I don't want to share mine."

Michelle grabbed her glass. Trevor held the door open while balancing the tray in his other hand.

"I'm just glad you had one for me too."

"Really, since you crashed the party and all."

Michelle gave him a peck on the cheek before stepping outside.

Danni shrugged and followed.

"I'm ready to jump in that pool before we eat."

27

Despite the late hour, the air was thick with humidity. It stuck to my skin, as if I'd bathed in some sort of lotion. I walked slow, trying not to stir up the gravel. The women were probably asleep, but I wasn't sure.

She was here. I knew she'd arrived early that afternoon. Seeking comfort from her friend or possibly making plans to get back into the singles scene, find herself a new man.

It was too bad my aim had been off that day, but I knew right away it was better the way it happened. She was hurt by the loss of her fiancé, her torment extended. Pain from the loss of a loved one—the very reason I sought revenge.

She now knew the kind of pain I'd suffered, and she deserved it. I smiled to myself and nodded, knowing I would inflict the same pain on her family when she was gone. They should suffer as I had. They could only blame her.

The bitch.

Something flew at me. I bent, dodging out of the way, and nearly let out a yelp in surprise. It was a bat. I took a deep breath and tried to calm my hammering heart.

Get this job done, and get the hell out.

The lights were off in the house. I edged around the side but didn't see any sign of the women in the back either. My timing was good. Too much partying on the weekend, so they'd gone to bed early. Good. The work could be done without too much fear of being caught.

The smell of citronella candles lingered at the back of the house. The moon reflected off the water in the swimming pool. It pulled at me. I could float around and take a few leisurely laps.

Maybe after I finish with the car. I'll deserve a little skinny-dip then.

I snorted and wiped the sweat from my brow with the back of my hand before turning toward the front of the house to get the job done.

"Don't mess this up, boy." Mama crouched next to the Scout and watched me work. "She'll go sailing off the mountain, you do a good job."

The thought made me smile.

"Yes, she will, Mama. Yes, she will."

Mama rocked back on her heels and cackled.

Danni was deep into a good dream. Later, she couldn't remember what it was other than Rick was in it and she was happy. Michelle was shaking her shoulder.

"Get up, chick. Come on. Want to go into town and play reporter with me?"

"Huh?" She wiped at her eyes and sat up. "What? What time is it?"

"It's almost two. I've got to go. Just got a call that Bloomington City Hall is on fire, and Brett's got nobody but a photog at the site. You know this kind of shit always happens in the middle of the friggin' night on the weekend. Want to go? Might be exciting."

Michelle sat on the side of the guest bed, tying her tennis shoes. She was already dressed in jeans and a purple blouse.

"Come on, Danni Deadline wouldn't want to miss out on this."

"Ugh, I should have never told you Paul calls me that. But, okay. I'm game, sort of," Danni mumbled while yawning and crawling from beneath the covers.

"Well, get with it girl. I'll be in the Jeep ready to roll in about two minutes."

She grabbed a pair of jeans out of her bag and pulled them on.

"Let me get dressed, and I absolutely have to pee first."

"Well, if you must," Michelle hollered while rushing out of the room.

"I must."

She pulled her sleep shirt over her head, threw it on the bed. Snatching a bra and a fresh top from her bag, she headed to the bathroom.

With a pair of tennis shoes in one hand and her leather bag in the other, she opened the front door and bumped into Michelle coming back inside.

"You're going to have to move your Scout, or we'll have to take it. It's parked behind me."

Danni bent down and slipped on her shoes.

"We can take it."

"Oh, good. Can I drive?" Michelle lifted her eyebrows.

"Sure."

Danni dug the keys out of her purse and dangled them from one finger. Michelle grabbed them and pulled the door closed behind them.

"I love these old Scouts. Never driven one, though. They were built to compete with the Jeep. Seem tougher to me. Always wanted to get behind the wheel of one."

"Have at it. You know that windy-ass road better than me anyway."

She climbed into the passenger side.

Michelle adjusted the driver's seat.

"You short-legged little freak."

"What, Amazon woman?"

"Wow, I would have thought it'd be a stick shift."

"Nope. This is a Scout II. '79 with all the extras. Even has air conditioning. I wouldn't be driving it otherwise."

Michelle pulled to the right, made a loop, headed down the driveway, and out onto the road.

"This thing is nice. One of the first SUVs."

"Rick said that too. It was his uncle's. He didn't have much family, but he loved his uncle. Kept it and fixed it up after he died. He babied it. Drove it on the weekends for fun and once in a while to haul stuff."

"He did a nice job with the interior. Love the leather seats."

Michelle ran her hand along the bench seat between them.

"He liked it mainly because of its simplicity. 'Nothing fancy. Just a good box with wheels, and built tough.'" Her deep voice mimic sounded nothing like him.

Michelle snorted. "Good box with wheels. I like that. Yeah, this thing looks nothing like the SUVs on the road today. You don't hardly see them anymore either."

"Nope. I don't think there's another one around here. Maybe sitting on blocks in someone's backyard."

The woods were dense and dark. With no moon, it was like driving through a cave. Only the trees along the edge of the road were visible.

"Huh. The brakes seem a little spongy."

"Really? Spongy?"

"Yeah, a little. Maybe it's just me not used to them." Michelle pulled a water bottle out of the cup holder straddling the axle hump in the floorboard. "Brett says the fire is in the back of the building. Isn't consuming the whole structure, but still, it is city hall and might be really flaming up by the time we make it to town. He wants me to get it on the Web as soon as possible. It's too late for this morning's edition. Have to go in Monday's paper."

What looked like a fox darted across the road as Michelle sped up on a straight stretch.

"I bet the mayor's had to get out of bed for this."

"Maybe he'll be in his robe." Danni snickered and grinned.

It had been a while since she'd been out on a news story. It felt good.

They rounded a curve and headed down a steep incline. The shoulder disappeared on their left in a precipitous drop to the valley hundreds of feet below.

"God, these brakes. Shit." Michelle pumped them.

"What?"

Michelle leaned forward. "They are not working at all."

The Scout gained speed.

"Geez, not good. This is *not* good!" Danni clung to the door handle with her right hand. "Oh, God."

"We're not going off that cliff. Shit! Shit! Shit!"

The words came out in a screech as Michelle steered toward the ditch on the right.

They plunged into the gulley. The Scout traveled about thirty feet, throwing Danni's shoulder against the door as they bumped along, still gaining speed on the slope. The front end hit something solid with a jolt that threw her forward and then back against the seat when the vehicle went airborne for a few seconds. It landed in the roadway sideways, then slid toward the other side of the road and down the embankment they had hoped to avoid.

She gripped the dash as the Scout rocked its way down the side of the hill for what seemed like miles, and she sang a long repeated "oh" that grew louder with each bump.

Michelle's scream came in waves between a screech and a whimper.

The downhill momentum ended with a jerk as a tree branch hit the windshield causing it to burst, spraying glass over them and coming just short of ramming into Danni's face. All motion came to a quick stop.

Danni let out the breath she hadn't realized she was holding, then tried to get her mind around what had happened.

The vehicle had landed on a steep slant, the driver's side against a large tree. Michelle was still, slouched against the door.

Danni reached up and turned on the interior light, then shook Michelle's shoulder.

"Hey. Hey. Michelle. Talk to me."

She felt a pulse at her wrist. There wasn't any obvious injury, but Michelle must have smacked her head on the side window.

A whirring noise came from the motor. She turned the ignition off and listened to the silence. Closing her eyes, she took a deep breath and tried to calm herself.

"Shit. What do I do now?"

She opened her eyes. The headlights were still on, but she couldn't see much outside the car. Her bag was lodged beneath Michelle's legs. It took some prying to get it loose. She dug around in it and found her cell phone. It had no bars.

"Dammit."

She shook Michelle gently by the shoulder again. "Michelle, Michelle. Come on. Talk to me."

Michelle stirred and moaned.

"Hey, girl. Come on. Wake up. You okay?"

Danni gripped Michelle's arm and patted her hand. Michelle whispered a moan but didn't make any sense.

Dammit.

What should she do? If she stayed in the Scout, nobody would likely find them. They were way off the road. There was no choice but to try to get back up the hill where she could get a cell phone connection to call for help.

"I'm going to have to crawl out of here and climb up to the road, see if I can get some cell service. Do you hear me?"

She stuck the cell phone in her back pocket. Michelle's eyes fluttered, then closed.

"You're okay, but don't move. I'll be back as quick as I can. God, I hope you're hearing me."

Michelle took in a breath but didn't open her eyes.

Danni bit her lip, fought the tears that wanted to come, and patted Michelle's arm.

"I have to go for help."

She reached for the door handle, then had another thought. Maybe a flashlight would help. The glove box popped open as soon as she touched the handle. *Go figure, gloves in the glove box.* There was also a flashlight. *Always prepared. Thank you, Rick.* She put on the work gloves and wedged the flashlight in the back waistband of her jeans.

"Sorry, girl. You're going to have to sit here in the dark or you'll be crawling with bugs."

She switched off the interior light and reached around the steering column to switch off the headlights. The door and part of the dash were curved in on Michelle.

Flipping on the interior light again, she looked down at her friend's legs and still couldn't tell much. With the flashlight she could see that her legs looked okay. They weren't penned in from the crumpled side of the Scout. *Little miracles.* She ran the flashlight up and down her friend's body. There was no blood, nothing she could see. Still, something had happened to Michelle, or she'd be more coherent. Danni flipped off the interior light again and returned the flashlight to her waistband.

Because of the incline, it took both arms to push the door open. Holding it with her feet, she turned back to Michelle and stroked her arm once before climbing out of the Scout. Once she landed on solid footing, she tried to get her bearings. Getting back up to the road might be tough. As gently as possible, she closed the door. The car seemed braced firmly against the tree that had stopped its dive, but she didn't want to test that theory.

She pulled the flashlight out and turned it on. The hillside had few small trees. The kudzu had likely strangled them out. The beam from the flashlight didn't reach the road. It surely couldn't be far. The accident had happened so fast, she wasn't sure how close they were to the road.

She turned around, bent over, and leaned inside the open window, shining the flashlight on her friend.

"Sit tight. Don't move. You hear me? Do *not* move."

Michelle grunted but didn't open her eyes.

A few steps in she realized the climb would be harder than anticipated. Her feet were already tangled in the kudzu vines. Her heart hammered at the thought of what might be lurking in the mess. Good thing she'd put on tennis shoes and jeans, rather than the sandals and shorts she'd worn the day before. The hillside was as dark as a movie theater. With the flashlight tucked in the waistband of her jeans again, she moved her cell phone to the front pocket and started the climb. She forced herself not to think about what she was doing. *Just move forward, move forward.* Sucking in a deep breath, she tried not to cry. She had to do this, and she could do this. There was no choice.

The kudzu was thick and hard to maneuver through, but not as dense as she'd seen it in other places. Sometimes it looked like a lush carpet. The vine could swallow structures and objects in its wake. At least it gave her something to grab on to and pull herself up, but her feet felt like they were tangled in a thick spider's web.

She didn't want to think about snakes. There had to be some and who knew what other creatures crawling in the mess. She forced herself to concentrate on the goal, reaching the top. That's all that mattered.

Get to the top, and use the phone.

She had to get help.

"Baby steps, almost literally, baby steps," she muttered to herself.

Each time she pulled a foot up, she felt a creepy tangle of vines she had to shake loose. After climbing for several minutes, she stopped to catch her breath and used the flashlight to get her bearings again. The road still wasn't visible. Looking back toward the Scout, she saw that she hadn't gone as far as she thought.

Dammit.

"I'll be back, Michelle. Do not move!" she hollered.

A scurrying noise in a tree on her left made her gasp. She aimed her flashlight in that direction but didn't see anything. It wouldn't do to worry about it anyway. Tears came to her eyes as she tried to catch her breath. There'd be no crying. There was no time for that and no choice but what she was doing. She tucked the flashlight away and began climbing again.

Hang on, Michelle. Just hang on.

The incline made her bend forward and grab at the intertwining strands of greenery. The humidity was high, despite the early morning hour. Sweat rolled down her back and between her breasts. One good thing was that there was no doubt she was going in the right direction. Up.

The woods smelled musty, and the humidity amplified the odor. Not good for her allergies. She had to stop herself from rubbing her eyes. There was no telling how much pollen, mold, and other woodsy crap was on her hands.

Her foot caught on a rock, and she fell forward, her face plunging into the sticky vines.

Well, so much for keeping the woodsy crap out of my eyes.

She pushed herself to her knees, yanked the bottom of her T-shirt up, and wiped the sweat from her face. Taking a deep breath, she fought the tears, tucked a strand of hair back, and struggled to her feet.

Keep going. Just keep climbing.

The road couldn't be far.

"Baby steps, for sure. Can't take bigger ones," she muttered to herself.

Most of the way, she kept her head down, concentrating on the next step, but the longer she climbed, the more she could make out in the darkness. When she got to a big tree, she stopped again, put a hand to her lower back, and stretched, then leaned against it with one hand and pulled out her flashlight with the other. The crest of the hill wasn't far. She couldn't see the car for a minute, but she swung the light back and forth, held it higher, and found a glint that had to be it. She'd climbed at least a hundred feet up, if not more.

She wiped the sweat from her face with her T-shirt again, then switched off the flashlight, pulled off a glove, and pulled the cell phone out of her front pocket. *Still no bars.* She put it back, put her glove back on, and continued climbing. Michelle needed help *now.* There was no telling how badly she was hurt. Danni pushed herself faster.

Her foot slipped on another rock, knocking it loose and sending her forward, but she managed to stay on her feet. The road was another ten or twelve feet up. Breathing heavy and ignoring the sweat, her jeans sticking to her legs, she struggled up the hill as fast as possible.

When she finally reached the gravel shoulder, she stood, then bent forward again, holding herself at her knees, struggling to get her breathing under control. It slowed enough for her to stretch and arch her back. She was stiff and achy, but she had to hurry.

Michelle was still down there. Down there alone.

Removing the work gloves, she tucked them under her arm and pulled out the cell phone.

No bars. Shit.

A few steps up the hill, she stopped. Would she be able to find the exact spot where she'd come out of the woods?

With the back of her wrist, she wiped sweat from her forehead. Taking the flashlight out again, she tried to see the car, but it was too far. She laid the gloves on the shoulder of the road and topped them with a baseball-sized rock she found a few feet away. The gloves probably wouldn't get up and walk away, but she was taking no chances.

The moon finally peeked out from the clouds but still didn't provide much light. A slight breeze picked up as she trudged up the hill as fast as her tired legs allowed. With her cell phone in hand, she watched for a connection.

Come on, stupid phone. Bars. Bars.

How far would she have to go? She hated leaving her friend stranded down in the woods, hurt and alone in the dark. God, she hoped Michelle didn't try to get out of the car. It was pinned against the tree pretty solidly, but if she got out, she could go the other way if she wasn't thinking. It couldn't be far from where the Scout had come to a stop to where that hill dropped off the mountain's edge.

A rustling noise in the weeds next to the road made her freeze. Yeah, there were squirrels and skunks out there, but there were also bobcats and mountain lions, probably even a bear or two. Maybe it was her imagination. The dark woods stared back at her. She began walking again but heard noise off to her left. Cat-like eyes stared back at her a few feet off the road, the reflection of the dim light giving them an eerie glow.

Her heart thumped. She was afraid to move.

She had to. Michelle needed her.

The rustling hadn't been that loud. It couldn't be a mountain lion. It would have already leapt out at her and attacked.

Or would it?

Maybe it was best not to know. Might be just a stray cat. Turning, she started walking. Slower at first. No sense in startling the kitty. Her heart was beating fast. She tried to control her breathing and keep walking. The brush rustled again.

The cat, however big and wild it might be, was keeping pace with her a few feet off the road.

She shifted her steps to the right side and continued to move up the hill. The more distance between her and her watcher the better.

The cat moved with her but stayed hidden amid the brush and rocks. Keeping pace ten or fifteen feet from the pavement, its tracking was apparent by the occasional shift in a branch or rock. There was no kudzu on the upper side of the road. The pavement had created a sort of dividing line or stop bar for the creeping vines.

She tried her cell phone again and stopped.

Bars. Thank God.

Ignoring the cat, she called 911.

A sliver of sun peeked over the mountaintop when the rescue squad finally made its way down to the Scout. Danni had a hard time keeping the tears from flowing while she paced at the side of the road, staring down at the scene below.

The daylight revealed how close they'd come to going over the mountainside. A cliff overhang was another fifteen to twenty feet beyond the oak that had put an end to their downward plunge.

There was no word on whether Michelle had ever regained consciousness or on her condition. Danni didn't want to even think of what could have happened. The Scout had hit the tree right at the driver's door, causing a massive dent that had to have injured the driver.

"She was wearing her seatbelt," she told a young paramedic who'd been down to the scene and then come back up for more equipment before they could get Michelle out of the vehicle.

"Yes, ma'am, but an older rig like that doesn't have any airbags. Really, though, you'd need one on the side to help in this case, and there ain't many new vehicles even got those yet."

He pulled a big black case from a compartment near the ambulance's rear wheel and slung it up on his shoulder.

She grabbed his free arm. "Is she, um, is she going to be okay?"

"We can't tell much. But she's alive. We'll get her to the emergency room for a full eval. They'll know more."

Shifting the pack on his shoulder, he made his way back down the hill.

She shuffled from one foot to the other while watching the rescue squad work around the vehicle to pull Michelle out and load her on a stretcher. Four emergency workers eventually picked up the stretcher and started the climb. The top of Michelle's head was all that was visible.

When they finally managed to get up to the shoulder of the road, Danni rushed to her side, but Michelle's eyes were closed. The only option was to stay out of the way.

"Where are you taking her?" she asked a first responder who loaded equipment into a fire truck.

"Lovely County Regional. Should be there in about twenty-five or thirty minutes. Might have brought in a copter for this one, but no place to land it up here." He shouted over the sound of the siren from the departing ambulance.

She nodded and stared while he continued to load up gear. Fear had stopped her from climbing into the back of that ambulance, but now she wasn't sure what to do. Her car was in town. The Scout was wedged against a tree off the side of the mountain. The only choice would be to go back to Michelle's, see if she could find her keys, and take her Jeep into town.

"Danni."

The voice startled her. She turned around quickly and nearly fell.

"Careful there." Ben Sizemore grabbed her elbow.

She pulled her arm back and massaged her forehead.

"I'm okay. You startled me."

"Sorry about that."

He took a step back, removed his county Stetson, and tucked it under his arm.

A couple of county deputies had climbed down to the Scout and were now standing around it talking. Their voices drifted up the hillside, but what they were saying was a mystery.

"I have to ask you something." Ben took a deep breath. "Had Michelle and you been drinking?"

"No." She knitted her brow and looked up at him. "Well, yesterday afternoon. She had a margarita. But it was early, and we didn't even have wine with dinner. We were too tired. Why would you ask me that?"

"Well, you know, the car's halfway down the mountainside there, and I'm kind of doubtin' there was much traffic out here at two in the morning. Hit a deer or what?"

She put a hand on her hip.

"For your information, the brakes went out on Rick's Scout."

"Went out?"

"Yeah, you know, they wouldn't work. She was pressing the pedal, and nothing happened. We went in the ditch on that side." She pointed over her shoulder with a thumb. "Hit something, I'm guessing that boulder there."

Just up the hill, a yellow tabby cat sat atop the rock, licking one front paw. Danni snorted.

"Geez, he sounded much bigger when he was stalking me."

"Huh, who?"

"The cat. Oh, nothing." She raked her fingers through her hair and tucked it behind her ears. "Anyway, it hit the rock. Then we went sideways back on the road, slid off the edge over here, and plowed down the hill. Thank God for that tree."

"Really. Pretty deep drop-off within spittin' distance." He switched his Stetson from one armpit to the other. "Where were y'all going at that hour of the morning anyway?"

"Really? You're going to question me like I've done something wrong?" She rolled her eyes.

Ben shrugged.

"Well, for your information, Michelle got called in on the fire at City Hall."

"Oh, yeah, heard about that. Wasn't much of a fire. They were trying to figure out a cause, last I heard."

"Hmmm."

She swatted at a fly that circled her head.

"Having any trouble with them brakes before this?"

She cocked her head to one side. *Have the brakes been acting up?*

"Not that I know of. I hadn't driven it but once or twice prior to the last couple of days, but I've been using it to move some stuff back to my place off Watson. Seemed like a good idea to drive it up here. The road's so rough going to Michelle's. She lives on County Road Twelve Eleven. It's gravel and not well maintained."

"I know the road. Nice up there."

"Yeah, she's got a heck of a view. But a rough drive."

"That it is."

He pulled a white cotton handkerchief from his back pocket and wiped the sweat off his forehead, then put his hat back on.

"Think the rough road could have knocked something loose on the brakes?" she asked.

Ben looked down the hill where the other deputies were making their way back up to the road.

"Not likely, but I don't know. We'll have to get a look at it. A tow truck's on its way. We'll haul it to the county impound lot, maybe get someone to go over it."

She nodded.

"You need a ride?"

"Not sure I want to get in that cruiser after the interrogation I got. But I guess it is what it is."

"Just a ride, Danni."

"Okay. I need to get to the hospital and see what's going on with Michelle." Her throat caught, and she looked back down the hill. "God, I hope she's okay. I can't believe she was the one driving. I shouldn't have let her. This is my fault."

Ben patted her shoulder.

"Now you know that's not so. I doubt your friend would think it's your fault. Things happen. No rhyme or reason."

She shook her head and blew out a breath.

"These belong to you, ma'am?"

A deputy with a red face and a round belly held up her bag and Michelle's backpack.

"Yes, well, uh. Yes, I'll take them," she stammered.

"You boys good with me taking this young lady on in to the hospital?" Ben asked. "She's wantin' to be there for her friend and might not be a bad idea for a doc to give her a look over too."

The chunky deputy nodded. "We'll catch up with ya later."

"Tow truck'll be here any minute," said a taller deputy who wiped sweat from his face with a cotton handkerchief.

"They get it up off the hill, have 'em take it to the county impound yard," Ben said.

The two deputies nodded in unison.

Ben held the passenger door for her and closed it once she was settled. While he made his way to the driver's side, the small white pickup she'd seen the day before passed, heading up the hill. The driver slowed and gawked at the scene as he went by.

Danni wasn't talkative on the way into town. She couldn't think of anything but Michelle. She wished she could turn back the clock to take the other car or at least put herself behind the wheel.

Ben seemed to understand and didn't press her for conversation. He parked off to the side in the emergency vehicle lane at the hospital and went with her to find out about Michelle. A medical technician had taken her down for an ultrasound. They didn't know anything yet.

Danni paced in the emergency room's waiting area—one hand on her hip, the other twiddling a strand of hair. Ben sat at the end of a row of chairs against the wall. His eyes moved with her back and forth parade.

"She's alive. At least she's alive," she muttered, then sobbed. Catching her breath, she said, "Oh, God, please don't let it be bad. This is all my fault."

Ben stood up and rushed to her, taking her by the shoulders. He pulled her around to face him.

"You can't blame yourself. This is not your fault. You hear me?"

But he was wrong. This *was* her fault. Her vehicle. Her stupidity for parking behind Michelle. Her suggestion they take the Scout. Her agreeing to let Michelle drive. Her fault. Her fault. Tears ran down her cheeks.

"But it is. I should have never have let her drive. She's not familiar with the Scout. She didn't know the brakes would fail."

"Did you? How could you have known? Nobody could have known." Ben held her against his chest. "Nobody could have known. This isn't your fault. Now stop it."

She nodded and tried to control her sobs.

"Let's calm down, have a seat, and wait to see what the doctor has to say after this ultrasound." He pulled out his handkerchief. "You can use this, but it's not exactly clean. Has my sweat all over it."

She took it and dabbed at her eyes. "Thanks."

How could she sob so much now, when she didn't shed a tear for Rick for weeks? She knew the answer. She wasn't numb now. She was just guilty.

"Come on, let me buy you a cup of coffee or some breakfast? You haven't eaten."

Ben nodded toward the end of the room.

"No, thanks. I'm fine. I don't drink coffee anyway." She handed him back his handkerchief and pointed to a box of tissues on a table at the end of the line of chairs behind him. "Please."

Ben smiled, tucked the handkerchief in his back pocket, picked up the box, and handed it to her.

"Thank you."

She pulled out two tissues and blew her nose, then blew out a breath.

"There we go. Now, how about a soda, okay?"

She nodded.

With an arm draped across her shoulders, he guided her to the area where vending machines filled up a corner facing three round tables with chairs. He pulled out a seat for her, and she took it while he turned to the soda machine.

"What do you like?"

"Diet Dr. Pepper. Need some caffeine."

He put money in the machine and handed her the can that clunked out at the bottom.

"Thanks."

She popped the can open and watched him stir a cup of coffee that looked more like chocolate milk by the time he loaded it down with several packets of instant creamer.

The pneumatic doors whooshed open, and a young couple with a crying baby rushed in. The mother held the child, who kicked and bucked against her shoulder. They talked to the nurse at the reception station briefly and were hustled back to the treatment area.

The only other person in the waiting room was an older lady in one corner reading a paperback. A television hanging on the wall above her head flickered with The Weather Channel, the volume silent.

"Maybe I should see if they're done with the ultrasound, if they know anything yet."

She bit her lower lip and pushed her chair back. Ben put his hand atop hers.

"Wait. Let 'em do their work. You gotta relax. They know we're waiting here. They'll come find us when there's something to tell."

She nodded, sighed, and pulled her chair back up to the table.

"She's probably going to be fine," Ben said.

"Yeah, I hope so."

Another couple came in with a whoosh from the automatic doors. The man, bearded and dressed in khaki shorts and a Pink Floyd T-shirt, hopped on one foot and leaned on the woman's shoulder. She had long brown hair in a thin braid draped over a shoulder and wisps of straggling hair ringing her face. Dressed in jean shorts and a thin white tank top with a bright-green bikini underneath that matched her flip-flops, she helped him to a chair before talking to the receptionist.

"They're really not too busy for an emergency room," she said and took a drink of her soda.

"No, they're not. Not for a weekend anyway. I've seen it much worse."

"Ben, you asked me about the brakes. You think someone messed with them?"

She played with the tab on her soda can. He didn't answer for a few seconds.

"I doubt it. Seemed odd, though, they went out all of a sudden like that. Usually, they're squeaking, getting kind of soft when you apply 'em. You get some warning long before they fail on ya."

134

"Hmmm. I don't remember thinking there was any issue, but I haven't been driving the Scout on a regular basis. Maybe Rick knew they needed maintenance and planned to take care of it. We had a lot going on with the wedding and getting settled in the new house. He never mentioned anything about the brakes." She wiped at her bottom lip with her thumb and index finger. "But he was like that, just taking care of things and me not knowing they needed it or that he'd already done it."

They both turned when a woman in a white lab coat with a stethoscope around her neck came through the treatment area doors, leaving them swinging behind her.

"Deputy Sizemore?"

"Yes." Ben stood up.

"I'm Doctor Simpson. I wanted to update you on Ms. Putthoff."

"Yes." Danni stood up.

The woman turned toward her. "Are you family?"

"A good friend. I was in the accident with her."

"Well, she's probably got a broken collarbone. We're getting an orthopedist to come in, take a look at that, and make decisions on how to proceed. Also, we've done an ultrasound to see if there are any internal injuries. She's got some bruising on her left side that's pretty severe, but we're not seeing anything. And we've ordered a CT scan to confirm the head injury isn't causing bleeding. It's a fairly significant bump."

"Is she conscious now?" Danni asked.

"She is."

"Can we see her?"

"Shortly. We're taking an X-ray of her collarbone, confirm it's broken."

"So not too bad then?" Ben said as he tossed his empty cup in the trashcan a few feet away.

"What we know so far is not too bad. We need to look at that bump on the head, but I'm not seeing anything alarming. Just being cautious. Considering that I heard she nearly drove her car off a cliff, I guess not too bad is a good way to put it." The doctor smiled.

Danni took a deep breath and blew it out.

"When she's out of X-ray and assigned to a room, I'll make sure they let you know."

Dr. Simpson nodded and left.

"See, not too bad." Ben raised his eyebrows and smiled. "Now let's get you a quick exam to make sure you are okay."

31

Danni waited in front of the hospital for her dad. Ben had been called away, so she was stuck without a car. She leaned on the building, her head tilted back against the brick. She didn't have any injuries from the accident, but her body ached. Tired didn't come close to how she felt.

Michelle would likely need surgery on her collarbone. She had a concussion, and although Dr. Simpson wanted to keep her for a day or so for observation, Michelle should be fine. It was best to get some rest—go home and take a nap herself and come back later.

She rolled the back of her head against the wall, closed her eyes, and let the sun warm her face.

A mechanic needed to look at the Scout's brakes as soon as possible. Could someone have done something to cause them to go out? Why? She'd forgotten about the flat tire. The air had been deliberately let out. There was no doubt about that. But why? Was it meant to frighten her, make it so she couldn't be comfortable in her own home. A garage would be nice. She took a deep breath and let it out.

Rubbing her eyes with the balls of each hand, she wished her dad would hurry up. It wasn't even noon, but she was ready to go to bed and call it a day. She could have walked the mile and a half to her house, but she was too tired.

A horn beeped. Her father's Ford Explorer rolled to a stop next to her.

"About time," she muttered and walked around to the passenger side of the truck. "Thanks, Dad."

She dropped her bag on the seat, pulled the door closed, and secured her seatbelt.

"Where we headed?"

He put the truck in gear but waited on a woman and two young girls to cross in front of them.

"My house. Bruno's there. I need to feed him, and I desperately need a nap."

"Tell me what's going on, Sis."

Her father, always supportive of her, listened to the whole story, then patted her leg.

"My God, Danni, you both could have been killed."

"I just wish Michelle hadn't suffered the brunt of it. I was so scared she was seriously hurt when I climbed up that hill in the middle of the night. I blame myself. It was my Scout. Well, Rick's, but still. I should've been driving."

"Oh, honey, you can't blame yourself. Michelle wouldn't want that, wouldn't say that."

He pulled to the curb in front of her house. She opened the truck door but stayed seated with one arm stretched out, holding it ajar.

"I know, but I hate that she's the one who got hurt. Maybe if I'd been driving."

"You can't 'maybe' it away. Maybe God had a plan there. Maybe she was better able to handle that Scout when the brakes went out. Maybe, if you'd been driving, you would have gone off that mountain ridge. Maybe you'd both be in worse shape. Maybe you wouldn't be here to support her as she heals."

"I hadn't thought of that. I guess you're right."

She let go of the door, leaned over, and kissed his cheek, then grabbed her bag and pulled herself out of the truck.

"You need anything from me before I go?"

"Nope, I'm good."

She stood, holding the door open.

"You look tired. Better take that nap. It's been a long night."

He thumped the steering wheel with one thumb. She snorted.

"You were just jumping my butt for sleeping too much. Now listen to you."

He rolled his eyes. "That was different, and you know it."

"Okay, Dad. No worries. I'm headed to bed as soon as I feed my dog and give him a little love."

"Where's your car? I can't leave you here without a car."

"It's at the other house. I'll figure it out. Too tired to worry about it now."

"Okay. Holler at me if you need a ride."

"I will."

She shut the door. He pulled away from the curb but stopped and rolled down the window.

"Hey, Lizzie wants you to give her a call."

"Okay, I'll do that."

She stood on the top step and waved before opening the door on the screened-in porch.

Bruno barked while she unlocked the front door. The doggy door let him into the utility room off the back porch but not the rest of the house. She let him in and reached down to pat his head.

"Hey, Buddy, how's it going? You miss Mommy? No jumping."

He didn't listen, of course, and continued to jump up on her legs. Excitement overrode any training she'd tried. At least he was getting better about jumping up on other people. She fed him and was about to take a shower when the doorbell rang.

It was Trevor. He nearly knocked her down before she had the door open all the way.

"What the hell?"

With one hand gripping the doorknob, she waved the other arm, as if ushering him in.

"That's what I was going to say." He stood in the center of her living room, breathing hard and glaring at her. "You look fine. Weren't you with her? How'd you manage to come out without a scratch and my girlfriend is in the hospital on the verge of dying?"

"What?"

"She couldn't even talk to me. She's all bandaged up, broken bones, concussion. I don't know yet what all is wrong with her, and I hear you're to blame, nearly killed her!" he shouted.

"Now, look here—"

"Look here, my ass."

"I didn't nearly kill her. For your information, she was driving."

Danni slammed the door shut.

"Yeah, why's that? I heard your brakes were bad, so I guess you had her drive. You want to kill yourself, have at it. You don't have to take anyone else with you."

He took a step toward her.

"Look, asshole." She moved toward him, the anger building inside her. "I didn't know the brakes were bad. She wanted to drive my Scout. I didn't force her to do anything."

"Sure, since she can't tell us anything, I'm supposed to believe *you*." He stuck a finger in her face, pointing on the last word.

"What do you mean, she can't tell us anything? She was talking fine when I left the hospital. Certainly wasn't on the verge of dying. Not even close. They want to keep an eye on that concussion and decide for sure if they want to do surgery on her broken collarbone. Nothing life threatening." Danni pushed her hair behind her ears with both hands and tried to concentrate on slow breaths and controlling her anger. "Yeah, it was a bad wreck. We slid down the hill, nearly flipped the Scout, and she's got some injuries, but she's going to be okay."

"What the hell's wrong with your car?"

He wasn't letting up.

Danni didn't say anything for a few seconds but looked him in the eye. She could see the hatred pouring out of him. There was no doubt that this was more emotion than the guy had ever shown Michelle.

"I don't know yet what happened with the Scout, but the brakes went out. They were fine earlier in the day, then nothing when Michelle was driving." She sat down in the wooden rocker. "I'm going to have a mechanic look it over and try to figure out what happened. It was Rick's Scout, and honestly, I don't know when he had it serviced last or had the brakes checked. But I've been driving it the last couple of days, and it's been fine."

"Sure, sure." He walked toward the door, then turned and pointed at her again. "I think you better stay away from her. I don't know what's up with you, jealously or whatever, but I don't want you near her. You hear me? I don't want you near her."

Danni was tempted to grab that finger and twist it. Instead, she shook her head and rocked casually, as if she didn't care what he had to say.

"Michelle is my best friend. I'll talk to her any damn time I want. Now, Mr. Don't Know Shit, I think it's best you get out of my house." She stood up, and this time she did the pointing. "You can leave."

He put his hands on his hips but didn't move.

"She was out when I left the hospital, but I'm going back up there and wait for her to come to, and we're going to have a little talk about the company she's keeping."

"Go right ahead."

She stomped to the door and held it open. He didn't move.

"I'll tell you another thing," he said. "I don't believe a word of that story you told us yesterday about your fuck up in Little Rock. Everybody knows what you did, all for the sake of a big byline. You may have Michelle snowed for now, but I'll make sure she gets the real story."

"Get out. Get out now!" Danni shouted.

As soon as he was on the porch, she slammed the door shut. She heard the screen door slap closed and burst into tears. As ridiculous as he was being, what if he was right? Was it all her fault?

The room was dark when Danni's ringing cell phone woke her. It was Michelle.

She sat up in bed, rubbed her eyes, and pushed Bruno to the side. He sometimes slept right up against her.

"Hey, how are you feeling?"

"I'm actually pretty good."

She let out a breath. "I'm so glad. I was worried, but I was so tired I had to get home and get some sleep. Had planned to come back up there, but I think I slept longer than I expected. What time is it?"

Michelle laughed. "It's almost eight thirty. Visiting hours are over soon anyway. Don't worry about it, chick. I'm good, and you needed the sleep, I'm sure."

"Boy, did I. Still wasn't expecting to sleep this long." She moved the phone from one ear to the other and swung her legs off the bed. "Have they given you any information? How's the head and your collarbone?"

"Yeah, I talked to the doctor this afternoon. They're going to keep me through tomorrow. Head's fine, but they have me set for surgery in the morning to fix the collarbone. I guess, where it broke and the way it's broken, it needs a pin or something. They want to go ahead and get it done, then release me. Probably get to go home tomorrow afternoon."

"Wow, that's great. I can come give you a ride home. A *safe ride* home. I'll bring my Subaru or maybe the Lexus."

"Oh, you poor girl. Down to two cars," Michelle teased.

"I know. It's such a rough life."

"Hey, Danni."

"Yes?"

"I want you to know that I don't in any way, shape, or form blame you for this. You couldn't have known about the brakes, and if you did, I know you wouldn't have let me drive, wouldn't have even driven the Scout up there yesterday."

"Thanks for saying that. I've been beating myself up about it."

"Well, Trevor came by here a while ago. He was ranting and raving, blaming you. I sent him on his way. Told him I wouldn't hear it. He was being unreasonable. This was no way your fault. He said he'd been by and given you what for."

Danni stood and stretched. "That he did."

"He had no right doing that shit, and it was stupid."

"Honestly, Michelle, he was kind of an ass."

She laughed. "He can be that."

"Glad we agree, but I've never seen him like that. He must care for you more than you realize."

Michelle snorted. "I'm not sure that's the case. His ass hasn't even been up here to see me but about ten minutes today. If it were me, I'd probably be at his bedside. Well, maybe not after this experience. I'm rethinking the whole deal with him. I sure don't know why he went off on you."

"Don't let what happened with me influence your relationship. I think he just doesn't like me. Remember, I've known him for years, but we've never really been friends. He pretty much ignored me in the newsroom in Little Rock."

She didn't tell Michelle that she always thought he was a pompous jerk, but maybe her friend was figuring that out on her own.

"We'll see. But my heart's not going quite so pitter-patter for his sweet ass like it was."

Danni laughed. "Okay."

"So, I'll see you tomorrow?"

"You bet. I have an appointment with Terry Butler in the morning, but give me a shout when you're ready to go."

"See you then, girlfriend."

"See you."

She tossed the cell phone on her bed and went to find something to eat. Her frozen burrito was cooling when the doorbell rang.

It better not be that asshole again.

And it wasn't.

She opened the door to Lizzie and ushered her into the kitchen, offering her a frozen burrito.

"You sure you don't want one? Not the most elegant of meals, but it works."

Lizzie declined, so she poured them each a glass of ice water and sat down at the table with her plate.

"Well, you'll have to excuse me. I'm starving."

"Go ahead and eat. Sorry to come by so late. Just wanted to tell you how much Josh and me appreciate you helping us the other day at the courthouse."

Lizzie reached down and patted Bruno, who, for once, hadn't jumped up on a guest. It was good to see her cousin looking better. She didn't appear to have gained any weight, but her hair was less frizzy, and she didn't have any visible sores on her arms.

"How is Josh?" Danni asked.

Lizzie's eyes welled with tears.

"Thank you for not telling Uncle Addison and your mom. Josh is lucky to be gettin' a job there. They fired him at the landscape business. I guess you already know that."

"Yeah, Dad told me. He's happy to have Josh."

"Josh was out there yesterday, ready to bust his balls and do a good job. So grateful. Guess he'll probably have to own up to all this crap to Uncle Addison eventually, but we'll see. We ain't wantin' to add more burden to your family with your mom having such a hard time and all."

"Really?" Danni asked. "I thought she was doing better."

"I don't know. She seems better to me, too, but something's up with your dad. Josh and I been talking 'bout it. He seems sort of depressed."

She put her fork down.

"I've been just too absorbed in my own problems. I haven't been paying enough attention."

"He'd holler at ya if he got too deep and needed help. I'm sure it'll be fine," Lizzie said.

Danni knew better. Her father wouldn't reach out unless it was a last resort.

"Yeah, I'm sure it will too. Anyway, you think Josh will stay on? Dad has been wanting him to come work at the cemetery for years."

"As long as he doesn't end up in jail." Lizzie pouted and wiped at more tears. "Oh, Danni, he's just the best thing ever to happen to me, and look at the mess I got him in. He's been so good about it. Probably should have left my butt a long time ago, but he's stuck with me." She sniffled. "Lot a good it's done him."

"You two will get through this. It's hard to see that now, but it will pass."

The sound of the neighbors laughing next door wafted through the open kitchen window as Lizzie wiped at her eyes with the back of her hand.

"He's got a court date next week. Our lawyer's trying to tell them that it's not Josh's, cuz it mighta been in the truck when we bought it. I figured it was mine, but I really can't remember losing any. I was holdin' on to that stuff pretty tight. Really, I doubt I would have lost any of it. That part of it was botherin' me from the start but figured it had to be mine. When the lawyer found out we got the truck a couple a months ago, he said we might be able to claim we didn't know it was even there. He's tryin' to get the cop to talk about where he found it and if it coulda been there a while."

"That sounds promising."

Danni took a drink of her ice water.

"He says that Josh not testin' positive for any drugs helps the case too. You know, they assigned him a new lawyer."

"Maybe it will all work out. Who's the new public defender?"

"Bill Carpenter."

"Carpenter's not a public defender. How'd you get him?" she asked.

"I guess they was too busy, and Josh said he got the case somehow."

"Really? Well, you lucked out there. He's got a good reputation. Great criminal lawyer."

"Anyway." Lizzie stood up. "It's getting late, but I wanted to stop over and let you know we can help you move, if you need. We got Josh's truck back from the cops."

"Oh, if you've got the time tonight, can you give me a ride to the other house? I'm kind of stuck here without a car."

"Sorry about that awful wreck. Your dad was telling me all about it. You weren't hurt, right?" Lizzie asked.

"No, I'm fine. Poor Michelle got really banged up, but she's going to be okay."

"I'm glad you're both okay. And you bet, on the ride. I can run you over there."

"Since you're being so generous, I was hoping to get more packed and moved in the next couple of days. Would you have time late tomorrow afternoon to help with that too? I have a meeting in the morning. Then I need to pick up Michelle and give her a ride home, so it might be late afternoon."

"Sure. I'll get Josh's mom to take care of Shane. Probably better off there than with his awful mama anyway." Lizzie wiped her nose with the paper towel wadded up in her fist.

"Now, Lizzie, stop that. You're getting off that stuff. That baby will be fine. He's lucky to have a mother who loves him so much." She patted Lizzie on her shoulder and pushed her frizzy mane behind one ear. "Cheer up. You'll get through this."

Her cousin pursed her lips and nodded. "And I ain't *getting* off that stuff."

Danni raised her eyebrows.

"I'm *off* that stuff." Lizzie smiled. "Off that stuff forever."

"Good." She grabbed her bag. "Let's go get my car."

33

Danni had a hard time getting back to sleep after Lizzie left. She tossed and turned to the point that Bruno finally stood up on the bed and yipped at her.

"Sorry, boy."

She sat up, threw the covers to one side of the bed, and got to her feet, sliding into a pair of flip-flops.

"Time for an old bad habit to comfort me," she muttered while shuffling off to the kitchen.

Bruno followed at her heels.

It took some digging, but she found her plastic butter dish in the back of the freezer. There were two cigarettes left in an old package of Salems that must have been in there since last year. Rick had convinced her to give them up, even though she only smoked one, maybe two a day.

"Perfect," she said.

There wasn't a lighter anywhere, but under the kitchen sink she found the long stick lighter used to ignite the grill or the water heater if the pilot went out. She plopped down in an Adirondack chair on the small back porch and lit up, being careful not to set her hair on fire with the awkward lighter.

It felt good to lean back in the chair and exhale. Bruno curled up on the rag rug at her feet, letting out a grunt as he did.

"Awful day. Huh, boy?"

She rubbed his back with her toes. A yellow bug light a few doors down and flashes from fireflies were the only light, but a block over, there was still plenty going on. A band from one of the local bars played a soft rock-and-roll montage muffled by the trees and distance.

God, how she ached for Rick. Damn that Billy Tom Viney for taking away the love of her life. Anger sent a shiver through her body. She pounded her fist on the arm of the empty chair.

"Screw you, Billy Tom Viney. I hope you rot in hell!" she screamed.

A light went on next door. She squeezed her eyes shut, but the tears still streamed down her cheeks. It took a few minutes before she got control of herself. She wiped at her face with the bottom of the oversized T-shirt she'd worn to bed, then pulled out another Salem and lit it.

Baby steps. Baby steps. I hear you, Dad. I hear you.

More than an hour later, she pulled back the covers and crawled into bed. Bruno snuggled up behind her in the crook of her legs.

"Just you and me, boy," she mumbled and closed her eyes.

34

"Let's not get too deep into this discussion until the investigation team gets here," Terry Butler said the next morning when Danni came through his office door and immediately started asking questions. "I'll just tell you that we've got satisfactory evidence against him or Mr. Viney wouldn't be cooling his heels in a county cell as we speak."

Tired from tossing and turning most of the night as she tried to sort out why Viney had gone after Rick, Danni had a hard time standing in one spot. She moved from foot to foot.

"Come on, Danni. I can see you're struggling with this situation, and I don't blame you for that." Terry stood up and came around the desk. "Let's take a seat over here and wait for Burns and Nelson. They're on their way over from the sheriff's office right now."

"I don't want to sit down. I want some answers." She nearly spit the words. "Are you sure Viney killed Rick?"

Terry nodded. "Let's calm down a bit here and talk to the detectives."

She plopped down on the leather couch against the wall and clutched the overstuffed arm.

"How about I get you something to drink? Bottle of water? Soda?"

He sat in one of the armchairs across from the couch.

Before she could answer, the detectives arrived. Both of them towered over Terry and were nearly matching in dark suits, but one wore a deep-blue tie with yellow suns and moons decorating it, while the other wore a plain, light-gray tie. They both looked to be in their early fifties.

Terry stood.

"Danni, this is Detective Nelson and Detective Burns."

The one with the bright tie nodded first, then the other. She nodded back at them. They each took a chair, and Terry moved to the opposite end of the couch.

"I was telling Danni here that we have plenty of evidence against Mr. Viney, and we believe we have the right man this time. We don't normally give the victim's family details of the evidence in this manner, but this is a special case. Rick was one of us here at the county." Terry turned to Danni and nodded. "We all know we've had some issues with this case. Doubts about Viney at first, and then, of course, the confession by Mr. Lendo. Consequently, I feel that it's appropriate to include Rick's fiancé in this rundown of where we stand on the investigation."

Detective Nelson, whose thick, bushy eyebrows appeared to have a permanent furrow, leaned forward with a hand balanced on his right knee.

"Mr. Viney had a set of the same brand of heavyweight carbon fiber arrows with fixed blade broadhead tips, along with a compound bow that looked like it had its fair share of use. The whole family, four boys, all used compound bows—do a lot of target shooting. Billy Tom also had a record of threats against Rick Turner, including one threat documented by this office in an outburst at the front desk after the suicide of his brother."

Danni bit her lip. "But I thought he had an alibi."

"His alleged alibi was the making of methamphetamine." Detective Nelson pulled a pocket notebook from the inside of his suit jacket and flipped a few pages. His knuckles were almost as bushy as his eyebrows. "He stated that he was with a John Sugget, who will not substantiate Mr. Viney's claim that they were together at the time of Rick's murder."

Detective Burns opened a black portfolio-type notebook on his lap.

"We also have a statement from a guy who had the pleasure of bunking with Billy Tom during his first couple of days at the county inmate inn. This upstanding citizen says Billy Tom admitted he wanted to kill Rick over what happened with his baby brother, and that doing it with his compound bow was quote 'the best ideer ever' end quote."

He shut the notebook and winked at Danni. She ignored him and met Terry's eyes.

"But a jailhouse snitch isn't much of a witness? Is this enough? What do you think, Terry?"

"Well, I think it could be stronger, but we'll get there. We're on the right track. This is the guy, Danni."

Terry put his feet up on the coffee table and crossed them, knocking aside a stack of magazines.

"There's more shit piled up against this guy already." Detective Burns held one end of a fist to his month in a smothered burp. "Excuse me." He opened his notebook again. "Well, we got his girlfriend, a real piece of work on her own, but she's saying he wanted revenge against the county officials, in particular against Mr. Turner. We also have this."

He pulled a photo from his notebook and tossed it on the coffee table. It slid to the other side and nearly fell to the floor, but Danni caught it with the slap of her hand on top of it. She held her hand in place and stared. Rick's smiling face peeked at her between her spread fingers.

"What?"

Lifting her hand, she gasped.

It was a picture of a big, round bale of hay with a target shape spray-painted on it. Rick's photo hung in the center. Three arrows stuck out of his chest, and one was centered on his forehead. Danni picked it up and stared.

"What? Where did you get this?"

Terry leaned over and snatched the picture from Danni's clutch.

"Danni, are you okay?"

She didn't move and didn't answer.

"Sorry for shocking ya there, miss." Burns closed his notebook. "That's a target practice set up that Billy Tom used behind his girlfriend's house."

Danni jumped up and ran from the office, holding a hand to her mouth. The women's room was ten to twelve feet up the hall. She barely made it, pushing the door open and throwing herself to her knees just in time.

Afterward, she retrieved her bag from Terry's office, told him she couldn't talk about it. She was fine and would call him later.

She sat in the car with the air conditioning blasting in her face for several minutes before she could drive herself home.

35

A moonless sky had settled in after a hard, quick rain that left the streets wet and reflected the streetlights. I watched and waited for the next one on my list.

Gerald Yell had turned out the lights in his second-floor apartment and left with friends more than two hours before. There were four of them. If he returned alone, I'd get my chance.

It was too bad. I'd actually liked the guy. His quirky sense of humor had caught me off guard more than a few times. And boy was he talented. Always winning awards for his photography.

It couldn't be helped. He had to pay for what he'd done.

"Got that right, boy. He's gotta pay. Just like all the rest," Mama whispered.

I closed my eyes and leaned against the rough brick wall. The wait could be hours, but I had to be prepared.

And I was.

I had both a knife and a handgun with me.

The knife was my preference. Gerald would suffer more before I killed him. Inflict a lot pain. Make sure he knew why he was being punished. With the gun, I'd have to aim for the heart or head, then make a run for it. There was no silencer on it, so I'd draw some attention. The guy lived downtown. There were people everywhere. With the knife, I could kill him quietly, get back in the car, and be gone.

What worried me was the guy's size.

I'll have to catch him by surprise.

Through thin plastic gloves, I fingered the smooth leather sheath attached to my hip and thought of the bloody mess I'd made the first time. Preparation was the key. I'd brought extra clothing and shoes and parked the car at the back of the city lot far from any lights. If all went well, I could toss the knife, my clothes, and gloves in a plastic bag before climbing in the car. I would dump the bag far from here.

Lingering in the shadows at the edge of the five-story building, the stench from the dumpster behind me was nauseating. A car honked as traffic streamed past on the busier cross street nearly a block away. The traffic stopped, and the crosswalk sign lit up. The tall, muscular figure held a phone to his ear as he made his way through the crosswalk. He was alone.

Smiling to myself, I stepped back farther into the shadows and waited.

"Yeah, you bet. See you tomorrow."

Gerald's husky voice was unmistakable.

I drew in a breath and held it as the guy stopped on the sidewalk right in front of me. He pocketed his cell phone, then reached for the opposite hip. Keys jingled, and he moved forward, not even glancing toward the shadowed side of the building.

When Gerald climbed the front steps, I scurried out and silently came up behind him. He entered the building and was about to shut the door, but I pushed it hard and knocked him against the wall.

"Hey, what the hell?"

Gerald's stunned expression turned to recognition as he spun around.

"Sorry there, bud." I grinned and shut the door. "Didn't mean to surprise you. Wow, Gerald, right? Long time, no see. You live in this building?"

"Yeah, man. What are you doing here?"

He held his hands on his hips and eyed me suspiciously.

"Well, got some friends live upstairs. Just moved in."

154

"Ah. Didn't know they'd rented the place out yet." Gerald turned, picked his keys up off the floor, and started toward the stairs. "Well, good to see ya. Next time be a little more careful barreling through the doorway."

I chuckled and scrambled after him.

"You bet. Sorry."

About halfway up the flight, Gerald stopped and turned back to me.

"Hey, aren't you going to take the elevator? They're on the fifth floor, aren't they?"

"Yeah. Just thought I'd get some exercise and see where your place is. Been a long time and all."

Gerald gave me a half nod and started back up the staircase.

"Second floor. Had the place for years. Not a bad flat, really. A little outdated, but cheap rent for downtown." Gerald stopped in front of his apartment door at the top of the stairs and turned back to me. "Super's kind of an asshole, but hey, lousy job. Right?"

"I guess so." I smiled.

"Anyway, tell your friends welcome to the building." He turned, put his key in the lock, and turned the knob. "Good to see—"

Before the sentence was out, I rammed into his back and shoved him into the doorframe, holding the knife against his throat.

"Inside, now," I growled.

We moved in unison into the apartment. I kicked the door shut behind us. The place smelled of stale cigarettes and an unattended litterbox.

"What?" Gerald squeaked without lowering his jaw into the knife.

I pulled the knife back, leaving a thin slice along his throat. Gerald clutched at it and spun around. Blood seeped between his fingers.

"What the hell?"

"Tracey, that's what. You bastard."

I stepped toward him, thrust the knife into his belly, and yanked upward as Gerald's eyes bulged and stared at me.

"You remember? My little sister."

Gerald pressed both palms against his abdomen and tried to say something, but it came out a gurgle as blood sputtered between his lips.

"Yes, you. You need to be punished for what you've done. She didn't deserve that. It ripped her heart out for everyone to know what had happened, to know she'd been made a fool of, she'd been betrayed and dumped. She's gone now because of you and the others. My sister killed herself, and this is my payback for her."

I spit the words out and watched as Gerald took his last few sputtering breaths.

Smiling, I shut off the lights and heard a cat meow from the bedroom. I peeked to make sure the hall was clear before sliding out the door and back to my car.

36

After crying herself to sleep on the couch, Danni was starving when she woke less than an hour later. She hadn't heard from Michelle yet but called the hospital and was connected to her room. It would be at least noon before they released her. She sounded a little groggy still from the surgery. Danni assured her she'd be there to pick her up.

With a grilled cheese and a cut up apple on a plate, she made her way to the front porch. Bruno followed. He sniffed every corner of the screened-in porch while she rocked back and forth on the swing and nibbled on a corner of the sandwich.

"Maybe we should take a walk, buddy. Clear our heads."

Bruno cocked his head to one side and looked at her like she was nuts.

"Yep, I might be. I am, after all, talking to the dog."

Bruno yipped.

A little more than thirty minutes later, she walked past the front steps to the *Bloomington Daily Times*. Brett Penderson, editor, was a tall man who wore Levi's, pressed into a crease down the front of each leg, cowboy boots, and a button-down shirt with a tie. Today was no exception. He descended the steps as she walked by.

"Ah, Danni, I've been hoping you'd come by."

He stepped off the bottom step and leaned against the iron rail.

"Well, I've been meaning to, but one thing after another, you know."

She pulled on Bruno's leash to let two young girls pass on the sidewalk.

"I'm really sorry for your loss, Danni. I know you've heard that a hundred times the last few weeks, but what else can you say at a time like this?"

She shook her head and waved a hand at him. "No need."

"So, I understand you were also with Michelle when the accident occurred."

"Yes. It was a rough night."

"I'm sure it was. Sounds like you girls were awful lucky." He shook his head. "I talked to her this morning before the surgery. She'll be out a week, if not longer."

"Yes, she will. I'm going to pick her up here shortly."

"That's good. Well, I hope you're ready to take me up on that job offer soon. I can put you to work right away, if you like. I've got a beat just opened up. You wouldn't have to work general assignment. Ever cover education?"

"I've never covered it steadily, but I've written plenty of school stories, attended many a school board meeting."

"I'm sure you can handle it. Got a reporter moved out of state. She covered higher education. You can take that beat, or we can put you on the Bloomington School District and move Barry over to higher education."

Danni bit her bottom lip and squinted as the sun peeked out between the leaves of the huge oaks the spanned the front of the red brick newspaper office.

"Either one, I suppose. I need a little time before I can start. I'm in the process of moving and getting things settled."

She watched as Bruno hiked his leg on the brick edging along the sidewalk.

"You take your time. We can manage for a while."

"I appreciate that and won't leave you hanging too long."

An older model Ford truck rumbled by, its exhaust leaving a stinky gray puff of smoke in its wake.

"Danni, I certainly hope that, if they prove he's guilty, they fry this Viney guy, maybe his brothers along with him. They need to get what they deserve, all of them. Nothing but trouble. Bunch of druggies. Now they're protecting a killer."

She nodded. "Thank you, Brett. I agree."

"It's sounds like an awful way to go. I took up archery a few months ago, and I know the power of a compound bow. It can reap a lot of destruction."

The flowerbeds bordering the steps up to the building teemed with color. She stared at the swaying blossoms and didn't meet Brett's eyes as she responded.

"I guess I've seen the power of a compound bow firsthand myself."

"Yes, yes, you have." He put a hand on her shoulder for a few seconds then pulled it back and stuck it in his pocket. "I haven't actually been hunting with my bow yet, just target practice with one of our reporters who introduced me to the sport. I hate that someone would use the weapon against another human being."

She nodded, not sure how to respond.

"We use the practice course at Arrow Dynamics. It's enjoyable and relaxing, not to mention decent exercise." He paused and turned toward the steps, grabbing the iron handrail that ran down the center. "Well, sorry to go off on a tangent there. I better let you get on with your day."

She pulled on Bruno's leash to distract him from a squirrel he'd spotted.

"I'll see you soon about the job," she said.

"Certainly."

Brett turned and headed up the sidewalk toward the downtown square.

37

Danni took Bruno home, fed him, and left him in the backyard with the doggy door open into the utility room. She grabbed her keys and phone, noticing she had an alert for a couple of voice mails. One was Paul, her former editor. He'd heard about the wreck and wanted to make sure she was okay.

Shit.

She needed to have a talk with him but wasn't ready yet to tell him she planned to take a new job.

The other three calls were from Ben Sizemore asking her to call him back. He sounded a little frantic by the last one. She hit the call return button, but it went to his voice mail.

"Hey, Ben, it's Danni. What's so urgent? Call me back."

It wasn't more than a minute later before her phone buzzed. She'd just backed the car out of the driveway.

"This better be important. I'm answering while I'm driving, and I've already been in one wreck this week." She chuckled.

"It is. How soon can you come down to the county shop? We need to talk." He sounded all business.

"I might be able to in about an hour, but I can't stay long. I'm going to pick up Michelle and give her a ride home. She's had her surgery and doesn't need to go on any big missions. What's going on?"

He hesitated. "We'll get Michelle home. Bring her with ya. You know where the shop is?"

"I've been down there a time or two. Behind the Road Department facilities off South Seventeen."

"I'll see you as soon as you can get here. Don't mess around."

"Well, all righty then," she said to an empty phone.

What the hell was that about?

He was always so polite. It was odd to hear him be so short with her, especially when he wasn't offering any explanations.

Michelle sat in a recliner in her hospital room, a bag at her feet, when Danni arrived. She was bandaged around her shoulder with one arm in a sling, her thick mane pulled into a ponytail atop her head. Waves of blonde flowed around her face. In a bright-orange and yellow sundress with a halter top that showed off her abundant chest despite the bandage, she looked ready to take on the day.

"How do you do that?" Danni asked. "I always look like I threw myself together, at best. You just had surgery and spent nearly two days in the hospital, but you still look so put together and gorgeous."

"Oh, shut up and come here. Let me give you a hug, but only a very gentle one."

Danni laughed. "Of course, very gentle."

Michelle stood, and Danni wrapped her arms around her, leaning forward to keep from pressing in too close.

"How you holding up?" Michelle asked.

She pulled back and nodded, pushed out her bottom lip, and blew at her straggly bangs.

"Okay, I guess."

Michelle patted her shoulder.

"Let's get out of here then."

"Yes, let's."

Michelle smiled and handed Danni the plastic bag with a Bloomington Regional Medical Center logo.

"I am starving. Haven't had a decent meal since Trevor's steaks the other day."

A nurse pushing an empty wheelchair came in and insisted on escorting Michelle out in it.

"Hospital policy."

Danni got the car and pulled it up to the entrance. Once Michelle was loaded and they were heading out of the parking lot, she told her about the strange conversation with Ben and the need for a pit stop at the county shop.

Danni pulled into a drive-thru and picked up a couple of chicken sandwiches on the way to meet Ben. As hungry as she claimed to be, Michelle could only eat half her sandwich and tossed the rest back in the bag when they came to a stop in front of the big metal shop building.

"I think I'll just sit. Leave the air on, and holler if you need me."

Michelle lowered her seat back a little and closed her eyes.

There were five extra-large garage bays on the structure, and one of them stood open. Ben and the two detectives Danni had met at Terry Butler's office stood right inside the door. Rick's Scout was up on a car lift inside it.

Detective Nelson, wearing a bright-yellow tie with a pattern of multicolor beach umbrellas, nodded as she approached. His partner looked up but went back to writing something in his portfolio notebook.

"Danni, how are you?" Ben asked and gave her a quick hug.

"Good, good. What's up with the Scout?"

"Well, it looks like the accident wasn't really an accident." Ben nodded toward the vehicle. "Someone's been messin' with your brakes."

"What? Why would someone do that?"

Detective Burns closed his notebook.

"Well, Miz Edens, that's something we're trying to figure out. We're wondering if maybe that arrow that got Rick might have been meant for you."

She looked from him to Ben and back again.

"How could that be? Why? What makes you think that?"

Detective Nelson hitched up his pants and bent down a little to step under the car. Pointing up with a small pen light he'd pulled from the inside pocket of his blazer, he said, "The brake line has been compromised deliberately. Whoever did it put a small hole in the line for the front brakes and a bigger one here in the rear line. By the time you went off the side of that hill, there wasn't any brake fluid in the vehicle."

Danni stared, a puzzled look on her face.

"That way they wouldn't go out right off the bat," Ben said. "You'd have had some brakes for a while, at least. Somebody knew what they were doing, for sure." He held a hand on her shoulder. "You okay?"

She didn't respond. Instead, she bent over a little and moved under the car.

"Where's it cut?"

Detective Nelson showed her.

"You don't think that could happen from a rock on a gravel road or something? I've had a flat tire from a sharp rock before."

"No. Tires will do that because they're grinding into the gravel. A rock flying up under the vehicle wouldn't have enough leverage against a heavy duty line like this." He moved the pen light to focus on the front. "And this one here is a clean slice. It's possible to get a leak in a line from wear and tear, but that usually happens at the connection points, not in the middle like this. This was deliberate."

Nelson clicked off his light and stuck it back in his pocket.

They moved out from under the Scout.

Danni bit her lip.

"Why do you think Rick's killer could have been after me?"

"He may not have been. But this brake thing is kind of an odd coincidence so soon after he was killed."

Burns stuck his notebook under his arm.

"You want to come sit down?" Ben said. "We've got a breakroom over here. We need to talk a little bit."

Danni pointed toward her Subaru. "I've got Michelle in the car. Just picked her up at the hospital. She needs to get home."

"You two were together when this happened, right?" Nelson asked.

"Yes. Actually, she was the one driving the Scout."

"Probably ought to have her in on this conversation as well then." Nelson raised his bushy eyebrows.

"Breakroom's got air conditioning and a soda machine," Ben said.

"Okay. Let me see if she's up to it. She just had surgery to repair a broken collarbone this morning."

Michelle had her eyes closed but wasn't asleep and agreed to come in and talk with the detectives.

"What the hell? Who would do that?" she asked once they were seated around a big folding table with cold cans of soda in front of each of them except Burns, who stirred multiple packets of sugar into a cup of coffee.

The breakroom smelled of pine cleaner. It had a stained concrete floor and mellow blue paint on the block walls. Vending machines, a side-by-side white refrigerator, and a small row of cabinets lined a wall of the room. A line of windows looked out on the Street Department facilities, and a big window air conditioner was mounted in the wall. It hummed nonstop while pumping a definite chill in the air.

"Now, to be clear here," Burns said, "we don't know for sure that these incidents are related, but it seems that someone was pretty determined to cause an accident for you. We have to assume the brake lines were tampered with while you were at your friend's house, so they likely followed you up there and took advantage of the steep roads you'd have to take back to town." Detective Burns ran his thumb around the edge of his black portfolio, flipped it open on the table, and pulled an ink pen from the center. "I want you to go through your day before you arrived at Miss Putthoff's house."

Danni told them that the only people she'd really been around before that were her parents.

"On Friday night, Dad helped me move a few more things from the new house back to my place off Watson Street. I spent the night there.

We had to go by the cemetery and get his compressor. Saw my mom for a few minutes, but that was it."

"What'd ya need the compressor for?" Ben asked.

"Someone had let some air out of one of the Scout's tires."

Burns looked up from his notebook.

"Someone tampered with your tire at your house? When did this happen? The night before the accident?"

"Yes, but I assumed it was a kid. Things like that happen occasionally. The house is just a block off Watson Street. College kids and drinking, well, you know." She smiled.

"True, but school doesn't even start up for weeks. Campus is pretty empty right now."

Detective Nelson rolled his soda can between his two index fingers.

She frowned. "Still, most of the patrons at the bars are the younger crowd. Could be unrelated, a random prank. It's happened before."

Ben took a deep breath and let it out. "Maybe so. But the brakes had to have been messed with up at Michelle's house. Otherwise, I think the trouble would have happened earlier."

"Let's talk to the mechanic again and confirm that. Maybe the tampering happened sooner," Nelson said.

Burns nodded. "Michelle, you were driving, correct?"

"Yes."

"How did the brakes feel to you, and when did you get the first indication there was an issue?"

She looked at Danni and back at the detective.

"I thought they felt a little weak when we pulled out of the driveway, but it was less than a mile later when we started down that big hill that I knew there was a definite problem."

"She said something about them feeling spongy. Then it seemed like there were no brakes at all," Danni added.

Burns took a few notes, then held the pen up and twitched his mouth to one side.

"Had anyone else been at the house that day?"

Michelle nodded. "My boyfriend, Trevor. He's a reporter too. Works at the *Daily Times* with me."

"We'll want to talk to him. I'll need contact information."

Michelle rattled off his number. "But he wouldn't have done this. I know he wouldn't."

"What about that electrician?" Danni asked.

Burns looked at her.

"Electrician?"

"There was someone who claimed to be lost, came by the house. Was supposedly an electrician on a service call but couldn't find the place he was looking for." She leaned forward. "I didn't see him. She answered the door."

"He seemed harmless. Kind of frustrated at being lost." Michelle shrugged. "We were getting ready to cook out when the doorbell rang. I've never seen him before. Wanted to know if he was at the right house. Can't remember what the name was he was looking for."

"What was he driving?"

"A pickup with some kind of funky tool thing on the back. Like a camper shell, but toolboxes that opened on the sides. Had red writing on the door and a logo like a lightning bolt. I didn't read it, pay any attention to it." Michelle threw herself against the back of the chair, then winced with pain. "Christ, I was the only one who saw him, and I didn't pay any attention to the name of the company."

"We should be able to track it down anyway." Burns thumped his pen on his notebook. "Might not be connected."

They went over the rest of Saturday evening's events. Michelle was adamant that Trevor wouldn't hurt anyone.

"He'd have no reason to do this anyway. I hardly know the guy," Danni said.

No need to tell them he was an asshole and about his hissy fit over the accident.

"We'll still talk to him. Maybe he saw someone outside the house when he left." Burns wrote something down and looked up. "You said he left at nine o'clock? Just about dark this time of year."

"Yeah, it was probably nine, maybe a few minutes after. It had been a long day. We were exhausted, so he went on home."

Michelle ran her fingers along the edge of the bandage around her shoulder.

"Is there anyone who'd have a bone to pick with you, Danni? Any problems at work could've got someone really mad at you?" Nelson asked.

"No. I'm not even working right now. Haven't since before Rick's death. I'm changing jobs anyway."

"Maybe Paul's really mad you quit." Michelle giggled, then covered her mouth with her hand and looked around. "Sorry, that was a joke."

Everyone was silent.

Danni took a long swig of her Diet Dr. Pepper, then put the can down. Surely they were wrong. This couldn't be happening.

"Any chance this could have been aimed at Rick? The brakes messed with before he was killed?" she asked.

"I don't think so, but we'll discuss that with our expert. With the kind of tampering that happened here, it's likely that the fluid drained out quickly. We're pretty sure it happened within hours of your trip down the mountainside." Nelson stood up, gathered the empty sugar packets from the table and put them in the cup, then tossed it in the trash. "I'm betting that Rick wasn't the one who was supposed to be killed that day on the dam. I think this could be a second attempt on your life, Danni."

She tried to swallow a lump in her throat.

"But what about Billy Tom Viney? He doesn't even know me. He'd have no reason to want me gone."

"We're going to look into it," Burns said. "We don't know for sure the two incidents are related. Nelson, here, may be jumping to conclusions. I don't think we need to be assuming anything." He closed his portfolio and stood up. "Danni, we're going to let you take your friend home, but we want you to be careful, be on your toes, and let us know if there's anything else suspicious that happens."

"You're going to just send her on her way?" Ben stood up so quickly his folding chair fell over backward. "What if someone's really trying to hurt her, maybe trying to kill her? She needs some protection. Her fiancé was just murdered."

"Now, Deputy Sizemore, we really don't know—"

"What do you mean you don't know? Someone did this deliberately. We know that much, and that's enough for me. I bet. You just wanna wait for another try?"

Ben slapped the table, then crossed his arms across his chest.

"Calm down, Ben. I'm fine. I'm not going into hiding or getting a bodyguard or something." Danni glared at him. "Really, let's let them do some more digging. I bet this isn't connected. Terry Butler seemed pretty sure that Viney's responsible for Rick's death."

"But they haven't even found those screwed up brothers. Randy and Rudy are still out there somewhere. They could have done this."

Nelson cleared his throat, then said, "Let's not overreact here. We'll investigate further. See what we can find out and go from there."

"Well, you better get busy and figure it out." Michelle pulled herself out of her chair, pushing off the table with her one good hand. "Danni, I need to get home. I feel another pain killer calling my name."

The only one still seated, she looked up at the others.

"I guess Michelle is safe. There's no way this was really someone out to get at her?"

Michelle snorted. "No, Danni, it was your car. The guy just seems to have bad aim."

39

Ben was still fuming, but Danni assured him she'd stay in touch and let him know if anything else happened. Burns and Nelson promised to contact her with more information as their investigation proceeded. The three of them stood next to the raised Scout, watching while she pulled out.

Michelle braced her elbow on the passenger door and rested her head against her palm.

"I can't believe someone did this to us. Why would they?"

"I don't understand it either."

She pulled the Subaru to a stop at a traffic light and looked over at the next car. A redheaded toddler in the back waved from his car seat. She smiled.

"Maybe they're wrong." Michelle sighed. "We'll have to see what comes of it, but I'm worried for you. This was aimed at you, not me."

They drove in silence for a while. When Danni glanced over while driving past the exit for Westover, Michelle was asleep.

She turned off the radio and thought about the possibility of a stalker. She'd had problems with one before when investigating a scandal that had someone pissed at her snooping. Rick had been there to protect her. They'd gotten so close during that time. He would sort through this bullshit and help her figure out what to do now, if he were only here.

She took a deep breath, let it out, and swallowed the lump in her throat. He'd tell her to be careful but assure her, too, that she could handle anything.

Who would do this and why?

The sun had faded behind thickening clouds, casting the day into a dull gray. What had been a slight breeze increased the farther south she drove. She wound around the mountain until she came to the spot where they'd gone off the road. With Michelle still asleep in the passenger seat, she pulled to the side of the asphalt, parked, and got out.

The kudzu and small trees were flattened in a path down to the tree where the Scout had come to a halt. It was terrifying to think how close they'd come to going over the ridge and plummeting down the mountain. What had she done to piss someone off to that extent?

She picked up a jagged piece of red plastic, probably part of the tail-light to the Scout. Funny, but the shape of it resembled a handgun. She let it fall between her fingers back to the gravel shoulder of the road. A shiver of fear ran up her spine, and tears came to her eyes.

A faint meow from behind her drew her attention. The yellow tabby cat she'd seen the night of the wreck sauntered toward her.

"Hey, buddy. You lost?"

She crossed the pavement. The cat turned and trotted up the hill, jumping atop the boulder that she suspected the Scout had hit. It sat down, thumped its tail on the rock, and stared at her. One of the ears was absent a good chunk off the tip. He looked scrawny, and some of his fur was missing in blotches.

"I bet you've been abandoned way out here in the middle of nowhere. I used to have a kitty, but I had a friend who was allergic, so I gave him away. He lives on a big farm in Missouri now with all the mice he cares to chase."

She talked in a soft voice and approached the cat slowly. He—well, maybe she—didn't run off and let her pick it up.

"Would you like to come with me? You'll get a good meal, see if we can fatten you up."

She stepped up out of the ditch at the shoulder of the pavement and turned at the sound of a vehicle coming down the hillside. It was the white pickup she'd seen that night on her way to Michelle's.

Shit. She'd forgotten about that. Might have been something she should have mentioned to the detectives.

The guy in the pickup slowed and stared at her when he passed. She didn't recognize him. He looked to be in his early forties, with dark hair. It was long, pushed behind his ears, and looked greasy. He had a goatee and a tattoo band on his left tricep, maybe a barbwire design. His skin was dark, like he worked in the sun a lot.

The truck sped up when it passed her. Mud covered the license, but she could see the first letter was a "P." But there was more in the back of the truck.

She let out a shriek.

The cat jumped from her arms and ran off in the woods.

A bow with a pack of arrows attached was mounted on a gun rack in the truck's back window.

The wind howled, and the clouds burst open before she made it back to the car.

Rain pounded against the windshield and the hood of the car. The tops of the trees leaned to and fro in the wind. Danni was surprised Michelle didn't wake up while they were bouncing along the dirt road to her house. Small rivers of water were already meandering through it and the ditch was filling up. She parked and waited for the rain to slow before waking Michelle. It wouldn't be good to wait too long before heading back to Bloomington, not with the weather conditions.

Michelle stirred and rubbed her eyes.

"We're home. Geez, I need a drink. It feels like I've been eating cotton balls."

Danni chuckled. "Better stick to the light stuff with the meds you're on, though."

"Hell, water sounds good right now." Michelle moved her seat to sit up straighter. "Waiting on the rain to slow down?"

"Yeah, but I can't wait for long. Looks like the road is deteriorating as we sit here. This is a bad storm." Danni flipped the wipers back on and jumped at a sudden flash of lightning, followed by a clap of thunder. "I hope it quits by the time I get back to town. Lizzie's supposed to help me move some things to the house."

"I hope so too. I don't mind getting a little wet. There's no hail. Let's just make a break for it."

"I have an umbrella. You take it, keep your bandages from getting soaked, and get in the house. I'll bring your purse and the bag from the hospital."

"Okay, Danni. You're a doll."

She took the umbrella, opened the door, and ran like a mad woman the fifteen feet or so to the small covered porch.

Danni followed. Thunder rolled just before she pulled the door closed.

"Phew, that's a soaker." Danni ran her fingers through her hair and then twisted it to wring out some of the water. "I'm going to try to get back into town. You going to be okay?"

Michelle flipped on lamps at each end of the sofa, sending a warm glow across the dark living room.

"You bet. I'm planning to get out of these clothes and go to bed here shortly. I can sleep like a baby in a storm. Mom's just down the road. She'll be up here this evening with a plate for me for dinner if she has to slog it down here in her big rubber hip waders. She already promised. I think she even made me a strawberry cake."

"Cream cheese icing?"

"Of course."

"Maybe I *should* stay for cake." Danni smiled.

Michelle had changed into a blue fluffy robe. She offered her a towel.

"Hey, do you know a guy that drives a little white truck? Dark hair, goatee, seems a little creepy. Maybe lives around here."

She bent over and fluffed her hair with the towel.

"Sounds like Randy Carlisle. He lives up the road a ways. Works on cars, piddles around in his garden, but he doesn't seem to have a job other than that. The place was his mom's, but she died last year. He and a sister used to both live there with the old lady, but I think the sister got the hell out of dodge a couple of years ago. Weird family." Michelle eased down on one end of the couch and curled her legs beneath her. "Why?"

"Just saw him there at the crash site. He drove by real slow, staring like I was some kind of freak show on the side of the road. Gave me the creeps."

She put the towel over the back of one of the dining room chairs.

Michelle nodded. "Sounds about right. He gives me the creeps too. What a weirdo."

"Odd thing is, I saw him the other night on my way up here."

"What? You think he had something to do with your brakes? Honestly, Danni, I think he's a little retarded. I'm not sure he'd hurt a fly."

Danni opened the door and looked outside. The rain was letting up a little. Without turning back toward Michelle, she said, "He's got a rack in the back window of that truck with a compound bow hanging from it."

"Well, you find a lot of those around here. If you're worried about him, have Burns and Nelson look into it."

She turned back to the room, keeping a hand on the doorknob.

"I might do that. Randy Carlisle, right?"

"Yep." Michelle leaned her head against the back of the couch. "I seriously doubt he's the guy, but have him checked out. He'd certainly know how to screw with someone's brake line. He's always got a car up on jacks in his driveway. Lots of people use him for repairs. I never have, but I've never had any real issue with him either. I think his mother went to the Westover Baptist Church. Mom's mentioned her before in regard to church."

Danni rolled the doorknob back and forth.

"But she's gone now?"

Michelle nodded. "About a year ago. Had a heart attack or something pretty sudden. Mom liked her. Might have even gone to the funeral."

"I don't think I've ever seen the guy in my life. Surely he wouldn't do this as a random prank. You think he's got something against you? Maybe messed with the Scout thinking it was yours?"

"I doubt it. He knows what I drive. Glares at me every time he sees me on the road."

"He's weird about that, huh? He drove by and just stared at me the other night, and then today on the side of the road."

"I think the guy has no life. A woman that's not family is something to gawk at. Kind of creepy, but harmless." Michelle pulled a green throw from the back of the couch and spread it over her legs. "I bet they'll find out he wouldn't hurt a fly, just doesn't know what to think of females."

"Okay. I'll talk to the detectives about him. The staring spooked me, then I saw the compound bow." Danni picked up the umbrella leaning against the doorframe. "Weird."

"Yeah, weird." She yawned. "Thanks for the ride home."

"You going to be okay? If you need anything, call me."

"I will on both counts."

Danni stepped out on the porch and popped the umbrella open. The rain still came down, but not as heavy. At least the lightning and thunder had stopped.

By the time she got to Bloomington, she'd driven out of the storm. Everything was dry.

41

Danni loaded the boxes nearly as quickly as Lizzie could fold them together and secure the bottoms with packing tape. She started with kitchen supplies, then the home office, and moved on to the bathroom.

"Dang, the entryway's already crowded with these things." Lizzie stacked one on top of another to clear some walking room. "Maybe I better start carrying some out to the truck."

"Okay, that's fine if you want. Take the ones on that side of the entryway. That's what I'm most likely to need." She pointed to the far wall. "The rest can wait a day or so, if we don't have room."

"We can make a couple trips today if you like."

Danni pushed hair out of her eyes with the back of her hand.

"I'll tell you what. Let's load the truck and the Lexus, and we'll make one trip with the rest of my essentials. I'll get the rest when I move furniture. I need to box up some stuff in the bedroom, and we'll pretty much be done packing."

The low rumble of a lawnmower running nearby grew louder when Lizzie opened the front door.

"I'll just stick all these full ones on the porch, then start loadin' the truck."

"Okay. Thanks. I might be upstairs when you come back in."

Danni grabbed a couple of empty boxes and made her way upstairs. She packed the contents of her dresser and went downstairs to get more empties. Most of the boxes that were stacked in the entryway were gone. The floor was littered with leaves from the dead plant on the side table. She picked the dried-out plant up to take it to the trash and noticed the white envelope she'd left there days before. Curious, she sat the plant back down and opened the envelope.

A note in blue ink with plain block letters said, "I MISSED!"

A small drawing of an arrow ran beneath the words.

The note slipped from her fingers and fluttered to the floor.

Danni dropped to the bottom step, clutching the staircase rail.

"Oh, God," she sobbed. "It should have been me."

It took several minutes to get her sobs under control, but then she realized Lizzie hadn't come back inside. There wasn't a sound but the distant mower.

"Lizzie?" she called.

She swung the door open. Two boxes were stacked on the front porch.

Her stomach turned over with a feeling of dread.

"Lizzie?" she called again.

Her cousin's green pickup was parked in the driveway. A box lay on its side on the concrete behind the truck, its contents of pasta and canned goods spilled out across the drive.

"Lizzie!" she screamed and rushed across the lawn to the truck.

Her cousin lay on her back beside the pickup, one ankle tucked at a funny angle beneath the other leg. A thin red line of blood meandered toward a box of spilled spaghetti noodles splayed out on the white concrete.

An arrow was embedded in her chest.

I stood in front of the open back door of my car and lowered the compound bow to my side. The girl had gone down with one shot. I smiled and placed the bow in the backseat, shut the door, climbed in front, and started the car. I took one last look at the crumpled body next to the truck and wondered if she felt her head slam down on the concrete.

The silence of the kill was satisfying. The only sound was canned vegetables rolling across the driveway afterward, then the *rat-a-tat* of a woodpecker in a nearby tree continuing his task.

The guy mowing his lawn three doors up didn't even look my way when I drove past leaving the cul-de-sac. The freshly mowed grass had a sweet smell that reminded me of home.

"You did a good job mowing our grass, takin' care of everything around the house for me and Tracey all those years. Such a good son, good, good son."

Mama patted me on the knee as I made the turn at the corner and left the little subdivision.

"Thanks, Mama. I try to do what you want, make you proud."

She laughed. "Oh, you're making me proud, boy. So proud."

I wasn't sure who the girl helping her move even was, but I knew the bitch would suffer, knowing it was her fault.

The heavy rains and thunderstorm revived the night that Lizzie died. The cloudy sky and intermittent rain lingered the next day as well.

Danni had wanted to curl up in her old bed at her parents' and stay again, but the thought of a killer running around trying to ruin her life forced her to make other plans. She couldn't just hide out until whoever it was came for her. Life was going to have to go on.

The sun was finally peeking out between clouds when she pulled into the courthouse parking lot two days after Lizzie was killed. She rode the elevator up to the third floor with a deliveryman pushing a dolly loaded down with four cases of printer paper.

Janet, an older woman who always wore her silver hair pulled into a tight bun atop her head, came around the receptionist counter, led the deliveryman to the supply area, and asked Danni to wait a minute.

She put her brown leather bag on the counter, tapping her short nails against the wood finish. Where was Kendra? A copy of the *Daily Times* was spread out across the desktop. She smiled to herself. She'd soon have a byline in the paper. To the side of the newspaper was a small dish of paperclips, a stapler, and a bobblehead Bill Clinton.

Was that Rick's?

Twice she'd left in a hurry and hadn't taken his things. Once because of Mr. Lendo's confession, and the last time after getting sick to her stomach over the photo of Rick on the archery target. Kendra had probably picked it up to play with and hadn't put it back.

"Where's Kendra? Y'all didn't run her off already, did you?" she asked Janet when she returned to the counter, a sweet, fruity perfume surrounding her.

"Oh, no, no. She's at lunch." She plopped down into the office chair, gripped the desk with both hands, and pulled herself forward. "Sorry, Danni, to hear about your cousin. I hope they find this guy, whoever it is."

"Thanks. Me too." She nodded toward Terry's office. "He in?"

Janet waved Danni toward the hallway as she picked up the phone. "Lovely County Prosecutor's Office . . ."

She pulled her bag off the counter and headed to Terry's office.

Her hand gripped the doorknob, but she froze before twisting it. She heard a muffled noise coming from behind her in Rick's office. Letting go of the doorknob, she turned.

The light was out and the door slightly ajar. Someone was crying. It was a soft, muffled cry, but definitely a cry. She pushed the door open and stepped inside the office. The box she'd been packing when Mr. Lendo stormed down the hallway was still on top of his desk. She flipped on the light.

Kendra was curled up between the high arms of the small loveseat, clutching her phone. She sat up and dropped her phone to the floor. Danni stared at it.

The screen was filled with Rick's smiling face.

"Danni." She dabbed at her eyes with a wad of tissues clutched in one fist. "I'm sorry. Did you come to get the rest of Rick's things?"

Danni stared at the picture and didn't respond. Kendra followed her eyes to the floor and jumped to her feet, snatching it off the floor.

"I, I'm sorry." She held the device to her chest and looked up at Danni, tears streaming down her face.

It didn't make sense. The girl didn't even know Rick.

What the hell?

She stared at Kendra, a puzzled look on her face.

Kendra plopped down on the sofa and put her face in her hands. The phone fell to her lap.

"I'm sorry. I'm so sorry. I can only imagine what you're thinking," she muttered.

"Why don't you tell me what I should think? I get here and find one of Rick's toys on your desk. Then I come in here and you're crying your eyes out over a picture of *my fiancé* on *your* phone. How'd you even get that picture? Let me see it."

Kendra handed her the phone. "I, um, I took it. It's not him. It's his picture."

"I know it's not him. It's just a picture," she snarled.

"I mean I took it of a picture of him. The one in the waiting room."

She looked up. Her eyes were bloodshot and her cheeks blotchy.

There were framed photos of Terry and the assistant prosecutors hanging in the reception area. The picture on Kendra's phone was definitely the same shot and looked as if it could have been taken through glass.

"Why?"

Danni tossed the phone back on the couch next to the girl.

"I liked him. I've always liked him. I think I loved him. He didn't know, Danni. He didn't have a clue. There wasn't anything going on. You'll have to believe me. Please don't be mad." Her eyes pleaded with Danni.

"What do you mean? You only worked here a week or so before he was killed. Are you nuts?"

She gripped the back of an armchair that faced the small loveseat.

"I knew him before. I'm sure he didn't recognize me, but we used to go to the same gym. I'd watch him workout. Then, when I came to work here, it seemed like it was meant to be." She shook her head and looked down at her lap. "I'm sorry. It was wrong. I know it was."

"I just don't understand."

"When I found out about you, well, I remembered you from the newspaper. Then, when I met you, I just, I don't know. I couldn't help but like you."

"But you're still hung up on him?"

Kendra looked around the room, then met Danni's eyes.

"I guess that, since he died, it's just been hard to get over it. He seemed so perfect. So very perfect."

"Well, I can't argue with that." Danni pursed her lips. "Did you know my cousin, Lizzie?"

"Who?" Kendra looked confused.

"What's going on here?"

Terry stood in the doorway, a puzzled look on his face.

Kendra jumped to her feet and smoothed out the front of her cotton dress with her palms.

"Nothing really. We're just talking. That's all."

"She was going to help me box up the rest of Rick's stuff, but we got sidetracked," Danni said.

Kendra took in a deep breath, let it out, and nodded in agreement.

Terry looked from one of them to the other, his brow knitting in a frown. His gaze finally rested on her.

"Danni, we need to talk."

"I have to get back up front." Kendra slunk toward the door and turned back to her. "Let me know if you need some help."

Terry tugged at the knees of his black dress pants and sat down.

"Why don't you have a seat."

That didn't sound good. She sat on the edge of the loveseat.

"I know this has been hard. It's been hard on you."

He leaned back and pulled his right foot up, balancing the ankle against his knee.

"What is it, Terry?"

"We're going to have to drop the charges against Billy Tom Viney. He didn't do it."

She rocked back against the sofa.

"I had a feeling that might happen. He couldn't have killed Lizzie, and it had to be the same person."

"I agree. Viney's methamphetamine cooking partner, John Sugget, has finally admitted he was with him at the time of Rick's death. He got some pressure from the Viney family, and then I guess he saw Viney on television after the arraignment. He couldn't do that to his friend."

Terry took a deep breath and let it out. "Viney's brothers were questioned last night in Lizzie's murder, and they admitted that Sugget had the Viney family beating down his door, demanding he come forward."

"What about the picture Billy Tom used for target practice? What about his cell mate? It doesn't make sense now that Lizzie's . . . Oh, God." Swallowing the huge lump in her throat, her voice came out a squeak when she asked, "What do we do now?"

Terry lowered his foot and sat forward.

"The picture proves nothing but a lack of taste and common sense on the part of Mr. Viney. The cellmate apparently tried to take advantage of the situation and win some favors with the prosecutor's office. A common occurrence with jailhouse snitches, I'm afraid. And with your cousin being killed with the same type of arrow, it points to someone else."

"They both died because of me." She shook her head.

"You can't take the blame. But you are correct. It appears whoever killed Rick and then Lizzie was after you. The note you turned over to the investigators yesterday certainly points to that conclusion."

She stood up and walked around Rick's desk. The trinkets she'd once packed in the box were now scattered across the desktop. She grabbed the cardboard flap and stared at Terry.

"You know we'll exhaust all efforts," he said.

She nodded slowly. "I know."

Terry sighed.

"I guess you've heard that my brakes were cut deliberately."

She tossed the balls and a Slinky into the box.

"What? Your brakes?"

He pulled himself up out of the chair.

"Yes. The wreck over the weekend, not so accidental. Someone cut the brakes."

He wrestled his cell phone out of his pants pocket.

"Who told you that they were cut?"

"Ben Sizemore. I met with him and the detectives on Rick's case Monday afternoon. There was some talk of whether it could be related to Rick's death. I hadn't seen the note yet."

"There damn well should be some talk. Excuse me while I make this call. Don't you go anywhere."

Holding the phone to his ear, he walked out of the office.

Danni piled more of Rick's things in the box, including a couple of photos and two paperweights, then pulled a jacket and a tie from the hook on the back of the door. She folded the jacket and put it on top but held onto the tie.

It was one she'd bought him. She closed her eyes and ran it between her fingers. The soft fabric was a nice pale blue with thin gray stripes. He'd loved it.

She sucked in a breath. This was not a time for tears. It was time to find out who was truly responsible for killing Rick and Lizzie.

Folding the flaps together, she picked up the box.

Danni placed the box on a side chair in Terry's office. He was still on the phone, elbows on his desk. He pointed to another chair. She sat down and dropped her leather bag to the floor beside her.

"Okay, Detective. I'll talk to Miss Edens. We'll go from there."

He pressed a button on the phone and tossed it on his desk blotter.

"What?" she asked.

"That was Detective Burns. They're at a loss. Don't seem to have any suspects, anyone with a reason to want you dead. They want to interview you again." He steepled his fingers and rested them against his nose. "Burns asked me about your problems in Little Rock. I don't know where he came up with that, but he inquired if there could be someone related to the scandal that could have a grudge against you. Or anyone else you've maybe written about as a journalist who might be vengeful."

"Geez, I wish that would just quit haunting me. I lost my job, moved half a state away, and still can't shake it." She twisted her hair in a tight knot at one shoulder. "I don't know, Terry. You never can tell when someone's going to misinterpret what you've done, what was your job to do, and take the result out on you. I try to be fair as a reporter, but some people don't see it that way. You know how things went down with the old sheriff here."

He shook his head. "I know. I know. You weren't to blame, and no one with a right mind could say you were."

"That and the story in Little Rock about Ronnie Hudgens and his shenanigans with the Highway Department are the two biggest stories I've ever covered. One almost got me killed, and the other got me accused of libel and fired." She rubbed her forehead with her fingertips. "I love being a reporter, but maybe I shouldn't."

"I understand, Danni." Terry ran his fingers across the top of his baldhead, then leaned back in his chair and rested his hands across his belly. "My position as county prosecutor gets me in hot water at times, but when you love what you do, you have to take the bad with the good."

They sat in silence for a few seconds.

"Well, as far as Hudgens," she finally said, "he's now missing. Probably took off, left the wife without a forwarding address, and doesn't want to be found."

She let the knot of hair loose and tossed it over her shoulder.

"I heard about that." Terry rocked forward in his chair. "I also heard this morning that a photographer for the paper down there has been found murdered. Stabbed. Don't know if it's related."

"Who?"

"A Gerald Yell. Do you know him?"

She gasped. "Yes. And he was the photog that took a lot of the pics used in the Hudgens stories. Of course, he took shots for a lot of news pieces."

"It may not be related, but I thought you should know. He was found in his apartment. The place looked ransacked. They're trying to determine if he interrupted a robbery. He'd just returned from a night out with friends."

"Jesus. That's too much. Surely it wasn't the same son of a bitch. Poor Gerald."

Terry's office phone buzzed. He glanced at it but didn't pick up.

"I believe Detective Burns was right in assuming Rick's death was an accident and the archer was aiming at you. The note seems to prove that. The issue with the brakes so soon after his murder points to that conclusion as well. Then Lizzie, and now this photographer. It could be related to that mess in Little Rock."

"Shit. I was afraid you were going to say something like that."

"Maybe it's Hudgens. He could be on the run and on the chase to exact some kind of warped revenge."

She took in a deep breath and let it out.

"You need to be careful, Danni."

"Yeah, I guess so." She leaned over to pick her bag up off the floor, pulled it to her shoulder, and stood. "For now, I've got to go check in with my family. See what's happening with Lizzie's arrangements."

"Promise me you'll give Burns or Nelson a call. They might be able to sort some of this out and come up with ideas."

With the box loaded in her arms, she went to the door, then turned back to Terry.

"Hudgens wouldn't do this. I just don't think he would."

On her way out of the office, she stopped at the front desk, rested the box on the edge of the counter, reached over, and grabbed Rick's bobblehead.

Kendra gasped and then gave her a sheepish look.

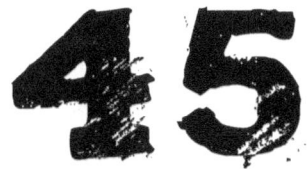

After picking at her food over a dinner with her family, Danni went back to her house and took a two-hour nap that evening. She woke up to darkness and a stiff neck. Bruno was curled in a ball next to her in bed.

A news alert from the statewide paper popped up on her cell phone. She couldn't believe it.

"Well, I guess that answers that. Don't you agree, buddy?"

Bruno cocked his head to one side and stared at her.

"Let's get something to munch on, and then we'll see what Channel Seven has to say about it."

Twenty minutes later, she sat cross-legged on the couch with a plate balanced between her thighs. She picked up the remote and flipped to the Little Rock station. The theme song to a nine o'clock show wound down.

It was the first story on the broadcast.

"Cleburne County officials report the discovery of the body of former Arkansas Highway and Transportation Director Ronnie P. Hudgens in a remote area along the shores of Greers Ferry Lake, north of Heber Springs. Hudgens was an apparent victim of a brutal attack, according to investigators on the scene. He lost his state position nearly three years ago after the discovery of a kickback scheme involving more than three Highway Department contractors. Hudgens was last seen June sixteenth at a family function in Little Rock. His wife reported him missing the following day. Cleburne County Sheriff Bob White said that definite leads in the death of Hudgens are being pursued. The body has been transferred to the state medical examiner's office in Little Rock."

The petite redheaded reporter turned to a male anchor.

"Well, Tom, all of Little Rock will be anxious to see how this one turns out."

"I'm sure you're right about that. And in other news—"

Danni's phone rang as the broadcast moved on to other topics. It was Michelle.

"Hey, girl. Did you see the news?"

"I did. I can't believe it. I wonder if his wife was involved."

She picked up the remote and muted the television, then massaged her neck.

"They say she reported him missing." Michelle yawned. "She's been keeping his disappearance active in the news. Of course, that could just be a cover."

"It could be. I don't know. Terry asked me if the sabotage of my brakes could be related to all that bullshit in Little Rock. I told him I didn't think so. There was no reason for Hudgens to come after me. But this is icing on the cake. I'm going to have to stew on this for a while and see if there's something I'm just overlooking."

She absently stroked Bruno's back as she talked.

"Hell, from what you told me, that asshole had his dick in anything he could catch wearing a skirt. He probably crossed paths with someone who didn't want to take his bullshit. Maybe with somebody's wife he should have avoided." Michelle snorted.

"I'll have to see what the *Republican Journal* reports in the morning. They'll have more information. Already put out a news alert, but it was brief."

"Okay, well, let me know if you find out anything. I'm going back to bed."

Michelle yawned again.

"Hey, how you feeling? Your mom still bringing you food?"

"You bet. More than I can eat. I'm good, just exhausted and already sick of this damned bandage."

"Ah. Take some of those pain pills. Life will be rosy."

"Oh yeah, real rosy. I just won't be conscious to know it."

Danni hung up, then massaged and rolled her neck.

What a week.

She was still processing Lizzie's murder and grieving for Rick too. She'd learned her brakes had been cut, and that Viney was actually innocent. She'd dealt with Kendra's infatuation with Rick, and now, they'd found Hudgens apparently murdered.

She pulled herself up from the couch and went to the kitchen. Half the omelet went down the disposal before she rinsed the plate and left it in the sink. She grabbed the fresh pack of Salems out of the butter dish in the freezer and the new lighter she'd put on the windowsill.

"Shall we partake a little, Bruno?" she asked the dog at her feet.

He yipped.

"I thought you'd agree."

Geez, talking to the dog a little too much. What the hell? At least I'm not hearing him respond.

She'd just lit up a cigarette when Bruno barked and jumped up on the railing below the screen on the driveway side of the porch.

"Nobody better be messing with my car!" she yelled nervously.

Could it be someone with even worse motives?

She pushed herself out of the Adirondack and went to the dining room to look out the window. A police car was parked under the streetlight in front of her house and what looked like an unmarked cruiser as well, but she couldn't tell for sure in the dark.

"Shit. What now?"

She looked down at Bruno.

The doorbell rang, as if in response.

Detectives Burns and Nelson, along with an officer she didn't know and another man in civilian clothes with cop hair, waited on the front porch.

"Can I help you?" she asked.

"Miss Edens?" the guy she didn't recognize in civilian clothes asked.

"Yes." She tried to hold a barking Bruno back with her foot. "Hush, boy. It's okay."

"I'm Detective Stevens. This is Deputy Wiles. And I believe you know these gentlemen." He cocked his head toward Burns and Nelson.

"Yes. Yes, I do."

She picked up Bruno.

"We'd like to speak with you about the death of Ronnie Hudgens," Detective Stevens said. "Sorry to come so late, but this is urgent."

46

Danni looked from Detective Stevens to the deputy whose uniform insignia indicated Cleburne County. Detectives Burns shuffled to the side, and Nelson acted like he didn't want to look her in the eye.

"Well, come in, I guess." She held the door open for them. "Let's sit in the dining room. I've got plenty of chairs in there."

The three detectives took a seat at the table, and the deputy sat in a chair in one corner.

"Give me just a minute."

Detective Stevens nodded. She carried Bruno to the back door and let him out.

"What the hell?" she muttered to herself, then grabbed her smoldering cigarette and took a deep inhale before stubbing it out and heading back inside.

"Now, what can I do for you?"

She pulled out the chair at the head of the table and sat down, folding her arms in front of her. Stevens snatched a pocket notebook from the inside of his suit jacket.

"First off, can you tell us where you were on June sixteenth and seventeenth?"

"I'm sure I was here. Well, at my other house. Rick, my fiancé, was still alive then." She frowned. "That was two weeks before he was killed. Yes, we stayed home that weekend. I think it rained. We watched movies. Now that I think about it, Bruno had a minor tumor removed that Friday. We did stay home and just babied him all weekend."

Stevens made a few notes, then looked up.

"Can anyone verify your location that weekend?"

She snorted. "Well, Detective, not anymore. My fiancé, you see, was killed. Someone shot him with an arrow while we were walking along the dam at Lake Louise by my other house."

"I've already informed Stevens here about your unfortunate circumstances," Nelson said. "I told him about the problem you had with your brakes and the accident that nearly killed your friend too."

"I understand your fiancé was murdered recently, and your cousin. Sorry for your loss, ma'am." Stevens thumped his pen on his pad of paper.

"I'm sure." She smirked.

"This is about another murder. But, now that you mention it, murder seems to be all around you these days. Doesn't it, Miss Edens?"

"You ain't kidding." Nelson stared at her and leaned back in his chair.

"What are you implying, Detective?"

With her arms still crossed, she rubbed her elbows and tried to keep her breathing steady.

How dare he imply that I had something to do with Rick's or Lizzie's death, or even my problem with the brakes.

"Miss Edens, did you have any reason to want Mr. Hudgens dead? Any lingering animosity you couldn't control?" Stevens asked.

She bit her lip. "I wouldn't wish death on my worst enemy. I'm not that kind of person."

"I understand you lost your job when Mr. Hudgens accused you of libel?"

He balanced his pen between two fingers and swung it back and forth.

"I did lose my job. And yes, he accused me of libel. I had proof of what I reported, but it went missing from my office. The witness substantiating the story also just happened to disappear and has since committed suicide, from what I understand."

She took a deep breath and wished for Rick—his hand in hers, here to support her, just help her deal with this shit. Exhaling, she continued, "But would I want him dead? Would I wish him any ill will? No, Detective, I would not."

"You've said."

Stevens continued to stare at her and swing the pen back and forth.

"I was here in Bloomington the weekend you're asking me about. In fact, I haven't been back to Little Rock since I left there more than two years ago." She stabbed the tabletop with each of the last few words.

He held his pen steady and cocked his head to one side.

"How might you explain some materials we found at the scene of the apparent murder that appear to belong to you?"

A wave of nausea hit. She swallowed hard and stared him down.

"I don't know what the hell you're talking about. Are you really accusing me of being involved in this murder?"

"Now, let's not get excited here. Nobody's been accused of anything." Stevens put his pen down next to the little notebook. "However, there are some issues we need to get cleared up."

She raised her eyebrows but didn't respond.

Ball's in your court, Detective.

"A notebook with your name on it and a mini cassette tape with a recording of an apparent interview you conducted, along with a number of documents, were found in a residence on the property where Mr. Hudgens's body was found."

Danni sat forward. "Documents? Like receipts for hotel rooms?"

"As a matter of fact, yes. I don't have a full tally of what they found, but there were some receipts. The materials were tossed around the scene. It was a little bit of a mess, maybe part of an argument fought over."

"Huh."

Just how much information do I have to provide this guy?

"Do you know how those materials got to that location if you weren't there?"

Stevens gave her that head cocked, wide-eyed inquisitive look again. She fought an urge to slap him.

"No, I don't."

"Do these materials sound familiar?"

"Yes, they do."

She slouched against the back of her chair and crossed her arms. He shook his head.

"Miss Edens, you're not helping yourself here. You need to be forthcoming about your knowledge of these documents and how they came to be found in this particular Cleburne County residence that just so happens to be the apparent scene of the murder of Ronnie P. Hudgens, a man you were accused of libeling in the statewide newspaper."

"Well, Detective, I'm a little concerned with the accusatory tone you've taken here. I will try my best to put those feelings aside long enough to tell you that, when I was accused of this supposed libel, a number of materials I had gathered in my effort to accurately report this story turned up missing. Those missing materials—which included my notes, recordings of a couple of interviews, and copies of some receipts and other documents—may very well be what you discovered at that scene." She bit her bottom lip and looked from one detective to the other. "How they got there? I have no idea."

Stevens stared at her, then closed his notebook.

"Miss Edens, we're gonna be investigating this further and will be in touch."

"That's fine, Detective. My answers will be the same then. I was not in Cleburne County and have no idea how anything connected to me ended up there." She stood and pushed her chair back up to the table. "You're welcome to see yourselves out."

The detectives looked at each other, then stood. Burns and Nelson pushed in their chairs, but Stevens sauntered out of the room leaving his where it sat. The deputy followed.

Stevens stopped midway through the living room and turned toward her.

"I assume you don't have any plans to leave town on vacation or anything."

She swallowed what she really wanted to say and answered politely.

"No, Detective. I do not. I have another funeral to deal with, actually."

He nodded, then walked through the door that Burns held open for him. Detective Burns also nodded before he closed the door. Danni stomped over to it and snapped the deadbolt in place. A shiver raced up her spine as she turned her back to the door and slumped against it. They couldn't seriously have any real evidence against her.

Stevens was rude and accusatory.

How dare he insinuate I was involved?

All he had was some of her work product that had been stolen from her. Someone connected with Hudgens had to have taken it from her desk back then, probably someone who gave it to Hudgens.

But why had it turned up now? And why had it turned up there?

A week went by without another word from the investigators. The morning of Lizzie's funeral, Danni's phone buzzed while she brushed her teeth. Terry Butler wanted her to come by his office to talk.

"I can't today, Terry." She looked at herself in the bathroom mirror with an exaggerated grin to examine her teeth. "I've got Lizzie's memorial service this afternoon."

"Okay. I understand. But tomorrow then? We need to discuss this. I don't want the situation with Hudgens to escalate."

She turned and propped her butt against the edge of the sink.

"You don't really think I had anything to do with that bullshit, do you?"

"No, of course not, but the Cleburne County authorities aren't as familiar with you as I am."

"I wouldn't kill anybody."

Well, there was a guy not that long ago that she seriously considered killing. She'd even aimed a gun at his head but stopped herself from pulling the trigger. Hitting him in the head with the pistol wasn't quite as exciting, yet it felt damn good. He deserved a bullet. Still, the concussion had worked for a temporary remedy. No need to get into that with Terry.

"I'm sure you wouldn't." Terry made a muffled sound of movement, as if he switched ears for the phone. "If you're uncomfortable coming to the office, would you care to meet me for lunch? It's important we talk."

They made arrangements to meet at Marlo's, a sandwich place downtown, for lunch the next day.

Danni forced herself to hustle into the shower. There were two missed calls from Ben, but she didn't return them. Talking with him about everything going on wasn't something she wanted to do just yet. She hadn't even told him about Randy Carlisle, Michelle's neighbor with the white truck. Thinking about his creepy stare sent a shiver up her spine.

What a weirdo.

Probably harmless, but someone needed to check him out. She was thrown off by the visit the week before, or she might have told Burns and Nelson about him then.

She made a point to concentrate on the family the rest of the day. They had a meal at the church after the funeral, where they sat around enjoying stories about Lizzie and mulling over family photo albums. Baby Shane tottered between the relatives, delighting everyone as much as possible.

Danni caught Josh alone when he snatched the baby up for a changing and took him to the church nursery. Josh was a few years younger than she was, and at least a year younger than Lizzie, but he was much taller than both of them. He often looked uncomfortable with his height, standing stoop shouldered and leaning forward most of the time. Carrying the baby to the nursery, he walked tall and proud.

"You doing okay?"

She held up the plastic wastebasket at the side of the changing table for him when he removed the soiled diaper.

"Not too bad, really. I'm going to miss her, of course, and maybe haven't got my head around it all yet, but I think it's going to be okay. I got this little guy to think 'bout. And . . ." He looked sideways, as if expecting someone to come walking up on the conversation. Then, in a soft voice, he said, "I think I may just get off on this drug thing."

"Lizzie told me your attorney is trying to work it out."

"He is. I never understood why she took that stuff. I never took it, and I'm glad for it."

"You should be. It's a horrible drug. I was proud of her for quitting. That's hard with meth. Really hard, I hear." She helped hold the squirming baby as Josh maneuvered him into a clean diaper. "You're a good man for sticking by her through all that, especially taking the blame for something that wasn't your fault."

"Thanks, but I told her no more. I think she understood that, was pretty darned scared about my getting busted."

"I know. Listen, Josh, and I mean this with all my heart. I'm sorry about Lizzie. I feel to blame. She was at my house, and it looks like it was someone out to get me all along. Whoever it is murdered Rick, now Lizzie, and probably cut the brakes on my car trying to kill me and Michelle both."

She picked up the baby and put him on her hip while Josh loaded wipes back in the backpack he used as a diaper bag. He threw the bag on his shoulder, shook his head, and looked her in the eye.

"Uncle Addison told me. But it's not your fault. The only one to blame is whoever took that bow and aimed at her. No one else. So, stop beatin' yourself up. She wouldn't blame you for this, and I don't. You've always been there for Lizzie and me. She knew it and thought the world of ya, Danni. Don't doubt that for a second."

She nodded. "Thanks for saying that."

"Meant it. Every word."

Shane reached for his dad with fat, wiggly baby fingers. Josh took him from Danni and tossed him in the air. Shane giggled.

"Let's go find some pie for this little guy."

He put Shane down, leaned over, and took his hand as the toddler staggered his way out to the hall.

48

Danni returned to the cemetery with her parents. She spent some time with her mother watching a movie and then went to find her father in the cemetery shop.

The shop was painted a dull brown with white trim. A six-foot privacy fence stretched out on each side and behind it, creating a yard for storing heavy equipment and miscellaneous materials for the grounds.

The thick wooden door stood open, and a fan hung from the top. Danni ducked under it. The shop area smelled of oil and sweat. The walls were lined with a wide workbench a little higher than waist level. Assorted tools and supplies were arranged on the shelves below or hanging on the pegboard lining the walls above it. One shelf had coffee cans labeled with masking tape and a marker listing their contents from nuts and bolts to zip ties and Weed Eater string. An old refrigerator stood next to a long rack where shovels, rakes, and other landscaping tools hung from pegs. A window at the back was ajar, and another fan faced out, creating a steamy breeze between it and the one hanging in the doorway. Exposed florescent bulbs hung above the workbench in a horseshoe around the edges of the room. The floor was concrete and stained in places, but swept clean of any debris. Her father was a stickler for keeping the tools put up and everything tidy.

A calendar from a local farm supply shop was pinned on the door to the garage area. A former groundskeeper had once switched it out for one with pictures of girls clad in bikinis. Her father had been none too pleased. The guy knew he'd messed up when he got assigned the job of cleaning out the fencerow at the back of the cemetery and a good case of poison ivy for his efforts.

Danni clasped her hands over her ears and waited for her father to stop the grinder. He held a long lawnmower blade to the machine mounted on a corner of the workbench. The sound was deafening, and sparks flew in a massive shower around him. After several minutes, he held the blade up, examining the edge, then laid it down, removed his safety goggles, and turned off the machine. She sat down in an old swivel desk chair with tattered arms and a seat pocked with duct tape.

"Hey, Dad."

He jumped at the sound of her voice behind him.

"Oh, Danni, I didn't see you come in."

She giggled. "I guess not. I didn't mean to startle you."

"Just caught up in my work here." He wiped his hands on a faded blue shop towel, then stuck one end in his back pocket, letting the rest of it hang loose at his hip. "Want something to drink?"

"Sure. Water's fine."

He opened the refrigerator and pulled out a couple of clear bottles and handed one to her, then leaned over and kissed her on the forehead.

"So, I hadn't had a chance to ask, but how's Michelle?"

"Not too bad. She was pretty banged up, but she's home now and going to be okay."

"Well, good. You getting settled at the house?"

He pulled a stool over next to her. Its legs screeched on the concrete floor.

"Yeah. I think that's the place for me. I like being in town, and I talked to Brett Penderson about going to work at the *Daily Times* here in a few weeks."

"Danni, that's great. I'm glad to hear it." He grinned.

"Anyway, I can walk to work from the house if they still want me after all the crap that's going on."

"Why wouldn't they? You don't mean Rick and your cousin getting killed? Why would they blame you, for God's sake?"

"Well, that might be part of it. I told them I want to get that all sorted out before I come to work."

Should I tell him I'm suspected of murdering Hudgens?

His once deep-red hair was now mostly gray, and new wrinkles had settled in around the edges of his eyes and across his brow. Caring for her mother in her mental state the last few years and running a business on his own were catching up with him. On top of all that, he spent too much time worrying about her.

Maybe it is best to hold on and not tell him more yet. Maybe after it is cleared up.

"Everything else okay, Dad?"

There had to be something bothering him. He'd hardly asked a question about the wreck. She'd expected an onslaught.

The corners of his mouth turned up slightly, and he nodded but didn't look at her.

"Not bad. Not bad."

Danni stared at him for a few seconds.

"Come on, Dad. What's up?"

He ran his fingers through his hair and took a deep breath.

"Well, Sis, I've got an offer on the cemetery. It's a substantial amount, would set us up pretty good for the future. Maybe I should sell, retire, and look after your mom."

Danni was stunned. She figured her dad would be working the grounds and managing the business for years to come.

"Wow, really? I had no idea you wanted to retire."

Her father had owned and operated the cemetery since she was too young to remember anything different. She'd grown up on the grounds, taught herself to ride her bike there, and later learned to drive his pickup on the gravel roads that were now covered in asphalt. She and her brother, Shane, had enjoyed summers filled with fun down at the pond fishing and chasing the ducks or playing Sardines with friends at night among the headstones.

"That's just it. I'm still closer to fifty than sixty. Not sure I'm ready to call it quits yet, and not sure what I'd do with myself if I did. The other problem that occurs to me is moving. Your mother might have a really hard time with that. She's still a long way from being right, despite the improvement, and you know how she gets confused with any change in her routine."

She nodded. He had been thinking this through, and she agreed with all his conclusions.

"But this offer's a good one. Might be hard to say no."

They both sat quietly for a minute, listening to the hum of the fans and sipping their water.

"When had you planned to retire?"

He scratched his chin and pursed his lips.

"I suppose I thought at one time your brother would take over the management, and I'd piddle around out here until I keeled over. Since he's been gone, I've tried to avoid thinking about it. With all the issues with your mom, I just wanted to stay busy, keep her stable, and keep on keeping on. Each day as it comes has been enough to consider. I don't suppose you'd want me to hang on and let you take over some day?"

She chuckled. "I don't think so, Dad."

"That's the answer I expected. So, I've been thinking about another plan that'd keep me going for a while and maybe get Josh a little more involved out here."

"Wow. You have been scheming. Josh has just started working here a few weeks ago. You sure he'd be interested?"

"No. Not sure of much. It's just an idea. I tell you, though, he's a good boy." Her father grinned. "He keeps his nose clean from here forward and he may be part of my future plan."

Oh, shit. He knows about Josh's arrest.

"His nose clean?"

"Don't you go acting like you don't know anything about it." He pointed a finger at her, then pulled it back. "I got it from good author- ity that boy was in some trouble. I'm hoping they weren't his drugs, as he's claiming, and he'll get out of it. Paid for the lawyer myself to make that happen. It's still a mess at this point."

"You hired his attorney? That explains Bill Carpenter being supposedly *appointed* to his case."

He grinned. "Josh doesn't know. He'd be embarrassed to think I knew anything about it, that I did that for him. He's a decent kid, just needs a break. Carpenter says the drugs were never his anyway."

"Oh, Dad, I think that's true. You're a good man to step in like that and expect no pat on the back for what you're doing. I hope it all works out for him."

"Me too. I want to keep him here. Especially now that he's lost Lizzie. He needs a little grounding."

"I agree. So what were you saying? Something about him and your future plan?"

She downed the last of her bottle of water.

He pulled a flyswatter off its hook on the side of the refrigerator and hit two in a row on the workbench before settling back on the stool.

"Well, what I'm thinking is that I might just build another house on the back lot here behind the shop." He nodded to his right. "Always thought that would have been better for us to be back there, rather than living up here in the front and having the office in the house. Give us more of a home life."

"You'd move Mom back there?"

"Yep. I think she could handle it. Let Josh eventually take over. What do you think?"

She grinned. "Dad, that's an awesome idea. I love it. You wouldn't have to move Mom away from the cemetery. You could keep working as much or as little as you want, as long as you want, and Josh would be great at running this place."

"Yeah, he might need me with more summers like this. Rain, sun, more rain. We can't keep up with the mowing." He raised his eyebrows and leaned forward on his stool. "Now, you wouldn't be giving up any inheritance or anything. I'd have him eventually get a business loan or maybe agree to give you a percentage of profits each year to compensate you for your share."

She smiled and shook her head. "Dad, you don't have to worry about me. Rick set me up pretty well. I've got two houses essentially paid off with the credit life we had on the new one. Plus a good insurance check coming, not to mention years of work as a journalist that, yeah, I know, doesn't pay much, but I'll put some away toward retirement as I go. I'm good."

"Credit life, huh? I had no idea you two had arranged that."

He stood and swatted another fly on the grinder handle.

"I didn't either, until recently, but too bad for that insurance company. They didn't collect much in premiums on it."

"I guess, then, I shouldn't give a second thought to that corporation wanting to buy this place. I thought it would be a good way to help you with your future."

"It's your decision, Dad, but don't worry about me in making it. I'm fine and going to be fine. You need to do what's best for you and Mom."

He kissed her on the forehead again.

"You're a good daughter. I love you."

"I love you too."

She tossed her bottle in a plastic recycling tub under the workbench, then stood and yawned.

"Me too," her father said and echoed her yawn. "It's been a long day."

"I'm going to head home and get some rest. Got a lot on my plate tomorrow."

"Guess I do too. Gonna see someone about starting that house. But first, I'll go give Josh a call and talk to him about moving in as soon as he's ready. We've got room, and no sense him being alone with his little one. Let me tell you, Patsy will love helping out with the baby. I think she gets a little bored just having to keep an eye on your mother. Best caretaker we've had for her though."

"I bet she'd love it." Danni grinned. "And Mom will too."

As she bent under the fan to leave, she felt the flyswatter hit her on the butt.

The following day, Danni walked the three blocks to the café located in the basement of a local gift shop just off the Bloomington Square. Her cell phone buzzed when she was about to descend the concrete stairs. The aroma of smoked meat made her stomach rumble.

"Miss Edens?" A cool female voice came through the phone.

"Yes."

"This is Ashley Burden from Channel Eight News. I understand that Cleburne County officials are in town to question a person of interest in the murder of Ronnie Hudgens, former director of the Arkansas Highway and Transportation Department."

She wasn't about to fill in the phone silence that followed.

What the hell? Now she was being questioned by a reporter, like she was an official suspect. *Damn that Stevens.* Her fingers tightened on the phone.

"Do you have any comment?"

"No."

"Well, I understand from an informed source that the person of interest in this case is you."

More silence.

She stepped aside for a couple to enter the restaurant.

Ashley sighed into the phone. "Can you tell me if that's true?"

"No."

"No, it isn't true?"

"I would have no idea if it's true."

Take the no and shove it.

"Have you been in contact with any authorities from Cleburne County about the murder? And do you know why they might suspect you?"

"Look, I think you're jumping to conclusions here, and I certainly don't have any comment."

"Did you kill him, Miss Edens?"

"Hell, no."

She huffed into the phone, hit the end button, and dropped it into her bag.

Dammit.

She backed up and slumped against the brick windowsill of the gift shop. What audacity by that detective to tell a reporter such a thing. It had to be him. Channel Eight was the Little Rock station. None of the local authorities would have a connection there.

With the back of her head against the window, she watched the clouds float against a bright-blue sky. This was not something she could control, not something she needed to worry about. Nothing would come of it because she hadn't even been there.

She stood, took in a deep breath and let it out, then looked up the sidewalk. Terry Butler tottered her way, reminding her of telling Rick how she thought Terry looked like Humpty Dumpty. It was his bald-head and round belly, not to mention his short legs, but sometimes he'd take off his suit jacket and reveal suspenders that added to the image.

His face was red. Beads of sweat lined his forehead and put a sheen on his bare skull.

"Let's get a table. I've got to get out of this heat. I need the exercise, but it's more equivalent to torture to walk the two blocks over here in this humidity."

"It is a warm one."

She removed her sunglasses as they descended the steps into the dark café.

The place had a unique atmosphere, with low ceilings and painted block walls crowded with antique-looking photos of unsmiling people and old trinkets and mirrors.

Terry pulled off his jacket before he sat down at a round table in the far corner. Sure enough, he wore suspenders, and they just happened to be bright red. He looked almost comical with his flushed face accented by a white dress shirt. He took a couple of deep breaths.

"We've officially dropped the homicide charge against Billy Tom Viney. He's still in custody pending his court date for the drug offense."

"I figured."

She opened her menu. Terry put his hand on her arm.

"Danni, I know you don't want to be alarmed, but I think it would be best if you take precautions. It really looks like someone has a vendetta against you."

She covered his grip on her arm with her other hand and patted it.

"I think you're right, but I can't for the life of me think who or why."

"We're working as hard as we can to figure it out."

"Thank you, Terry. I appreciate your concern. I'm not sure everyone is coming to the same conclusion." She closed the menu and set it aside. "Tell me what you know about this Cleburne County bullshit. I had a visit last week from a detective from down there, in addition to Tweedle Dee and Tweedle Dum, our local investigators."

Terry pursed his lips.

"I know, I know," she said. "They're not that bad, but this damn Detective Stevens insinuated that I had something to do with Ronnie Hudgens's death, and they were feeding right into it. He even had a cop along for the ride, like he was ready to put the cuffs on me and haul me off." She rolled her eyes. "I'm surprised they haven't been back to do just that."

"I heard they had interviewed you."

He handed his menu to the waitress, who had sidled up to the table with a tablet in hand. They each ordered the chicken sandwich special, and Terry added an order of fries to his. When the waitress left, they talked about the evidence found at the house where Hudgens was killed.

"It would have proven that I hadn't libeled him. Of course, his mistress disappeared too, and that didn't help my side of things."

Terry unwrapped his straw and plopped it in his soda.

"I'm sure I know the answer to this, but do you know who might have removed those things from your possession?"

"Of course not." She shook her head. "If I did, I would have gotten them back. It had to be someone with access to the newsroom, or someone who got access from an employee and knew where I kept my stuff, where my desk was."

"Any chance this Gerald Yell could be connected?"

She shook her head. "I don't know, but I don't see why he'd be targeted. He barely cared anything about hard news. Just took the pictures for us on the news side, but didn't like it. He was all about sports."

Terry nodded and took a drink.

"Have you heard anything more about his death?"

"Not a word. I definitely don't want anyone suspecting you of that as well."

She snorted. "That one should be easy to dispel. It just happened, and everyone knows I haven't left town the last few weeks with all hell breaking loose."

"That's true. Have you thought about hiring an attorney to represent you?"

"You think I need one? Don't you think that'd make me look guilty?"

"Not at all." He moved his glass to rest on top of a folded napkin. "But it would be prudent to have representation."

They both turned to look at the patrons at the next table when laughter erupted. It was some sort of celebration, complete with gag gifts that had the six women giggling.

"Hudgens had been missing for over a month. Why wasn't the body found sooner? And who's to say someone didn't leave my papers and stuff there since the murder happened? On top of that, it wouldn't make any sense for me to have done it and then leave documents that were clearly mine all over the alleged crime scene."

She sat forward and took a drink of her water, wiping the condensation she picked up from the glass onto a napkin.

"His body was apparently discovered in a shallow grave among a grove of trees near the house, but they believe the murder happened at the house. I'm probably not the one who should be providing you this information." He looked around the room, as if to see if anyone was listening. "But I'll tell you in confidence that they claim there is a bloody footprint on some of the paperwork that was tossed around the living room of the home."

"A bloody footprint?"

It sounded like a *Dateline* or a mystery novel plot.

"Yes. So they're convinced the paperwork was scattered about the same day as the murder, and the print is likely from the killer or an accomplice. You are correct, however, it wouldn't make sense for a killer to leave their own materials behind at the scene."

Terry smiled and looked up at the waitress, who presented him with a large plate loaded down with fries piled between the two halves of a thick sandwich. He immediately flipped open a plastic bottle of ketchup and squeezed some onto his plate.

The waitress, a young woman with her hair in a knot on top of her head that had three blue ink pens sticking through it, placed another plate in front of Danni. Hers had a sandwich with a bag of Lay's between the halves.

"I haven't been out of Northwest Arkansas since I moved up here," Danni said. "I certainly haven't been to Little Rock or even Cleburne County. But that weekend they think this happened was when my dog was recovering from surgery, and Rick and I stayed in the entire weekend. My alibi is dead."

Terry, who'd tossed his tie over one shoulder and spread a napkin across his lap, put his sandwich back on the plate and finished chewing a mouthful. Then he said, "There's likely someone who talked to you on the phone, or someone who stopped by. Right?"

"Well, I'd have to think about that. I'm sure I talked to Dad. I don't think he came by." She put a chip in her mouth and stared at the painting of a barn and a field of cows above the table. Surely she'd had contact with someone other than Rick that weekend. "I guess I need to get a lawyer."

"That's what I hoped you'd realize."

She shook her head and took a bite of the second half of her sandwich, then tossed the napkin atop the leftovers and set the plate aside.

"I've got Rob Wesley handling Rick's estate and all that garbage. I'm sure he'd probably agree to represent me on this too."

"I'm sure he would. He's a good attorney."

Terry drug a couple of fries through the remaining ketchup on his plate.

"I may not even need him." She sipped her water. "I hope."

"My concern here is the material they discovered that points to you."

"Me and you, both."

"I have to wonder if this isn't related to the issues you've been having lately, and it's some kind of vendetta. The tampering with your brakes, someone possibly trying to kill you, Rick shot instead, and the stolen materials turning up, as if it's an effort to make you appear to be guilty of committing murder." He wiped at his mouth again and placed the napkin on top of his empty plate. "It all could be related. Have you considered the possibility?"

"But what could I have ever done to piss someone off that much?" she asked Terry.

He stared at her for several seconds, then shook his head.

"One thing I have learned over the past twenty-seven years on the prosecuting side of the law is that you never know how a deviant mind works. Sometimes what they might think and act on is absolutely inexplicable."

50

A silver county cruiser screeched to a halt at the curb a few feet in front of Danni as she walked along the tree-lined street back to her house. She'd been daydreaming, and the swift stop caused her to jump. At least it was a police car and not someone trying to kill her.

"Geez." *Am I about to be arrested?*

Ben rolled down the driver's side window.

"Hey, Danni. I've been calling you."

"I know." She shrugged. "I just had a lot going on since Lizzie was killed."

"I know. I'm sorry about that. I came to the funeral but didn't stay afterward. I didn't want to intrude on your family."

"It's okay. The service was hard for everyone. She was so young."

She looked up to keep from bursting into tears.

"Let me give you a ride. Where you headed?"

"Home."

"Hop in."

He hit a button, and the car beeped.

She climbed in the passenger seat after he picked up a small stack of manila folders that she offered to hold, noticing he was looking for a spot to stash them.

"So I've heard you've had even more trouble comin' down on ya."

He pulled away from the curb.

"You could say that."

"Don't for a second think that I'd believe a word of it. I know you, Danni. I know your folks, and I'm sure there's nothing to this. Those Cleburne County guys'll figure it out too."

"I'm sure, but how far will they drag me through the mud before they do."

She'd probably be mentioned on the evening news out of Little Rock. Every reporter in town would be calling her. It could even put her new job at risk.

"Well, hopefully, it'll pass over soon. I'm a little worried about you."

He maneuvered a corner and pulled up to the curb across from her house.

"I've been meaning to call you but didn't get a chance yet. Michelle's got a neighbor I think you should look into. He's kind of obsessed with her. He may have cut the brakes to get back at her for turning him down. But, get this, he's also got a compound bow."

He turned in the seat toward her. "Who's this?"

"Well, I saw him on my way to Michelle's the day of the accident, and then I saw him again when I took her home from the hospital. His name's Randy Carlisle. Drives a little white truck. Think it might be a Chevy."

"I've heard that name. Mechanic, I think."

He thumped the steering wheel with his thumb.

"Yeah. Michelle said he works on cars for a lot of people down that way. Now that I think about the bow, I just wonder if he had some connection to Rick, maybe. He wasn't trying to hide the bow or anything, though. Seems like he would if he was involved in the murder. But then again, Michelle did say the guy was a little slow in the head. It really doesn't make sense." She sighed. "But not much does."

"Criminals aren't always the best baked cookies in the jar."

She snorted. "I don't know what his problem is, but he's definitely creepy. Just stared at me weird both times I saw him, and he was in the vicinity that day before the accident."

Ben pulled a pen off a ridge in the dash, took the stack of folders from her, and wrote the guy's name down on the front of the one on top.

"I'll look into it. Anything or anyone else come to mind?"

"Nope."

He stuck the pen back in the ridge on the dash.

"I know this Hudgens guy's body just turned up," he said. "Just wonderin' if the culprit could now be up here after you."

"I doubt it." She shook her head. "I don't see a connection. I'm assuming he was killed by his wife or somebody he screwed over in all that financial mess with the Highway Department."

Taking her bag from the floorboard, she slipped it over her shoulder.

"I can't imagine any connection with me. I know they found my stuff there, notes and interview tapes. Things taken from my desk at the newspaper when he accused me of libel. But he probably had all that shit all along, and the killer just stumbled onto it."

"I don't know. There could be something there." He thumped the steering wheel again with his thumb. "I don't like it. And from what I hear, this was a very brutal murder. Whoever did it pretty much gutted the guy."

She winced. "Really?"

"Really."

"I've not had any threats besides that note saying 'I missed.' I haven't even talked to anyone I knew down there since I left. I have a few friends on Facebook that I worked with, but that's it." She pushed open her door. "I need to make some calls, Ben. Thanks for the ride."

He leaned over the seat as she climbed out.

"You okay?"

"I will be. Just got to get through this."

"Look, Danni. Maybe you should go stay at your dad's or something. I'm worried."

"Hey, now, I'm good. Besides, he just got me out of there. Don't think he wants me hanging around again."

She knew that wasn't true. He'd welcome her back anytime. Especially if he knew what was going on. That might be the first call she needed to make. He didn't need to hear on the news that she was a suspect in a brutal murder.

"Well, listen, if you need anything, you call me. I'd come camp out on your front porch, if you want."

She laughed. "It's a little humid for that. You'd melt. I'm fine, and I'll be on my toes."

"Maybe I should check out the house before you go in."

"No, it's fine, I'm sure. Besides, I have Bruno. He hears a moth light on the window and barks. Don't worry."

He nodded, and she shut the car door.

Danni sat on her porch swing and rocked slowly. She couldn't keep her fingers out of her hair—twirling a strand until it was tight at her scalp, letting it loose, then twirling it again. Before Michelle could even say a word, Danni started talking into the cell phone.

"I need to talk to you." She took a deep breath. "I guess I should ask how you're feeling before I start in on my troubles. Sorry."

Michelle, on the other end of the phone, chuckled.

"I'm good. Actually, I'm feeling better. Mom's been hovering over me a little much, but what the hell, maybe I deserve to be babied. How are you, and how's the family?"

"Well, hmmm, it's okay. We're past the funeral now, so it's a matter of adjustment, mainly for Josh and her parents. I'm not sure where to start about everything else going on. Got time for a visit?"

"Sure, but Trevor's coming up this afternoon. He's taking tomorrow off and going to stay for a three-day weekend. But you're always welcome anyway. Just wasn't sure if you'd want to share my company. Something on your mind?"

Dammit. No, sharing her company with that asshole wasn't good.

"Ah, no biggie. I wanted to warn you that I may be on the news tonight."

There was a rustling on the other end.

"What happened now? Someone try to kill you again?"

"Well, no. And I'm not so sure anyone is trying to kill me. But I'm actually the one being accused of murder."

"No way."

"Yes, way. Cleburne County officials think I might be involved in Hudgens's death. They apparently found at least some of the materials I'd gathered on his case—my notes and at least one audio tape of an interview I did—at the scene where he was killed."

"You've got to be kidding. Why would you want to kill him? Bastard that he was, you moved on."

"Yeah, well, I guess there's enough there they think I could be out for revenge or something."

Michelle let out a heavy breath. "That's asinine. You weren't even there. You can prove that, right?"

"There seems to be some trouble on that front. Rick and I stayed home that whole weekend they think he was killed. It was right after Bruno's surgery." She moved the phone from one ear to the other. "So my only alibi is dead, other than Bruno, and he's being mum about it."

"Shit."

"Anyway, Terry thinks it will all come out in the wash. They'll be able to track my phone, but we both know that doesn't prove I was the one using it. I'm sure they'll argue that."

"Dammit, I was so busy at work, I don't think I saw you from the first of June until Rick died."

"No, and we were busy too. The wedding planning and all. I'm sure I made some calls at least. Surely."

"It'll be okay. There's no way anyone who knows you would think you'd do something like that. Honestly, girl, I don't think you've ever talked about that Hudgens like you hated him or anything. He did you wrong, cheated on his wife, took kickbacks, but we deal with scoundrels like that all the time in this business. No reason to hate him. You got a good story out of him." Michelle paused. "Well, I guess it was a good story until it got retracted."

"And that's the rub. I still didn't hate him. Blamed myself more than anything for not backing up my shit and not getting more sources and confirmation of the facts. Confirmation that couldn't be denied."

"So, what are you going to do?"

She sighed. "I'm going to call Dad and warn him about the news tonight. I had that idiot Ashley Burden from Channel Eight call, wanting a comment. She knows they've questioned me, so it's going to be a story. Probably at five."

"That bitch."

"Really. Well, no, not really. She's just doing her job."

"Funny to be on the other side, huh?"

"Yeah, real funny."

"You know what I mean, Danni. I can't believe this is happening."

"I know. Terry wants me to talk to a lawyer."

"Good idea."

"Anyway, Michelle, I just wanted to give you a heads-up before you saw it on the news. I've got some more calls to make."

"Okay, girl. You let me know if there's anything I can do. I'm still on the mend, but I can ditch the pain killers and head that way any time."

Danni laughed. "Thanks."

"And call that lawyer."

She hung up and watched two teenage girls in shorts ride past on their bikes, one weaving around the other as they passed on the street in front of the house, both of them laughing.

The next call was a little tougher. Her dad was obviously surprised but took it better than she expected, telling her that he'd stand behind her no matter what. Then he scolded her for not already calling the attorney.

Rod Wesley Law Offices was the last on her list. She made an appointment for later that afternoon. She had yet to meet Wesley, just talked with him on the phone about Rick's estate. He seemed to be on top of it, so she hadn't worried. Probably didn't have it in her to worry about it in those weeks after his death.

Thoughts of Rick brought tears to her eyes. It was funny how easily she could cry for him now. Tears hadn't come for weeks after he was killed, but her eyes flooded and a lump nearly strangled her, thinking of how much she needed him now.

52

With an hour until she had to leave for her appointment with the attorney, Danni sat down at the dining room table with two legal pads and a pen. Bruno stretched out on the rug next to her, sunning himself in the rays streaming through the window.

"Let's see if I can't outline what's happening here, approach it like an in-depth news story. What do you say, boy?"

Bruno just looked up at her and cocked his head to one side.

"I don't know if it will work either, but maybe, just maybe, I'm missing something."

Bruno yipped.

"Talking to the dog, and the dog's responding." She chuckled.

First, she made a timeline of what had happened over the past few weeks since Rick's murder, noting the accident and Lizzie's murder. She ignored the days of oblivion she'd spent trying to get past the pain.

She pushed that notepad aside and wrote "Little Rock" at the top of the other. Her memories of the Hudgens story, the interviews, the accusations of libel, and the newspaper's reaction to it all were as fresh as ever. It was amazing how pain could do that to the mind. Her hand shook when she thought about the argument she'd had with that pipsqueak of an editor the day he fired her. She could even remember thinking that his stupid wire rimmed glasses had so many fingerprint smudges on them that he could probably barely see.

Her stomach knotted and churned reliving her frantic search for her notes and documents. She'd sat on the floor in front of her desk with her head braced against her chair and realized the materials were gone. How could they have thought she'd just make up a story, make up the sources, not have anything to back up what was printed? How could someone have taken those things?

Gerald Yell's role in it all seemed so minor. He took some photos of the players, but other than that, he wasn't involved. She couldn't even remember him being there the day she was fired.

She took a breath, shook her head, and flipped a yellow page of the notepad. Could someone involved in that whole mess be making her life hell now? And why? Hadn't she suffered enough humiliation?

There were several people living in Northwest Arkansas that were in Little Rock when she was there. Could one of them be involved?

She wrote "Now in NWA" at the top of the blank page and then made a list starting with Matt Dodson. He couldn't be involved. Trevor was next. Doubtful that he was involved either, but he *had* been at Michelle's that afternoon the brakes were tampered with. She wrote "brakes?" next to his name and then "temper," remembering the day he'd stormed into her house and blamed her for Michelle's injuries.

Who else had she known in Little Rock that was in Lovely County now? Kendra had been there. Danni didn't know her, but she'd worked at the paper. The girl seemed like such a naïve young thing. Maybe she had unknown skills in archery. If so, her aim was off. There's no way she would have wanted Rick dead. Danni, yes. Rick, no way. She jotted the girl's name down and made a note of her crush on Rick. It didn't seem like she had enough backbone to go after dinner, much less someone she hated. Maybe it *was* her and she had help.

The list wasn't long, but she couldn't think of another name to add. She tore out the sheet and laid it on the table next to the other notepad.

At the top of the next sheet of paper, she wrote "Suspects in Rick and Lizzie's Murders," and first on her list was Billy Tom Viney, then his brothers. She noted that he was cleared of any connection, but the bastard deserved to be on the list just for his disdain for Rick displayed on his hideous target.

Randy Carlisle, the weirdo in the white pickup, hit the list. He also could have tampered with her brakes. She made a note of that and the fact that he was an archer, or at least owned a bow. There was no connection with Rick, or no link she was aware of. Maybe he'd been prosecuted or held a grudge for some other reason. Or maybe he'd been aiming for her, but she didn't know him either. If it was Carlisle, it made more sense that he might be aiming for her, missed, and then took another try at it with the adjustment to her brakes. But why? His name didn't ring any bells. She'd have to dig deeper in Mr. Carlisle's past.

She doodled a spiral on the edge of the paper. Who else? Who else would want him dead or maybe want her dead? Nobody else came to mind.

The next list was titled "Who Wants Me Dead?" and started with Kendra's name. There was no telling if the girl would really want her dead, but she would have liked her out of the picture so she could pursue Rick herself. No doubt about that. Could she have cut the brakes? That didn't make sense because Rick was gone by then. Hers was the only name on two of the lists so far, but Danni still went back to the thought that Kendra was harmless. She wrote "doubtful" and moved on.

Teresa Hillburn could go on the list. Her dislike for Danni was more than evident, but that was so long in the past. There was no way she would have tracked her down from Little Rock, unless she somehow got it in her head that Matt had moved to the area to be with Danni. Maybe. It seemed unlikely, but as they say, a woman scorned and all that. She made a note of Teresa's name and the Little Rock connection.

She pulled the paper from the pad and laid it next to the first list, then stared at the notes. Nothing made sense. There wasn't a name on the list that she could imagine having a reason to kill that made sense.

She added Trevor's name and a big question mark to the list. He was an ass, but he'd have no reason to come after her or Rick.

What to do now? Visiting with Matt at the *Business Bugle* might not be a bad idea. He was close and might know something about what happened in Little Rock. He'd stayed in the newsroom after she left. After writing "To Do" at the top of the next blank sheet, she made a note to see Matt.

She could always go to Little Rock and snoop around, try to figure out who had taken those materials from her desk, but that wasn't likely to prove anything anyway. She made a note of the possible trip and added a question mark.

"Press Kendra," she wrote next. Maybe she'd take that girl to lunch and see if there was anything there. It was doubtful, but adding another thing to her To Do list made it feel like she was moving forward.

Then there was Randy Carlisle. Ben was going to have him checked out. There was no connection between her and Randy, but maybe some connection to Rick. She made a note to ask Terry to check the records on that.

What else? Could she be missing something? She thumped her pen against the notepad, then put it down and pushed out her chair, but one more thought came to mind. Arrows. A visit to Arrow Dynamics might be worth it. She made a note.

She stood and leaned over the table, surveying her lists. Still none of the notes made sense. Nothing jumped out as a possible real clue to what was happening.

Dammit. This is useless. She threw the pen down.

"Screw this. I'm craving some fruit. Bruno, let's see what's in the kitchen. Then I'm going to see a lawyer and maybe get started on this To Do list." She reached down and rumpled the fur between his ears. "Want to share an apple with me?"

53

Danni answered her cell phone after debating about ignoring it through three rings. She didn't recognize the number, but the area code indicated the central part of the state.

Shit.

She moved off the sidewalk out of the sun next to the four-story office building.

"Hello, Detective. Are you enjoying your day?"

"Well, yes, Miss Edens. Every day is a good day here in the great state of Arkansas. I hope yours is just as enjoyable." Stevens's tone held the usual snide edge.

"Of course." *But it is likely going downhill fast.* "What can I do for you, Detective?"

"I have a few questions for you and wondered where we might catch up with each other this afternoon."

Yep, downhill with no brakes.

"Well, I'm actually walking into my attorney's office as we speak. Would you like to meet me here?"

She stepped inside the office building, and the cool air hit her, making her skin tingle. A rustling sound came from the other end of the line.

"Yes, ma'am, that will be fine. Give me specifics."

After she provided Rod Wesley's name and the location off the Bloomington Square, he agreed to be there in ten minutes.

Danni disconnected, dropped the phone in her bag, and slumped against the wall in the foyer of the law office. Frigid air from a ceiling vent streamed over her upturned face. It provided some relief from the sweltering heat she'd just escaped but didn't relieve her stress level.

If I'm arrested, will they take me all the way to Cleburne County? Probably. Shit. I'll have to call Michelle or someone to come get Bruno. This is not good.

She threaded her fingers through her hair. Her stomach clenched. Maybe she should have shared more of that apple with Bruno. It was not sitting well. She took a deep breath and let it out before pulling the door open to the inner office.

Rod Wesley was a square-shouldered guy with the kind of hair that should belong to a woman. It was thick with multiple shades of light brown and blond and perfectly swept to the side across his forehead. He wore a pale-green button-down shirt with the sleeves rolled up to just below his elbows and a dark pair of Levi's.

She sat across from him and watched a fly buzz in one corner of the window while Rod thumbed through the file on Rick's estate.

"I have a couple of documents you need to sign, and I need to gather some information from the Sheriff's Department, but I believe the payout on the insurance should come soon. Already filed for the credit life on the house. I assume you've made the July payment?"

Her gaze drifted from the fly to the attorney. She nodded.

"The August mortgage payment should be a mute issue, but I'll communicate with you if not. The life insurance company wants confirmation that you're not a suspect in the murder before they'll pony up. It's possible they'll wait for a conviction in his murder before they'll pay. However, it shouldn't play out that way if it's clear you're exonerated of any connection to the case."

"Okay."

She didn't care. She should, but couldn't make herself.

"He had two hundred and fifty thousand, but with double indemnity, it'll be an even half mil."

She swallowed. "What? Double indemnity?"

"Yes. In the event of accidental death, and believe it or not, the insurance industry classifies murder as accidental, the policy's payout is doubled." He pulled out a sheet from the file and stood up. "With this and the payoff of the home you two shared, you'll have just over nine hundred thousand in insurance compensation."

She stared up at him, her mouth hanging open.

"Mr. Wesley, I, uh." She sucked in a breath. "I can't take that."

He chuckled. "Oh, yes you can, and you will. Rick was very deliberate in his dealings. The will is settling out now, and you are the sole beneficiary. He was a good man and wanted to take care of you. Sign here, and call me Rod."

He put the document in front of her and handed her a pen. It was a blur. She didn't read it, could barely see the line where her signature needed to go. Her hand shook, but she signed.

"Now that that's resolved, shall we allow the detective who's cooling his jets in the waiting room in to discuss this other matter?"

She nodded. Rod picked up his phone and told his assistant to allow Detective Stevens in.

He strutted in and looked around, a scowl on his face.

"Trying to map out your defense already?"

Danni snorted.

"Detective, if you'll have a seat. Miz Edens and I were discussing another matter that had nothing to do with your farfetched idea that she was involved in some murder miles from here. She hasn't had an opportunity to explain in detail why she should be connected with this at all."

"Well, I sure as hell can tell you that."

Stevens yanked on a straight-back chair in front of Rod's desk and nearly tipped it over. He dropped into the chair, threw an ankle atop one knee, and slapped a manila folder on his lap.

Danni uncrossed and crossed her legs and shifted in her chair to face him. Raising an eyebrow, she smiled.

Come on, asshole. Let's hear why you're wasting your time with this investigation.

"Number one, Miss Edens has a clear motive. She lost her job due to pressure by Ronnie Hudgens to get her fired. He professionally embarrassed her by proving she had libeled him."

She rolled her eyes.

Stevens shrugged.

"That's how it played out. Number two. At the scene, a number of items were strewn about that evidently belonged to her and may have proven that his accusations of libel were, in fact, false. Although the murder apparently happened about two months ago, there's no sign that anyone else has been there, and some of the paperwork is smudged with blood that we now know belonged to the victim. That makes us think that whoever tossed the things around did it on the day he was sliced up."

"Any fingerprints? Any proof she was there?" Rod asked.

Stevens shook his head.

"That's it? I don't believe that proves anything. I want you to know that I take exception to the naming of my client as a so-called person of interest in this case if that's all the evidence you have. I assume you're not here to make an arrest?"

Holding back a smile was hard.

Stevens gripped the arm of the chair with both hands, then let loose and ran his palms over his thighs, as if wiping away sweat. He picked up the manila folder and waved it.

"Not yet, no. But I would like to get her to look at some photographs and confirm that these are some of her notes and things she alleges were stolen from her desk in Little Rock."

"I'd like to see those first and make a decision on whether my client needs to offer that opinion."

Stevens handed him the photos.

"This is the scene inside the cabin. Hudgens's body was found in a shallow grave on the property."

Danni shifted in her chair and took a deep breath. Rod flipped through the photos and then closed the folder, placing a palm down on top of it.

"Detective, I'd like to discuss these photos alone with my client. Then we'll make a decision on whether she'll provide any information regarding what is depicted."

"Um, okay. I guess that'd be all right."

"You can wait in our reception area." Rod nodded toward the door.

"I already been sittin' out there for a while. I'm not going to wait too long. Got it?"

Stevens stood up.

"I imagine this won't take but a few minutes."

He started to leave but hesitated at the door.

"If you don't mind, close the door please." Rod smiled.

Stevens rolled his eyes and shut the door.

She thumbed through the eight-by-ten color photos. The first shot revealed a smartly furnished living area with a bank of windows, a huge stone fireplace, and wooden floors. Papers were strewn about, some on a deep-green area rug, a couple on the coffee table, and several on the couch. A large manila envelope rested on the hearth with two cassette tapes stacked on top of it along with a notebook. It was upside down but looked the right size and shape to be a reporter's notebook. Even before she looked at the next photos, she was certain the materials were hers.

God, how she wished she'd had a digital recorder back then. A copy of those interviews would likely have been on her computer if that had been the case. Instead, the audiotape proof of the legitimacy of the quotes vanished when that envelope disappeared.

A close-up of a receipt on the floor had her telltale sketched star in the upper right corner in red. The total at the bottom of the page was circled, along with a line item stating "king room." It was a receipt from the Marriott in Memphis, where Hudgens supposedly traveled for a conference but in reality had a liaison with his girlfriend. She remembered that receipt.

Another shot showed several typed pages that appeared to be a draft of the story before it went to print. The next shot was more of the same but with notes in the margin that were clearly her handwriting.

Another showed a receipt with a dark smudge across part of it that looked like the imprint of the heel of a shoe—likely the blood evidence that Terry Butler had mentioned.

There was no need to look any further. She put the photos back in the envelope and handed it to Rod and nodded.

"It's mine. Rather, it *was* mine. It's definitely the paperwork and I'm sure the interview tapes stolen from me out of the newsroom in Little Rock."

"You recognize these notes and receipts?"

"Yes. I do. That one has my handwriting. I think the big envelope on the hearth was what I'd stored it in when the story was done. That's what went missing from my desk."

He pursed his lips. "I have to ask. Were you in Cleburne County? Do you have any idea how these materials would have ended up in this cabin?"

"No. I don't know that. I've ever been to Cleburne County, and I certainly don't have a clue how that stuff got there." She slumped against the back of the chair. "What does this mean? Will I be charged with this murder? It doesn't make sense anyway. Why would I leave my own belongings there?"

He shook his head. "I suppose they're surmising it was a fight. If they truly think it was you, they believe you left the scene quickly without considering the evidence left behind. If this is all they have, they're fishing, and there's no immediate chance you'll be charged. Let's talk to that detective. Well, rather, let me talk to that detective. I don't want you saying a word, answering any questions, unless I give you the go ahead."

She nodded. Rod used the phone and told his assistant to send Stevens back in.

Stevens stood behind the chair where he'd previously sat and gripped the back of it with both hands.

"Detective, Miss Edens agrees that these are her materials. She will cooperate with your investigation but is adamant that she was not involved with this murder. To the best of her knowledge, she doesn't believe she has ever been to Cleburne County. She was not at the scene when this murder took place and was not involved in any way."

"Can you explain how these things got there if she didn't put 'em there?"

"She has no knowledge of how they came to be in that location," Rod said.

"I'm not stupid enough to leave them there anyway. That doesn't make sense." Danni shook her head and puffed out a breath.

"You could have killed him and not known that stuff was in the house." Stevens shrugged.

Danni started to rise from her chair, fists clenched at her sides as she tried to control the anger.

"Now just a minute here." Rod motioned for her to stay seated. "The last time Miss Edens saw these materials, she packed them into a large manila envelope, which may be the one shown there on the mantel, and put them in a file drawer in her desk at her former office in Little Rock. When Mr. Hudgens made his false accusations of libel against Miss Edens, she discovered the envelope and its contents were missing."

Stevens turned to Danni. "Anybody down there able to verify that?"

She looked at Rod. He nodded.

"I made it clear to my editor that my notes, tapes, and copies of documents verifying the story were missing. He should be able to confirm that. It was a big scene the day I was fired, and I shouted to the entire newsroom that someone there was a thief."

"What's the editor's name?"

Stevens took a small notepad and a pen from the inside pocket of his suit jacket.

"Jim Dore."

"I'll talk to him." Stevens tucked the notepad and pen back in his pocket. "We also have some fingerprints we haven't matched as of yet." He turned to Danni. "I don't suppose I can convince you to come in and be fingerprinted?"

"Sure, if it—"

"Now wait a minute here." Rod stood up, sending his chair backward. He leaned over the desk like he might just crawl across it. "I don't think that's going to prove anything. My client has already admitted the materials found at the scene likely belonged to her at one point. We would expect to discover her fingerprints on some of those items, now wouldn't we?"

Stevens shook his head, his arrogance deflated in the presence of the angry lawyer.

"I figured as much when she asked me to meet her here. Just wanted to pose the question, see if we couldn't get some of this cleared up and move on with the case."

"We haven't said no to this yet." He looked at Danni and she nodded. "Miss Edens's fingerprints are likely to be found on her work product. If it's necessary, she'll agree to be fingerprinted for purposes of elimination. If that will help with your investigation."

"I'd appreciate that," Stevens said. "Can you come by the sheriff's office here in town and get that done?"

"It's getting late in the day." Rod looked at her with eyebrows raised. "I assume you can do that in the morning, Danni?"

"I can."

Rod put his hands on his hips. "We'll agree to the fingerprinting, but we'd like a concession from you, Detective."

"What's that?" Stevens knitted his brow and looked from Danni to Rod.

"We do not want to hear any more reports of Miss Edens being listed as a person of interest. If there's any further discussion of her alleged culpability in this crime, it better be accompanied by solid evidence that she's involved and an imminent arrest." Rod crossed his arms.

Stevens rolled his eyes. "After I get her prints, I'm planning to go back to Cleburne County. I'll let you know if there's any reason for me to come back up here and talk to ya."

"That's fine."

He handed the detective the file of photographs.

With a nod at each of them, Stevens left the office.

"I hope you don't mind supplying your prints."

Rod came around the desk and leaned against one corner in front of her.

"Not if it's going to help eliminate me as a suspect."

"That's what I'm hoping."

"If not, I guess, it is what it is."

\- \- \-

The clouds darkened, but the rain held off until Danni got home. She flipped on the lamp in the living room and let Bruno in, then dropped on the couch and stared at the ceiling. She wasn't sure whether to feel relieved after her visit with the attorney and Stevens or more concerned about the possibility of being arrested. Grabbing a throw pillow and shoving it under her head, she kicked off her sandals and put her feet up on the opposite end of the couch.

It all was a bunch of bullshit—bullshit that had her scared, angry, and probably headed for pure embarrassment after the evening news.

There had to be some way to prove she wasn't involved. The photos didn't make it look good. On top of that, there was no telling what the early evening newscast would have to say about it all. She didn't have a good feeling.

She rolled to one side and pulled the remote control off the coffee table. Her fingers tightened around it. It wasn't going to be pretty. If she turned it on and watched the broadcast, she'd have to put the remote down and maybe remove all small objects within arm's reach to avoid throwing something at the television.

What the hell can I do about it?

She hit the power button, changed to the right channel, and dropped her arm off the side of the couch, letting the remote slip to the floor.

The first story was about a drive-by shooting in North Little Rock. No one was hurt, but there were a number of pissed off neighbors. The front of a building had been sprayed with bullets.

Lucky neighbors.

The second story centered on some action by the governor's office to deal with ongoing and ridiculous problems in the state Department of Human Services, in particular the foster care system. It had always been terribly underfunded and caught up in politics that resulted in kids at risk. Then they went into a piece about a new exhibit at the Clinton Presidential Museum. The station went to commercial break. Maybe she had avoided a crisis.

After ads for three different kinds of medication, two of them for erectile dysfunction, the broadcast came back with a short preview of the weather segment, then cut to a reporter in the field. It was Ashley Burden.

Shit.

She stood in front of the Lovely County Sheriff's Office.

Thunder clapped and heavy rain came down as Ashley started to speak. Danni sat up, grabbed the remote off the floor, and pumped the volume button.

"Cleburne County officials tell us the Northwest Arkansas person of interest in the murder of former Arkansas Highway and Transportation Department Director Ronnie Hudgens has been ruled out as a suspect and is fully cooperating in the investigation. Detective Dennis Stevens declined to comment further on the issue, other than to say that he's returning to Cleburne County this evening to continue his investigation."

She let out a long sigh and sank back against the couch. Ashley had done her a favor there. She hadn't even mentioned her name.

54

I sat there shaking with anger.

Why didn't they list her as a suspect?

I'd planted the right seed and knew the state investigators were looking at her, but nothing. Nothing on the news. Her smart little ass still walked free.

Seeing her photo displayed on the screen would have been the cat's meow. I'd even set my DVR to record it.

They'd found that bastard's body and the things I'd left behind. She should be blamed.

"Mama, they think she did it. They have to think she did it. They're just not saying." The shout rang out in the empty room. "They're protecting her. They have to be. This isn't how I'd planned it."

I turned up the volume. They said there was a "person of interest" with no details of who or why.

But they knew about her connection to Hudgens, how she'd been shamed out of the job in Little Rock for her unprofessional conduct as a journalist.

I clapped my hands. "This isn't right."

"Yes, son, it isn't. Think they'll arrest her?"

His mother rocked back and forth in the wooden chair next to him—a pile of yarn in her lap, the knitting needles clicking as she went.

"They might, Mama. They just might."

"She deserves it."

"Yes, she does. Nobody deserves it more. Why aren't they arresting her? Why? Tracey deserves to be vindicated."

Tracey.

The thought of her stopped me cold. I sat back in the chair and watched as the news reporter moved on to something about the Little Rock River Market. Tracey should be here with us. Tracey should be thriving, living her life and thriving. She might have been famous by now if it hadn't been for that bastard. He'd stolen everything from her. She'd given up everything for him, and he hadn't deserved a bit of it.

I clenched the leather arms of the recliner and took a deep breath.

"There, there, my boy. Don't you worry. She's gonna get her just rewards for this."

I nodded. "Yes, Mama. Yes, she will. If it's the last thing I do, she'll get her just rewards."

The needles continued to click.

I closed my eyes and smiled, imagining all the ways that could happen.

55

The morning came too soon. Danni didn't want to move. Really didn't want to open her eyes. Bruno stirred around and probably needed to go out, but she ignored him until he panted in her face.

"Okay, okay. I'm getting up."

She pushed back the covers and stood. Her stomach flipped. With a hand covering her mouth, she rushed to the bathroom. It was probably just nerves and the fact that she didn't eat anything but a yogurt the night before. There was no time to be sick. Too much was going on. Thankfully, she felt much better after tossing up the little she had in her stomach.

Tea would help. She started a pot and grabbed her robe while it heated. The sky was overcast and unseasonably cool after the overnight rain. A cold front had moved in and pushed the humidity out. With the warm cup between her palms, she sat on the back steps and surveyed the gray skies. Bruno ran in circles around the yard. Returning to bed sounded like a great idea, but she had a list of things to accomplish.

"Mama's got to get going, buddy."

She stood up and stretched, then went back inside for some toast, a shower, and a call she wanted to make.

Michelle answered on the second ring but declined her offer of a field trip to the sheriff's office followed by a couple of stops for some needed snooping around. She was feeling better but expected Trevor to come up to spend the day swimming and lying around the pool.

"Remember? We talked about that yesterday. Come up when you get done with your running around and join us. You can even stay over if you like. I promise we won't have to get up in the middle of the night and plow down the mountainside." Michelle laughed.

"Ha Ha. Maybe. I don't know. It might be too late by the time I get done with all my errands. I don't want to be a third wheel anyway. You enjoy your Friday with Trevor."

She wasn't sure she was ready to spend any leisure time with him yet. They hadn't really spoken since he'd accused her of intentionally causing the accident.

After wrestling with the idea of wearing jeans, she finally decided on brown Capri pants and a simple white cotton shirt. She slipped on some sandals, put Bruno out in the utility room, and opened his doggie door.

Her cell phone rang when she turned the key in the ignition. Maybe Michelle had changed her mind and was going to blow off Trevor for the day. Not likely. After retrieving the cell from the bottom of her purse, it surprised her to hear Paul's voice.

"How's my favorite reporter?"

"I'm good. How are you?"

"Fine, just fine. But I'm hearing some concerning gossip about my Danni Deadline."

"Shit. I guess I should have called you, Paul. I've been making the rumor mill. Haven't I?"

Paul had been good to her since she'd returned from Little Rock, dragging her tail between her legs and looking for a job. She couldn't even get an interview with the *Bloomington Daily News* at that time. Brett Penderson wasn't editor then, and the previous editor wouldn't have anything to do with her because of the accusations of libel.

Paul nibbled on something. It was loud and likely one of his favorites—pork rinds. Why he couldn't stop while he made a phone call, she'd never know. But then again, she couldn't recall ever talking to him when he wasn't munching on something. His desk was always covered in crumbs and a veritable feast in snack foods.

"A Detective Stevens called me yesterday, asked if I'd talked to you on Saturday, June sixteenth? He said there were three or four calls that day between us. At least two from you and one back from me."

"Oh, really." *That's why Stevens backed off on his accusations.*

He apparently did track her phone usage that day.

"He wanted me to confirm I'd actually spoken to you. We don't talk that often on the weekends, but I remember that was the week before we put out that special environmental edition. Remember? You finished up late that Friday night and called me to make sure I got the copy you'd filed the night before. I think I called you back with a couple of questions."

"You're right. I remember that. I'd forgotten it was that weekend. And I think I even got in touch later that evening about boxing those figures on recycling."

"Yep, that was it."

"Thanks, Paul. I think that probably helped get me off the hook for murder."

There were clearly repeat calls throughout the day, and her cell phone must have pinged from the Bloomington area.

He laughed. "Really, what idiot would think you'd hurt anyone?"

"Not everyone knows me like you do, and I guess it was easy to assume I might have had a reason to go after Hudgens."

She felt a little vindicated when she thought about it like that. Hudgens was wrong to blame her, the messenger, for his own mistakes. He just happened to be a public figure and fair game for exposure. She was doing her job.

"But that was a long time ago, and my theory is that people like that usually suffer their own reward. Karma is pretty exacting at times."

"Yes, it is." He crunched a couple of times, then made a muffled sound, like he was taking a drink. "Listen now, Danni, I want you to know that I'm here for you. Come by and see me sometime soon. And, by golly, if you need some help, you better let me know."

"Thank you, Paul. I appreciate the faith in me. And I will get down there and see you soon. It's been a little crazy lately. I think all that crap about Hudgens is going away, but I have to go by and provide my fingerprints this morning."

"What? They're fingerprinting you?"

"Yeah. I'll have to tell you all about it when I see you, but Hudgens apparently had some of my work product. They want to eliminate my prints from any others they might have found. I'll give you all the juicy details when I see you."

"I'm counting on that. You doing okay otherwise? I heard about Lizzie. I'm awfully sorry. Seems like it's just piling up on you."

She sighed. "It's been tough, but it will be okay."

"Give my condolences to your family. And, Danni, when you're ready to come back to work, you know you don't have to go on to the big daily drama. You're always welcome here."

There was a crackling as he probably closed up the bag of goodies. He must have heard about her plans with the Bloomington paper. But, then again, he wasn't stupid and may have just assumed.

"Thanks, Paul. I'm not sure what I'm going to do yet. I might just take a more extended vacation before I go back to work."

"You do what you need to. I'm here for you, regardless."

"Thanks."

She hung up and backed out of the driveway.

56

Getting fingerprinted wasn't what she expected. It was amazing the things that technology had changed. Not that she'd ever had her prints taken before, but she knew what the process used to be like. It was all electronic now. No more messy ink to clean off your fingers. They rolled her fingertips across a digital reader, and the image instantly popped up on a screen. The prints would be forwarded to Detective Stevens in Cleburne County by email.

She was in and out of the sheriff's office in about ten minutes. A couple of deputies had to tease her a little, joking that they had a clean set of pink-striped prison scrubs ready for her after her prints were taken and that she'd like the pickle loaf sandwich they were serving the inmates for lunch.

Pickle loaf? Really? Do they still make that stuff?

The Subaru's air conditioning vent blew her hair in wild, dancing strands over one shoulder. She stared at a flowerbed teeming with a mix of red and white blossoms surrounding a small tree in front of the sheriff's office and twirled her engagement ring around her finger.

It was a relief to know that she was being cleared of the murder accusation but still troubling that Hudgens's killer might have tried to set her up. And the same bastard might be responsible for Rick's death, not to mention Lizzie's, and trying to kill her too. She glanced around the parking lot, but no one looks scary or suspicious.

What have I done to drive someone to that type of vengeance? Could I possibly deserve it?

It would be so easy to cocoon herself at the house again. Just stay in bed and dream of Rick and all she'd lost. But that wasn't helping, and she'd eventually have to pull herself out of it again. For no other reason than she couldn't stand the thought of her father worrying about her any more than he already did.

"More baby steps. None of this depression shit," she mumbled to herself.

After a determined chin up in the rearview mirror, she tucked her hair behind her ear, turned the vent to the side, and popped the car in gear.

Arrow Dynamics was just outside the Bloomington city limits. The gravel parking lot held a mix of cars and pickups, from clapped-out junk to bright, shiny new. A tall metal fence stretched out on each side of a long one-story structure. Between doors on opposite sides of the white building was a bright-red arrow with yellow feathers on one end and a silver tip on the other pointing to the entrance.

Danni opened the door to the brightly lit retail area and heard a familiar deep voice.

Brett Penderson yelled to someone who'd stepped outside another door as she came in.

"Go ahead and start it, get that air conditioner going."

He tossed some keys, and the door shut before he turned back to the clerk at the counter next to the exit.

She meandered around some display shelves and came up beside him.

"Well, hello, Danni." He held a soft vinyl satchel with a tube attached. "Have you decided to take up archery yourself? I wouldn't have guessed that."

"No." She smiled and looked over his shoulder at a display of arrows. "I was just coming to see what it's all about."

Brett looked her up and down. "I see. A good reporter does their own investigation when something tragic happens." He pursed his lips. "I've, thankfully, never been in your shoes, but I suppose I'd do the same thing."

She nodded.

"I've got to get to the newsroom, but anything I can do for you before I head out?"

"No, Brett. I can handle this."

"Danni, stay in touch."

"I will. I'll come talk to you about that education beat again soon."

"Good, good. I'm counting on it. I hear the other problem is all cleared up."

"Yes. I think so."

"Well, then."

He pulled the door open. She watched through the glass door while he put his satchel in the trunk that stood open on a red, sporty-looking sedan not far from the front of the building. He climbed in the driver's seat. The car turned left on the highway. Danni couldn't see anything but a silhouette of the passenger.

She clutched the grab bar on the door. Brett couldn't be involved, but it seemed that everyone she knew with archery skills became a suspect in her mind. He'd moved to Arkansas to take on the job more than a year before. He was still in Texas when she crossed paths with Hudgens and was fired from the *Republican Journal*.

Brett had said before that someone in the newsroom got him interested in the sport, but she didn't think he'd mentioned a name.

Who accompanied him just now? She should have asked.

"Ma'am?"

She turned to see a young clerk looking at her with a strange expression on his face. The lanky boy had a pockmarked face and wore a brown polo and jeans with a green camo vest outfitted with a number of pockets.

"You okay, ma'am?"

"Oh, yes, yes. Sorry. I sort of got lost in thought there for a minute."

She pulled the strap on her bag up on her shoulder and sidled up to the counter.

"Can I help you with something?"

She didn't respond, just scanned a wall covered with arrows of all colors and sizes behind the counter.

"Umm, if you're looking to get into bowhunting, we have beginner classes. We can also just let you try out our Robin Hood course, see if you'd like it. Our Apollo course is much tougher, and you'd need to have some experience to go on it. Are you experienced at bowhunting, maybe sport archery?"

She snorted. "No, no. I, well, I just wanted some information."

"What can I do for you then?"

"I wanted to find an arrow I've seen before. It was white with green and yellow feathers."

He turned from the cash register and looked at the display.

"Well, most of these come in a variety of feather colors. That doesn't mean a lot."

"Oh."

"Are you asking about that guy that was killed?"

She swallowed an instant lump. "Yes, actually, I am. How'd you guess that?"

"Had a couple detectives in here a few weeks ago asking about arrows with green and yellow feathers. They had photos."

"I see. And can you tell me if they figured out which arrow was used?"

The boy, he couldn't be much older than nineteen or twenty, bit his lip.

"I don't know if I'm supposed to tell anyone else about it. Are you a reporter or something?"

Perceptive little shit, even if he was young and obviously losing a battle with acne.

"Used to be. I don't currently have a job. This is personal. I'm not looking for a story. The guy that was killed, he was my fiancé. I was there the day he was shot. The same type of arrow was used to kill my cousin. She had a baby boy right at a year old."

"Oh, geez. I'm sorry."

"Thanks. I just want some answers, and the police seem to be struggling to find any."

He nodded. "Well, ma'am, you might need to talk to the manager, but he's out on the course right now."

"Did the manager visit with the detectives? Sounds like you helped them."

"Well, yeah, I did. I don't know if they eventually talked to him too. Not sure on that one."

"Okay, then . . ." She looked down at his nametag and back up at him. "Christian. Why don't you just tell me what you told the detectives, and we'll keep it between us. Think of it as helping me get some closure. Okay?"

Biting his lip again he said, "Okay."

"Thank you."

He turned back to the display and reached up to pull an arrow from the small brackets that held it against the wall.

"This is it. It's real popular. Heavy-weight carbon fiber rod with a fixed blade broadhead tip. No telling how many we sell. Got a good accuracy rate from a decent distance, durable, and it's pretty reasonable on price."

She took the arrow from him and rolled it between her fingers. It was the arrow. She sucked in a ragged breath and tried to stop her hands from shaking as she rolled it between her fingers.

"Any chance you gave them a list of people you know for sure bought this arrow?"

She handed it back to him.

"'Fraid not. Just too many that would be on a list like that."

They both turned as three men came in a back door. They went into another room, talking and laughing as they went. Two of them were teasing the third about missing the target and needing new glasses.

"What else did the detectives want?"

He turned and hung the arrow back on the wall mount.

"They asked about our membership list."

"You have members?"

"Yeah. They get a better rate on running the courses and a discount in here."

She leaned against her arms on the counter and watched the boy's attention shift to her neckline. Leaning over a little more, she asked, "Any names in particular that you remember them asking about?"

"I checked a couple for 'em, but really, I can't remember what they are. Sorry. I didn't write it down or nothing."

He absently squeezed his chin between his thumb and the knuckle on his index finger.

"That's okay, Christian. But would you mind checking a name or two for me. See if they're members?"

"You bet." He moved over in front of the register and pressed a couple of buttons. "Who?"

"Can you look for a Randy Carlisle?" She spelled out the last name.

"Let's see." He stared at the screen and repeatedly tapped a button as he scrolled a list. "I don't see that name."

"Want to check another one for me?"

"Sure."

"Kendra Carter."

He scrolled again. "Nope, don't see her either."

"Hmmm." It had been a long shot.

"Anyone else?"

"Yes. How about Trevor Daniel?"

He tapped the keyboard.

"Got a William and a Barry, but no Trevor. A slew named Daniel. I think that whole darn family comes in here."

"Okay, thanks. If someone comes to mind, can I call and get you to check for me?"

She smiled up at him and pulled herself away from the counter.

"You bet. I'm here Tuesday to Saturday, but not always the same times."

"Well, I'm glad I caught you here this time."

She smiled.

He grinned.

"Thanks again for the help, Christian." Even though it didn't really get her anywhere.

"Well, didn't do much good, really. Besides, whoever it is might be a customer but not a member anyway."

"I understand."

She pulled her sunglasses from her purse, waved, and left before she wasted more time barking up the wrong tree.

The *Northwest Arkansas Business Bugle* office operated from a strip mall on the north side of town. A string of bells attached to the door jingled when Danni opened it. Those might have been left over from a gift shop or whatever had occupied the space before. The tabloid should have changed it to a bugle sound. That would have been funny. Either way, it was effective. Three heads turned to see who had entered. One of them was Matt.

He grinned and walked toward her. The others went back to what they were doing.

Matt's cowlick was even more pronounced than she remembered, or he'd embraced it and styled his hair to accent the swoop.

"Danni, Danni, how are you? You look great."

He hugged her in a quick embrace.

"I'm good. How are you liking Northwest Arkansas?"

"Great. Lovin' it up here. Much better than Little Rock. Rat race got to be too much. Lovin' the traffic. People complain about it, but I'm like, 'This is nothing.' And, man, I really like getting out of the daily grind. This weekly thing is awesome."

She smiled. The daily grind had been her dream. A weekly seemed like a step down, but maybe he had a point.

"So, what's up with you? You looking for a job or something?"

"No, no. Well, maybe, but no. Not right now anyway."

She looked over his shoulder. It didn't seem like anyone was too busy. One guy had his feet on his desk, reading the paper, and another clearly scanned Facebook while he sipped on an extra large soda.

"I wondered if you might have time for a cup of coffee or a drink. I wanted to talk to you about something."

He grinned. "You bet. There's a coffee house in the next building. We can walk."

He draped an arm over her shoulder and guided her back to the door.

"You sure you're not too busy? I didn't mean to just drop in on you, but I wasn't far and thought I'd pop in and see if the rumors were true that you'd moved up here."

"Nah. We just put this week's to bed yesterday. Today's our breather. Just getting organized for next week, then I'm out of here. We have a Friday morning meeting and talk about the next edition, then everybody hits it hard Monday morning."

He held the door open for her. The coffeehouse smelled like cinnamon rolls. Matt didn't resist the tantalizing aroma, but she declined. He ordered one with his coffee and tea for her. They sat at a small round table in the front window.

He took a bite of the big gooey roll and grunted. She smiled and bounced her tea bag up and down in the water.

"So, what's up? I'm sure you're not here to talk about the rain coming in today."

He wiped at the corners of his mouth with a paper napkin. She glanced out the window. The sky was definitely graying up.

"No. I, um, well, I don't know if you've heard all the crap floating around about Hudgens and me."

"I heard they found him dead. The asshole. After what he did to you, I wouldn't blame you if you'd knocked him off." He snorted and opened his mouth for another bite but looked up at her, closed his mouth, and put the chunk of roll back on his plate. "Don't tell me you're the person of interest they've been talking about on the news."

She rolled her eyes. "One and the same."

"Shit."

"But I didn't have anything to do with it."

"Well, of course not, but do they think you did?"

"They questioned me, but now they've backed away from that idea. I think my cell phone saved my ass on that one. I wasn't anywhere near Cleburne County when it happened."

"Yeah, they can track a person pretty damn good with today's technology. A little scary, really."

"Tell me about it." She sipped her tea. "Anyway, the reason I'm here is sort of connected to it all. They found my notes—copies of documents and interview tapes from the piece I did on Hudgens—when they found his body. It's the stuff that was stolen from me at the *Republican Journal*. What I needed to prove that I hadn't libeled him."

"Wow, really? You think someone tried to set you up?"

"Maybe."

"I couldn't believe all that shit then. You know, I got a safe at home and now take anything important home and store it."

He licked his fingers, wiped them off, and stuck the wadded up napkin under the edge of his plate.

"Good idea. I wish I'd been that smart back then."

"Well, hell, you don't think about not trusting the people you work with."

"It was a big newsroom." She put her mug down and sat back. "I wondered, Matt, if you heard anything after I left. If you knew anyone who might have taken that stuff from my desk to help Hudgens or get at me for some reason."

He puckered his lips and looked out the window, watching a couple of women walk past.

"Don't be pissed at me."

He glanced back at her and sighed.

"What?"

"I should have told you back then, but I didn't think she'd really do anything. It all happened so fast. I knew something was going on, and the next thing I knew, you were gone. I heard later about Hudgens accusing you of libel and that you thought someone had set you up. I didn't know the details for a while." He took a deep breath and let it out, sputtering his lips in the process. "When I heard what happened, I asked Teresa if she did something. She denied it, but I wasn't sure. I wouldn't even talk to her after that."

"Teresa? Really? You think she didn't like me enough that she'd steal from me, make me lose my job?"

He nodded.

"I can't believe she was that jealous. She really had the hots for you. Hated that you and I teased each other, that we were friends."

She raked her fingers through her hair, tucking it behind her ears.

"That she did. But that wasn't it. Well, it might have been part of it."

"What do you mean?"

"She told me when you were writing about him that Hudgens's girlfriend was her cousin. I think they were pretty tight. Teresa was furious after that story came out."

"Oh, God."

She slumped against the back of her chair. It had to be Teresa. Their desks were, at most, ten feet apart in the Little Rock newsroom.

That bitch.

She'd taken her notes and documents and turned it all over to her cousin, or maybe given them directly to Hudgens.

Anger boiled inside her. Anger at the newspaper's editorial board for not believing her. Anger at Teresa for daring to steal from her, then sit back and watch her career fall apart as a result and not say a word. Anger at herself for not realizing it could be Teresa.

Why hadn't she recognized that the petty jealousy was just a small part of the woman's dislike of her? Why hadn't she pushed harder for an investigation of the theft, defended herself more? She'd walked away and shouldn't have.

"I hated that Jim Dore didn't have your back, Danni. He should have stood behind you as your editor. I had to get out of there after that. I couldn't stand working with her anymore either. The whole thing made me sick."

"Is she still working there?"

"Yep. She sure is. Jeff, my bud in sports, said she's dating Bob, the features editor. I heard she uses his clout and sits around the newsroom hardly churning out any copy, thinking she's hot shit, as usual."

Danni snorted and took a sip of tea. She had to get to Little Rock. Teresa might not talk to her, but then again, she might. Danni had to ask what she'd done with the stuff she took. It wasn't quite eleven a.m. Maybe she should go now. Waiting for Monday would kill her.

"Can you do me a favor?" she asked.

"Sure. What you need?"

"Can you call Jeff, see if she's in the newsroom today?"

He pulled his cell phone from the front pocket of his jeans.

"You bet."

"Make it casual. I don't want him alerting her, but I need to talk to her, and catching her off guard might be best."

She downed the last of her tea while he talked to his buddy in sports. It would be at least three before she got there, but she had to go. She had to.

"Teresa's there." He leaned back and stuck the phone in his pocket.

"You're the best. Thanks, Matt. I gotta go."

She stood up, pulled her bag up on her shoulder, promised to be in touch, and headed out to find answers.

58

Danni stopped by the house to check on Bruno and debated about taking her pistol with her. She didn't have a state conceal and carry permit, but something told her she might need to defend herself. Rick had been harping at her about getting proper training. At least she'd shot it a couple of times. It was a Walther P22. Not the most high-powered gun, but it would do. The good thing was, Rick had said, it held ten shots.

She grabbed a sandwich, a bottle of water, and a can of Diet Dr. Pepper, then headed south. The gun was tucked away beneath vehicle documents and a flashlight in the glove box.

It took a little over an hour to make her way to Interstate 40. The drive was beautiful through the Boston Mountains, despite the overcast skies. The rolling, lush green mountains and lack of billboards in south Lovely County provided a scenic backdrop to the interstate that had her thinking of Rick and their weekend hikes. They'd planned to start camping out—taking a tour of the state parks and a float trip down the Buffalo River—but their time had been stolen. Their future gone with the flash of an arrow.

She was now convinced it had started long before that day at the dam, when something much less important was taken from her.

Teresa had to be the one who stole her materials on the Hudgens story, but she had no proof. She might be stupid to go all the way to Little Rock looking for answers that may never come.

What will I say to Teresa?

Controlling her temper would be the main issue. Maybe she could sweet-talk her into confessing.

Probably not.

She tried to remember the last encounter she'd had with her. Mostly what she'd done was ignore the girl. Petty people don't deserve more.

After making a pit stop on the outskirts of Russellville, she passed the Arkansas Nuclear One facility and was in Little Rock an hour and a half later, without going more than ten over the speed limit.

It was a few minutes before three o'clock when she lucked out and got a parking spot in the small lot across the street from the three-story *Republican Journal* office building. Her cell phone rang. She didn't recognize the number and didn't answer.

Teresa's yellow Mustang was backed into a space in the corner. It could be two hours before the girl left the office. Probably not on a Friday afternoon, but there was the possibility. A call to the office about a minor accident with a parked car might just bring the driver outside. She debated about making such a call, then saw a bleach blonde coming toward her.

It was Teresa. A large black bag was slung over her left shoulder, and her right arm cradled a vase filled with at least a dozen red roses and greenery. She toddled forward in a short gray dress and a pair of black high heels. The girl grinned and seemed to be lost in thought, probably about the guy she had wrapped around her finger enough to send her flowers. Probably the sports editor Matt Dodson had mentioned.

Danni got out of her car while Teresa dug around with one hand in her bag, obviously oblivious to everything around her.

"Hi, Teresa."

Teresa looked up with a jerk and nearly dropped the vase. She leaned forward in a sort of lunge that sent a splash of water over the top, spilling onto her toes that stuck out of her obnoxiously high heeled shoes.

"Danni?"

Her eyes scrunched, but her brow barely moved in a semi-frozen, questioning frown.

Probably Botoxed.

"Yep, it's me." She smiled. "Pretty roses. Someone special, I'm guessing?"

Teresa looked around, like she was trying to figure out why Danni would be there or how she'd gotten there.

"Someone special?" Danni nodded toward the roses.

"Yes, well, he thinks he's special anyway," she said in a matter of fact reply that she'd probably repeated a few times since the flowers arrived at the office.

"Don't they all?" she said.

Teresa stuck her free hand back in her bag, digging for her keys again.

"What are you doing here? Trying to get your job back?"

She chuckled. "Uh, no thanks. I live in Bloomington now. I was just down here and thought I'd stop by the paper see if you have a few minutes to touch base with an old friend. How've you been?"

Teresa raised one eyebrow. "Good. You?"

"Not too bad. Thanks for asking."

Teresa hit the button on her key fob, and the car beeped.

"Really, Danni? Old friend?" Pulling the car door open, she stood back and eyed her up and down. "Were we friends? Really? You didn't even bother to say goodbye when you walked out of the newsroom."

"Well, I was a little stunned over the crap I'd just been through. I always thought we were friends. Not close friends, but friends, nonetheless." She cocked her head to one side and bit her lip.

Come on, bitch. Buy it.

Teresa twisted her mouth to one side and opened the driver's side door.

"Okay, sure." She leaned into the car and put the roses on the passenger seat, then put her black bag in front of the vase. She stood up and put one hand on her hip. "What do you really want, Danni?"

"You have a few minutes? I'd love to buy you a drink, talk a bit."

Teresa looked back toward the office and didn't say anything for a minute.

"I've got these roses. I can't leave them in the car. It's too hot."

"Let's go over there to Omar's. You can bring the flowers in. Might brighten up the place. We can catch up a little."

Teresa scanned the parking area. Probably wondering could she and should she get out of it. Curiosity must have won out.

"Okay, but I'm not taking the flowers in there. Let's make it short."

"You bet. Come on."

They walked the half block over to the neighborhood bar. Danni's cell phone rang again. She reached in her bag and flipped it to silent without even looking at it. She tried to ease the tension by asking about a few of her former coworkers who still wrote for the *Republican Journal*. Teresa obliged with tidbits of gossip.

Danni stepped up on the small concrete stoop in front of the bar and held the arched wooden door open for her. The place was tiny with a row of five booths that could barely hold four people, two small tables, and a long bar with wooden backless stools.

They took a booth near the front and ordered a couple of light beers. The small-talk gossip continued until the waitress, who looked like she could be on the other side of sixty, slid a cardboard coaster and a mug in front of each of them.

Teresa sipped her beer, sat it down, and cocked her head to one side.

"You going to tell me what's up? We both know we were never friends. I think this is the first beer we've ever had together that didn't include a pack of others from the newsroom."

Danni nodded. "No one would ever accuse you of being stupid, Teresa. I wanted to ask you about something that happened when we worked together. You probably already have an idea what I'm talking about and may have wondered why I never asked the question before now."

Teresa pulled her head back and leaned against the tall wooden booth bench, as if she didn't have a clue.

"Why did you take my materials on the Ronnie Hudgens stories?"

Teresa raised an eyebrow and took a long sip of her beer. She sat it back on the coaster and swiped her tongue across her teeth. After twitching her mouth to one side, she asked, "What makes you think it was me?"

"I've got it from a good source that you were the cousin of his former girlfriend."

The laughter came unexpectedly. Teresa smiled, threw her shoulders up and her head back as she laughed. A deep-throated chortle.

"What's so damn funny? That cost me my job."

"You don't have a fucking clue, do you?"

"I'm not sure what you mean?"

"That's what I thought." She looked around the small bar and then back at Danni. "I didn't touch your shit. And for your information, Miss Know It All, I wasn't the only one who cared that you were ruining the lives of people I loved just for a front-page byline on a story that didn't mean shit. Who cares if he was having an affair? He was a rich man long before he took that position with the Highway Department. The cush job and the power that came with it were just icing on the cake. I haven't met a man yet with that kind of money and position that didn't let his ego settle in his dick. A smart girl who can attract someone like him can use all that bullshit to her advantage. That's all she did. My cousin was no different than a thousand other girls. She just made the mistake of actually falling for the bastard."

Stunned, Danni cradled her beer between her palms and took a deep breath.

"I'm not going to sit here and defend that story any more than to say he was a public figure using public funds. He should have used his own money to pay for trips with the girlfriend. I had every right to report it."

Teresa leaned forward. "Hell, he was already going down over that kickback accusation. Sure, you had the right, but you didn't have to do it. Don't you see what you did? Do you know what it meant to his family to be accused of the affair and stealing on top of what was already going on?"

"Don't *you* understand the Fourth Estate? I thought you had a degree. This is basic Journalism 101." She rolled her eyes and pushed aside the beer she'd barely sipped. "There's an obligation as a journalist to expose what the taxpayer has a right to know. But I'm not going to sit here and argue the merits of my job with you."

Teresa pointed at her with her index finger extended over the beer mug she gripped with her palm.

"I may have been her cousin, but I wasn't the only family member working in that newsroom. I bet you didn't have a clue about that either."

Danni blinked and stared at her. "What are you talking about?"

"I figured." Teresa rolled her eyes. "I didn't take your shit, but I know who did."

It took a while to get the whole story out of her former coworker. Teresa eventually stormed out of Omar's, leaving Danni stunned by her revelations. She stayed and ordered a cup of tea and tried to get her emotions in check before she hit the road again. The person involved in the plot to set her up back then was still on a mission to ruin her life and had done a pretty good job of it so far.

When she got back to the parking lot, she found wilted red roses slung all over her windshield. She laughed and carefully brushed them off.

"You're a real piece of work, Teresa," she muttered to herself as she started the car.

59

Traffic was hell north of Little Rock. Weekenders leaving the city and others coming in for the nightlife had lanes in both directions jammed. Danni listened to soft rock on the radio and tried to sort out what she'd learned with what had happened in recent weeks.

Could it be that simple? And right before my eyes all the time? Why hadn't I figured it out when I was in Little Rock back then?

She had to be careful in assuming too much. There had already been way too much misdirection in pursuit of the killer.

It was well past dinnertime by the time she made it to Russellville. She pulled in to a McDonald's to use the bathroom, grabbed a chicken sandwich and a large Diet Dr. Pepper, and was back in the car in fifteen minutes. She ate her sandwich in the car at the back of the restaurant's parking lot.

Her cell phone rang with the same number she'd ignored three times now. She had to sort all this out in her head before she'd feel like talking to Stevens or any other investigator.

A bright-red cardinal landed on the wooden fence in front of her. Its less colorful mate landed next to it a few seconds later. They flapped their wings and bobbed their heads before taking off toward a grove of trees.

Danni wadded up her sandwich wrapper, wiped her mouth with a napkin, and stuffed the trash in the paper sack.

It'd take another two hours before she would get back to Bloomington. She needed to get home and talk to a few people as soon as possible. She grabbed the paper bag, swung open her door, and climbed
out, but was immediately slammed backward. A large black dog stood
on its hind legs, barking and pushing against the door so that it penned
her between it and the car.

"Jake, Jake, get back here." A guy in a Kansas City Royal's baseball
cap and all denim hollered and rushed toward her. "Sorry about that."
He grabbed the dog's collar and pulled it away. "He's usually pretty
friendly. Got shook up when you jumped out of the car so unexpected.
Don't think he knew you was there."

She took a deep breath and let it out.

"You okay? Sorry, really."

She nodded, still too stunned to say anything. The man pulled a
leash from his back pocket and put it on the dog.

"We been riding a while. Just trying to let him get a little exercise.
Sure didn't mean nothin' by it. He's really a good dog."

"No harm. I guess I should have looked before I hopped out."

"No, no. Not your fault at all, ma'am. Jake, you scared the nice lady."

Jake wagged his tail and cocked his head to one side, as if apologiz-
ing. Danni laughed and held out her hand, palm down so he could
sniff it. Jake sniffed, and she petted his head.

"You are a good dog. Sorry I scared you, boy."

"Well, after all that, he likes ya." The man grinned. "Sorry, anyway,
ma'am."

Danni managed a smile as the man took Jake to the grassy area on
the other side of the fence. She tossed the paper bag in the trash and
got back in the car. Her hands were still shaking when she took a long
drink of her soda. Her mind reeled with what Teresa had told her.

"Screw this," she said aloud.

She switched off the radio and picked up her phone. Detective Stevens didn't answer, but she left a message asking him to call her. She
bit her lip, then called Michelle. There was no sense in alarming her,
and it would be better to talk to her in person, but she wanted to see if

she was home and alone. It would be easy to swing by her house on her way north. Maybe her best friend could help her sort out the facts from assumptions and confirm if she was on the right track.

"Hey, girl."

"What's up? You sound a little down."

Funny how well she could read Michelle.

"Oh, just lonely, I guess. Been sitting here all day watching stupid-ass television, bored stiff."

"I thought Trevor was taking the day off to spend a three-day week-end with you."

"Oh, so did I, but I haven't heard from him, and I'm sure the hell not calling his ass to see what's up. Either you want this or you don't, dude."

"Good for you. Don't put up with that crap. You deserve better." *Good, she's alone.* They could talk. "Well, how about a little visit from someone who does care about you? I'm kind of lonely myself."

"Excellent. You can come share in this marathon of *Terminator* movies about to come on. Get us a little Arnold fix."

Danni laughed. "I suppose I can handle that. Got any popcorn?"

"You bet. A whole box of microwavable Orville with extra butter. Got plenty of beer and even some tequila, if you like."

"Hmmm. Maybe. Tummy's been a little touchy lately when it comes to alcohol."

She watched an old Chevy pickup pull up in the space next to her, took a deep breath, and let it out when she saw a compound bow suspended in the truck's back windshield. Damn, she was seeing those things everywhere these days.

"You're not getting sick are you?" Michelle asked.

"I don't think so. Just sometimes liquor appeals to me. Sometimes not."

"You've never been the lush I have. That's for sure." Michelle chuckled.

Danni switched the phone to the other ear. "That's an understate-ment."

"Hardee, har, har. What a friend."

"Well, this friend will be there in less than an hour."

"Great."

She tossed the phone back in her bag and turned up the radio, hoping that traffic had cleared out. It would be dark by the time she got to Michelle's.

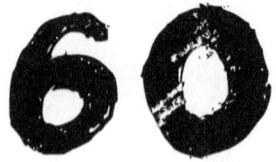

The house was dark when Danni pulled in the gravel drive. That didn't make sense. What happened to the *Terminator* marathon? She climbed out of the car and looked around. Michelle's yellow Jeep was the only other vehicle in front of the house. Had she gone to bed?

The half moon and a sky full of stars overhead provided a thin light, but the yard was mostly shadows from the trees that surrounded the house. She stood quietly next to the car and listened to a plane pass overhead and leaves flutter in the breeze.

Someone sobbed.

It sounded like Michelle.

What the hell?

The sobs grew more frantic. Then a man's muffled voice. Danni couldn't make out the words. Who was in there with her friend?

She slipped back into the car, opened her glove box, and pulled out Rick's pistol.

God help me if I have to use it.

Holding the gun at her side, she eased the door shut and tried to control her breathing. She edged over to the side of the house. Standing on her toes, she was able to see into the living room window. A faint light came from down the hall, probably the kitchen.

She inched along the wall, trying to avoid the holes dug sporadically around the yard by those diligent armadillos. There was rustling in the tall grass a few feet away. She froze. What if she ran into one of those creepy beasts or some other weird creature out here in the dark?

Whatever it was moved just beyond a row of bushes to her right. She couldn't see anything or anyone.

The sobbing started again.

Danni crouched under the dining room window and looked in. Michelle sat at the table in the adjoining kitchen, and next to her sat that creep Randy Carlisle. A gun and a thick piece of rope rested on the table between them. Michelle blew her nose. Randy didn't appear to be threatening her in any way.

Why was Michelle crying?

Why didn't she grab the gun?

Randy looked up toward the window.

Danni hunkered beneath the sash.

She moved the gun to her left hand and felt her back pocket.

Dammit.

She'd left her cell phone in her bag in the car and debated about returning for it. She moved that way, keeping hunched below the window frame.

A branch snapped on the other side of the bushes about twenty feet away. She froze, then raised the gun and listened. Her hand trembled, and the gun wobbled. She tried to steady it with her other hand.

Something moved in the bushes. They were only about shoulder high. If someone lurked there, they had to be crouched or crawling.

The rustling started again, and another twig snapped. Whoever or whatever had shifted to the end of the line of bushes.

A shape moved out in the open.

She held her breath, raised the gun with a trembling hand, and squeezed the trigger.

Nothing happened.

She gasped in a breath, the pistol shaking in her hand.

The gun's safety was still on. Rick would have scolded her for that. One of the first things he'd taught her.

"It's a good thing to have, but the gun is useless if you leave the safety on," Rick had said.

Leaning the back of her head against the siding, she watched the small doe leap off into the trees.

She closed her eyes and listened. Michelle had apparently calmed down. Inching along the side of the house, she moved closer to the back door. She might be able to hear what was going on from there.

A loud clatter rang out. Something fell over on the back patio. Danni stopped in her tracks. Was someone else creeping around trying to get a look in Michelle's windows? The sliding glass door rumbled open.

"It's a raccoon."

Randy Carlisle had a deep voice. Not what she expected from the creepy little guy. Danni had pressed her back against the side of the house when the patio lights went on. The door slid closed. She peeked around the corner.

The animal sat on his hind legs, his cheeks puffed out as he munched. The lawn chair with the bag of dog food on it from last week was toppled over and kibble scattered around it.

Michelle's sobs rang out again. She had to move closer to the kitchen to hear what was being said. She'd never heard Michelle cry like that before. She was always a stop-and-smell-the-roses, oh hell, pick-'em-and-throw-'em-in-the-air-while-we-dance kind of girl.

The raccoon dropped to all fours as Danni moved around the back of the house. He gathered a few kibbles of dog food and stood back on his haunches, eating.

"Stay over there, boy," she whispered.

He watched her with beady black eyes but didn't seem to care about anything other than the banquet spread out on the concrete.

Danni edged up to the sliding glass door. She couldn't go any farther without being seen, but she could hear.

"This is all my fault. I can't believe this," Michelle wailed.

"Just wait. They'll be here soon." Randy sounded like he was trying to calm her, not threaten her.

Who is coming soon?

The raccoon dug in the dog food bag. There was enough spilled on the patio to feed the fat critter for a couple of meals at least. Did he really need more?

The song "Dirty White Boy" rang out for a minute, then stopped. Randy began talking on a cell phone.

"Yes, she's here still. We're waiting for you."

She needed to act fast before his reinforcements arrived. Michelle needed to get out of there.

"Hurry up," he urged whoever was on the other end of the line.

Randy came back toward the door. Danni jumped away and plastered herself against the siding. He slid the glass door open.

She didn't breathe.

He stayed inside and slid the screen door shut.

"I don't know where he went. We've seen no sign of him." His voice faded as he walked farther into the room.

Who?

Danni peeked around the edge of the door.

"It's the second drive on the right once you hit her road. Front door's unlocked." He slapped the phone shut and sat back down. "They'll be here in about ten minutes."

Danni turned at the sound of crinkling. The furry little thief had half his body in the dog food bag.

If the front door was unlocked, she could go back to the car, get her phone, and come in that way. Or she could go in through the patio and catch Randy by surprise.

"This is my fault. My fault."

Michelle was more under control but still sounded frantic.

No time like the present.

In one quick jerk, Danni slid the screen door open and stepped into the kitchen. Both of them turned. She held the gun with two hands and aimed it at Randy.

"What the hell's going on here?"

"Whoa. Whoa." Randy held up his hands, like he was used to having a gun drawn on him.

"Danni, put that down." Michelle got to her feet and wiped at her face with the back of her hand. "I've seen enough guns tonight."

She lowered her weapon.

"I don't understand. What the hell is going on?"

Randy kept his hands up and stayed seated, his eyes wide.

"Why are you busting in here waving a gun around? Sit."

Michelle pulled out a chair and pointed at it.

"Why are you crying? What's he doing here? Did he hurt you?"

"No, no, nothing like that. He's here to help." Michelle shook her head and sat back down. "Apparently, he's got a habit he's going to have to stop, but in this case, it really helped me out. He's been checking on me occasionally when he sees I've got company."

Randy lowered his hands and eyed them each with a hesitant, embarrassed look on his face.

"Trevor was here, going berserk." Michelle took a breath and bit her lip, then went on. "He was yelling about you. Said you're out to get him and called you all kinds of names. He wanted to know where you were. Says you deserve to go to jail for Hudgens's death and somebody named Tracey. He was nuts, girl, nuts." She shuddered and sniffled. "Talked crazy, like he was carrying on with someone not even here. I think it was his mother. It was bizarre. What scared me most was that I think he'd been looking for you all over the place, said he was going to make you pay, Danni."

It must have been him on those calls she'd ignored.

"Where's he now?"

"Marshall Dillon, here, came busting in and threatened him with that pistol."

Michelle snickered and pointed at the gun on the table. Randy smiled.

"When Randy got on his cell phone to call the cops, Trevor ran out."

"It's not loaded. Not a bullet in it." Randy shrugged.

"You threatened him with an unloaded gun?"

"He didn't know it was no good." Randy grabbed the pistol, flipped open the barrel, and held it up. The chamber was clearly empty. "Nobody's shot this thing in years. I ran and got it when I saw he was gonna tie her up. Wasn't even sure I still had it in the truck, but sure 'nuf, it was there under the seat. Course I had to dig it out from under at least a dozen RC Cola cans. God, I gotta clean that thing out."

"He was going to tie you up?"

Danni finally took a seat next to Michelle and sat her pistol on the table.

"Yeah, I think he wanted to keep me from calling you. I told him I hadn't heard from you, didn't know where you were. He'd been to both your houses looking." Michelle ran a palm across her mouth. "I tried to tell the cops to look for him. Don't come up here. He's gone. But they wanted to come get a statement."

"She was so upset. I figured they best come on anyways," Randy added.

"Well, you might want to turn on a light out front. It's dark as hell out there." Danni pointed her thumb over her shoulder.

"I'll get it."

Randy got up. Danni slid her pistol off the table and tucked it in the back of her pants, pulling her shirt out and over it.

"No need for the police to know I've got this. I don't have a conceal and carry permit."

"I'm to blame for this." Michelle sniffled.

"Why? It's not your fault." Danni reached over and squeezed Michelle's hand. "This is all about that crap in Little Rock. It has nothing to do with you."

"Well, he wouldn't even be around if it wasn't for me."

"Bullshit. I'm pretty sure he's the one who killed Rick and Lizzie. He probably killed Hudgens too, and maybe even Gerald Yell, the photographer from Little Rock. He somehow blames me for his sister's suicide."

"He, he killed Rick? Lizzie?" Tears flooded Michelle's eyes.

Danni shook her head and swallowed.

"I just came back from Little Rock. Teresa Hillburn told me that Trevor was out to get me. That his sister, Tracey, was Hudgens's girlfriend.

She killed herself when Hudgens broke it off after my stories ran about the misuse of his state credit card. He holds me responsible for all of it."

"Oh, God. I'm sorry, Danni. I'm sorry. He's blaming you for something you didn't do."

Michelle wrapped her arms around herself.

"And you're blaming yourself for something you didn't do."

Michelle nodded. "Touché."

61

It took some convincing, but Michelle persuaded Danni to stay the rest of the night. Tension and worry kept her from sleeping much. The state police, the Lovely County Sheriff's Office, and the Bloomington Police Department were all searching for Trevor Daniel. Two county deputies stayed in a cruiser at the end of Michelle's driveway, just in case he returned.

She called Ben Sizemore at seven a.m. He assured her that everything was being done to find him. They suspected he'd gone back to Little Rock, but he hadn't turned up at his family home yet, according to the police down there.

When she got off the phone, Michelle's mother came in to round up her daughter and take her back to her house. Danni was ready to head to town anyway.

"I need a shower and some clean clothes," she told Michelle.

"Are you sure it's safe to go home?"

"Yeah. It sounds like the cops have been all over the place, so he won't be anywhere close. Ben says they're going by there every couple of minutes. They think he left town. Probably got scared and went back to Little Rock."

"I bet they'll get him."

"Are you okay with that?"

Michelle shook her head back and forth and rolled her eyes. "Absofuckinglutely! I sure do pick 'em, don't I?"

A horn beeped.

"Mom's getting impatient. I better get outta here."

"I'm going too."

Danni grabbed her bag and followed Michelle out. She tucked her pistol back in the glove box before she headed into town.

She called her dad on the way, but he didn't answer. Ben said the police patrolled by the cemetery several times during the night, but getting no response worried her. He might just be dealing with a Saturday morning service. It wouldn't hurt to check before she went home for that shower.

The wind picked up, and menacing gray clouds pushed out any hope of sunshine. It was turning out to be a very wet summer. Lightning flashed off to the north as she pulled up next to her dad's pickup in front of the cemetery shop. The door stood open, and the fan hung in the doorway. No other vehicles were around. There must not be any services, or the grounds crew would be on hand, despite the impending rain.

She ducked under the fan and stopped.

"Dad!" she screamed.

Her father sat in the old office chair. His chin rested on his chest, and his eyes were closed. His wrists were strapped to the tattered arms of the chair with zip ties, and his legs were bound with duct tape. She ran to him and crouched in front of him, jostling the chair. His head flipped backward, knocking into the grinder mounted on the workbench behind him.

"A grinder. Hmmm. That'd make a nice torture device," Trevor said behind her.

She stumbled forward and hit the chair again.

Her father's head dropped back to his chest.

Her heart raced, and she couldn't get a breath.

Trevor stood between her and the door, grinning.

"He's alive, just passed out from a little whack on the head. We could wake him up, though. Start that grinder. Take off an ear. He'd wake up, don't you think? Might be fun to watch *you* do it."

She sucked in a breath, closed her eyes, and tried to calm the rage and fear pumping through her. Opening her eyes again to face the situation, she pulled herself to her feet and backed up against the workbench. Her arms trembled.

"Uh, uh. Get away from there."

He pushed her to the side against the bench on the other wall. A coffee can filled with zip ties lay on its side on the workbench, along with a roll of duct tape and a pair of long metal scissors. Trevor picked up the scissors and waved them at her.

"I tell you what, though. I'll do you a favor. You don't deserve it, but I've got a little plan for a nice dramatic end to your sorry life. We'll leave Daddy here for now, and you'll have to guess what will happen to him when I return. Or maybe, if you're a real good girl, we'll leave him be."

"Please, don't hurt him. I'll do what you want." It came out in a whisper, her voice catching with fear. "He's never done anything to you."

Trevor threw his head back and laughed, then stopped and snarled at her.

"My sister never did anything to you. You killed her and then my mother."

"I, I only met Tracey once and didn't even know your mother," she pleaded. "You should have talked to me back then. Maybe we could have worked something out. Maybe I wouldn't have written that story."

"Now that's hilarious. We both know it's a lie."

"No, no. We could have."

"Bullshit. Nothing would have prevented you from going after that byline. You were looking for fame, for a prize, for your name on the front page with another bullshit story. My mother, my sister, they didn't matter to you. Nobody did!"

He leaned toward her and screamed the words. Spittle hit her cheeks. She turned her head and pinched her eyes closed.

"I didn't—"

"Sure you did. You meant to do whatever it took to help yourself. Screw everybody else. You were looking to make Daddy, here, proud of his only daughter."

He kicked the side of the chair, sending her father in a spin that left him with his head cocked to one side as it slammed into the wooden workbench.

Danni gasped. "Please."

"Yeah, sure, please don't hurt your daddy. Let's see how you cooperate, then we'll make that decision."

As he stalked back toward her, she noticed a dark-brown smear ran down the side of his gray button-down shirt.

Blood?

Oh, God, where's Mom? Is she all right?

Her pulse pounded in her ears. Tears streamed down her cheeks. She wiped at her face with the back of her hand.

"I'll do anything."

Trevor grabbed a handful of zip ties and stuck them in the back pocket of his jeans. He waved the scissors toward the door, then pushed her as she ducked under the fan. He led Danni around the side of the shop, the point of the scissors against her back. His gray Toyota was parked behind the building. He pushed her against the side of it.

"Hold out your hands."

He wrapped a zip tie around her wrists and snapped it tight.

"Now stand right there where I can see you. I need to get something."

A wave of nausea came over her as she watched him pull a compound bow from the trunk. It had four arrows mounted in some kind of sheath holder on the side. The feathers were green and yellow.

Her heart hammered in her chest and bile rose in her throat. She leaned over and threw up, then stood and wiped her mouth with the back of her hand.

Trevor laughed and slammed the trunk shut.

"Yes, Danni, I know how to shoot a compound bow. Actually, I'm pretty skilled with it. I suppose you've figured that out already. Penderson told you, didn't he? He said he talked to you yesterday when we were leaving Arrow Dynamics."

She closed her eyes, leaned against the car, and tried to hold back another round of nausea. Her body didn't cooperate. Thunder rolled, and big drops of rain hit her back as she bent forward and dry heaved several times before standing up again.

"Sounds like you're done. Come on, before it starts pouring." Trevor grabbed her sleeve and pushed her back toward the gate. "We're taking your car."

62

"I'm sorry, Mama. I'll make this right."

I tried to keep my eyes on the road but was drawn back to her stare in the rearview mirror.

She didn't understand.

She never understood me or tried to see things my way. It was always her way. I was trying to do what she wanted. Trying to be the good son she deserved. I could feel her eyes on the back of my head. I didn't even have to look in the rearview mirror to know she was giving me the look—the look that said she knew I could do better. The one that made me wince and wait for her to slap me. The one that convinced me she was ashamed.

Ashamed I wasn't better.

Better at doing what she wanted.

Better at making a good living.

Better at protecting her and Tracey.

Better at everything.

I wasn't her precious Tracey. I'd never be what she was to Mama.

"You should have finished her daddy off, boy. Made her watch. Maybe make her do it. She needs more suffering."

Her lips were pinched up in a tight pucker, her eyes glued on mine in the mirror. She nodded toward my passenger. I shook my head.

"Yes, Mama."

There would be no disappointing her again. I'd do what was necessary.

She rocked back in the seat and smoothed the front of her cotton dress.

"Good, good. You know what's best. Just step up and get it done this time."

"I will, Mama. I will. I'm going to make her suffer first. I will. She already lost the man she loved. She's not getting married and won't ever have his children or see the life she dreamed about. She took that all away from Tracey, and I took it from her."

Mama reached up and patted me on the shoulder.

"Good, son. Good. I'm proud of you for that. I know, I know. I was disappointed at first, but you're right. She's suffering cuz of it. Then her cousin." Mama laughed. "Killing them both was good. She doesn't deserve to be happy, maybe knows that now. Look at her. She's trying not to cry. Sitting there staring out the window. She ain't stupid. She knows you're gonna kill her." She laughed. "Did you see her throwing up? That was fear, boy. Fear, for sure."

She patted her chest and rocked in the backseat as she laughed.

I laughed too.

63

Danni sat in the passenger seat and tried to get her breathing under control. Trevor was ranting and raving like there was someone else in the car.

Mama? What the hell?

He wasn't just an angry asshole. He was totally nuts.

She considered jumping out, but she'd have trouble getting the door open with her hands bound. If what she suspected was true, jumping out of the moving car wasn't an option. She had to get through this.

"Trevor, I'm sorry."

"Shut up. We don't want to hear anything out of your mouth. Do we, Mama?"

He looked in the rearview mirror and nodded, as if someone was in the backseat.

Danni turned to look. Trevor backhanded her on the cheek.

"Keep your nosy ass out of this, Danni fucking Deadline."

She bit her lip and stared at the road ahead. He seemed to be driving toward her house, the house she'd shared with Rick. Her body shook with a silent sob, and she thought she might throw up again.

Trevor babbled on about payback and the pain he planned to in-flict upon her, his words becoming a blur, meshing with the rhythm of the windshield wipers. Rain beat against the car. Maybe she could somehow get to the gun she'd put back in the glove box. She needed something. All he had was the bow he'd put in the back of the Subaru and the scissors tucked under his left thigh. She still wore the long button-down shirt she'd put on at Michelle's that morning. It would cover the gun if she could somehow get it and stick it in her waistband.

"Mama thinks you're plotting some way to get out of this little predicament."

Trevor pulled into the driveway and reached over in front of her, pressing the button for the automatic garage door opener.

It rumbled up.

Rick's Lexus SUV was parked in front of them. Trevor backed up and pulled forward into the empty space beside it. He shut the car off and hit the garage door button again.

"Okay, let's go inside. I need a drink." He started to get out, and she reached for the door handle. "No, wait. You sit here until I'm ready. Don't want you running in the house ahead of me."

He climbed out of the car and went to the back to get the bow.

"I thought about doing this up at the dam." He called out as he fiddled with the keys. "Take you back to where you lost your great love. But, well, you know, this wonderful weather we're having."

She reached forward and opened the glove box. Holding it halfway closed with her knees, she reached in with her bound hands and felt for the gun.

The back of the Subaru popped open.

"Got any apples? Maybe we could have some fun. You can see how good I am. Put one on your head and let me aim."

He laughed and slammed the rear hatch down.

She eased the glove box closed and held her breath. There was no time. Trevor yanked open her door.

"Okay, let's—"

"Let's nothing. Get back."

She aimed the pistol at him. This time she'd remembered to flip the safety off.

"Put down the bow. Put it down, now," she snarled.

His mouth gaped open, and he backed up against one of the bicycles mounted with a bracket to the wall.

"There's no way you'd get that thing loaded and shoot me before I'd have a bullet in you, no matter how good your aim is. So put it down or drop it."

She pushed the car door closed with her hip and held the gun with both hands.

He bent at the knees and laid the bow on the concrete floor next to a small puddle of rainwater off the car. When he stood, his eyes shifted to the roof of the Subaru.

Danni glanced that way, then met his eyes.

He lunged forward and grabbed the scissors he'd left on top of the car.

She pulled the trigger.

Danni made her way across the cemetery grounds in search of her father. The sweet smell of freshly cut grass and the sound of a mower humming made her smile. She had loved using the gas-powered trimmers when she was a teenager just because she could get lost in her thoughts while she worked.

She found him at the pond. He sat on a wooden bench, a pair of gloves on the seat next to him and a rake on the grass at his feet. A wheelbarrow with a pile of brush was parked closer to the bank.

"Hey, Sis. Come sit with me."

"Sit I will, and that's all you're supposed to be doing."

She pushed her sunglasses atop her head, bent and gave him a hug, then sat down.

"Oh, believe me, a little concussion won't slow me down. And besides, Josh isn't letting me do much anyway."

She chuckled. "He's just trying to keep you from hurting yourself. I'm so glad he found you when he did."

"Me too. Good kid. He wasn't even supposed to be working Saturday, rain coming down the way it was and all."

They sat in silence for a few minutes, watching the geese swim in circles and honk at each other.

"How are *you* doing?" He put a hand on her knee and patted it.

"I'm fine. Good, actually." She smiled and clasped his hand. "I have some news."

"Josh told me. Said Trevor Daniel is alive, still in the hospital, but headed to jail in a few days."

"Well, yeah, there's that too. I can't believe I shot him. I'm a terrible shot, but that's not for long. I've signed up for shooting lessons."

"Really? Well, I hope you never need them."

"Me too, Dad. Me too. Still, it's better to have the skill. I don't ever want to feel helpless. Thinking about taking archery too."

"Archery? Why would you do that?"

She sighed. "I don't know. I think it's better to know that which I fear. Maybe take the fear away."

Her father nodded and pursed his lips.

"Maybe I'll come join you on that. Always thought I might enjoy it. Targets only, of course."

"Of course, and that would be fun. I'd love to take lessons with you."

"It's decided then."

"Yep. I'll get us signed up."

A goose waddled out of the pond and pulled its legs underneath it to take a seat in the shade beside the wheelbarrow. She lowered her sunglasses back to her nose.

"Anyway, I'm glad Trevor's not dead, even if he deserved it. Not sure how I'd feel about killing someone. And by the way, he confessed to killing Ronnie P. Hudgens and Gerald Yell."

"Well, good. I'm glad they solved that mystery. Took suspicion off you. I tell ya, if he'd harmed your mother or you, I would have tracked him down and shot him myself."

"I bet you would. Honestly, I thought I'd killed him at first, until he started moving around. I could have shot him again, but I just took those zip ties and strapped him to Rick's bike. He wasn't going anywhere with his hands tied to one wheel and his feet to another, not to mention bleeding all over the place." She swatted at a mosquito on her arm. "I still haven't been able to get over to the house and clean up the garage floor. You don't think about the mess left behind when stuff like that happens."

"I can help you with that."

She shook her head. "No you don't. You're not helping with a thing. I can take care of it."

He shrugged and turned as a loud goose honked and took off after another one, both of them flapping their wings and flying a few feet off the water as they left the pond and headed up the side of the hill where Josh worked at something with a rake, the riding mower parked nearby. He stopped to chase off the geese.

"I got him convinced to move in with us," her dad said. "He and the baby are going to take your room until the house out back is built. The contractor will start on the new place in the next week or so."

"That's great, Dad. I'm glad to hear it."

"You don't mind?"

"Mind what?"

"That I gave away your room."

She snorted. "Heck, no. I'm happy things are working out this way. You need the help. It's time to let that happen, Dad. And besides, Josh deserves a break."

"He's been cleared on the drug charges. Convinced the prosecutor those drugs were in the truck when he bought it."

"That is great news."

"It certainly is. I made him take the truck down and get it detailed, make sure there's nothing else in there. I guess he knows I'm aware of what happened now. Didn't say anything, but he let me pay for the detail." He picked up the leather work gloves and slapped his thigh. "I'm glad to have him on board. Good to have family around."

"How's Mom handling it?"

"Good. She doesn't know about the house yet, but she's enjoying the heck out of that baby, I tell ya. Think she'll love having him around all the time."

"Is she? That's good. Wonder how she'd feel about another one."

He looked over at her with his brows pinched together. "You're kidding."

"Nope, not kidding. Surprised as all get out, but not kidding. Had an official test this morning. Should be here right around Christmas. Rick left me a special gift. A very special gift."

She twirled her engagement ring and smiled at the tears gathering in her father's eyes.

A chorus of honking geese exploded, as if shouting for joy.

- THE END -

ACKNOWLEDGEMENTS

The supportive community of writers in the Ozark Mountains has my deepest respect and gratitude for the encouragement that keeps me going. I would likely still be hammering away at my keyboard but never daring to let anyone get a glimpse at my words without that support. I especially want to thank Duke and Kimberly Pennell at Pen-L Publishing for believing in me and never wavering in their faith that my work could find an audience. They've gone well beyond my expectations to get *A Lovely Murder* in print and in a way that makes me so proud to be a part of their team.

As for that Ozarks writing community, in addition to the Pennells, I want to thank Linda Apple, Jan Morrill, Russell Gayer, Nancy Hartney, Alice White, Ruth Weeks, Jessica Nelson, Julie James, Meg Dendler, Jim Davis, Jennifer Murray-McClain, Brenda Black, and all the members of Ozarks Writers League. I also owe a big thanks to author Velda Brotherton as well for all her encouragement to keep pushing forward and find my voice.

And I'd like to thank my #1 beta reader and husband, Lloyd, who never doubts my talent but is also ready to offer criticism when duly deserved.

My acknowledgement of those who've supported my work would not be complete without mentioning my two daughters: Sara Glenn and Hillary Stone. They hold my writer's heart. I would never have dared make my dream of being a writer come true without their support and encouragement. They make a couple of fine beta readers as well.

And thank you with all my heart to my readers. It's your decision to keep turning the page that keeps me wanting to pound out more suspense and thrills for your enjoyment.

ABOUT THE AUTHOR

Lori Ericson grew up in her family-owned cemetery and spent years as a newspaper reporter but isn't sure which experience helped more to shape the dark stories that spill from her head. The author and her husband, Lloyd, live in Northwest Arkansas with their rescue dog, Charlie, where she drags them both off to walk through old cemeteries occasionally. Lloyd insists those walks occur during the daylight hours.

A Lovely Murder received The President's Award and First Place in the Unpublished Manuscript contest from Ozark Writers League in 2015. *A Lovely County,* the first novel in the Danni Deadline Thriller series, was published in January 2015. Look for *A Lovely Grave* in 2017 from Pen-L Publishing.

CONNECT WITH LORI AT:
Subscribe to her Blog at: LoriEricson.com
Email her at: LoriEricson.author@gmail.com
Like her on Facebook: LoriEricson
Follow her on Twitter: @Author_Ericson

Dear Readers,
If you enjoyed this book enough to review it for Goodreads, B&N, or Amazon.com, I'd appreciate it!

Thanks, Lori

Find more great reads at
Pen-L.com